CHAPTER ONE

I'm sitting in the graveyard with my best friend, Zen, when he spots a ghost.

'It's over there,' he says. 'In that tree!'

It's not a ghost. It's a plastic bag. But I don't say this to Zen. Instead I fix him with a serious look and say, 'Let's get it!'

We jump off the bench and run through the graveyard, laughing as we dodge between the graves. Out at sea, thunder rumbles and dark clouds cover the sky like a blanket. There's a storm coming, but we don't care. We've got a ghost to catch.

While Zen leaps around, his shirt untucked and his shoelaces undone, I find a long stick and start whacking the bag. Eventually it floats to the ground and Zen snatches it up.

'Is it dead?' I ask.

Zen rolls his eyes. 'Sid, it's a ghost. Of course it's dead.'

But it turns out it isn't because suddenly it attacks me and it doesn't stop until I pull the bag off Zen's hand and stuff it in my pocket.

Ghost hunt over, we go back to doing what we always do after school: sitting on the bench, eating crisps and making up stories about the people buried in the graveyard.

'OK,' I say, nibbling on a Wotsit. 'So Iris Tiddy over there was famous for her pilchard pasties and she was going out with Harry Thompson.' I point at a headstone with 'Harry Thompson, Gone Fishing!' engraved on it. 'She loved him because he caught the biggest pilchards in town.'

'It was an unusual relationship,' says Zen, 'because Harry was born one hundred and ten years after Iris died.'

I laugh, but my voice is drowned out by an enormous clap of thunder. It's followed by a flash of lightning.

'Awesome,' I say, as goosebumps prickle my arms. 'Zen, can you smell the lightning?'

'I can't smell anything,' he says. 'I'm too scared.'

And that's when I notice he's huddled down inside his hoodie. Zen's been scared of storms ever since his dad told

him about this man who's been struck by lightning seven times.

'Well, it smells amazing,' I say. 'Like snow and sparklers mixed together.'

'I'll take your word for it,' he says, then we watch as the black clouds roll closer. Soon fat drops of rain are speckling my face and glasses. When another bolt of lightning lights up the sky, Zen decides he's had enough.

'I'm going home,' he says, grabbing his rucksack. 'You coming?'

'No, I'll stay for a bit longer.'

'Suit yourself,' says Zen. Then he runs down through the graveyard pretending to be struck by lightning seven times as he goes. I join in too, and when he finally disappears through the gates I'm lying on the path.

I pick myself up and sit on the bench. And then . . . everything is quiet.

I keep very still, watching and listening. Snails stretch their way across wet headstones, rain falls and birds peck at the gravel. Water drips from the trees and the stream bubbles past me towards the sea.

I watch all this, then get up and wander along twisty

paths, trailing my fingers over lichen and picking my way between headstones that stick out of the ground like teeth. Some have fallen over completely and are lying, half buried, under moss and mud.

But not my mum's grave. That's perfect. The best in the whole graveyard.

I crouch in front of it and clear away some dead leaves. Dad made it himself by carving all Mum's favourite things into a tree stump: there's an owl, a fox, shells, beetles and a lightsaber. There's even a shark's fin rising out of the top. I touch the fin each time I visit and now it's smooth and shiny.

Not only is Mum's headstump (as Dad insists on calling it) the best in the graveyard, it's also got the best view. From up here I can see all of Fathom: the narrow streets and ice-cream-coloured houses; the seafront with its harbour wall that stretches out to sea like a giant snake. I can even see the model village where, right now, I know Dad will be sitting inside the red-roofed kiosk tidying up souvenirs and thinking about our tea.

It's fish-finger sandwiches tonight. My favourite.

I stand up and take one last look around the graveyard. Every bush and tree is swaying wildly with the wind.

Then I see something strange. There is a clump of ivy over by the sea wall that's standing dead still, not moving at all.

I wipe my glasses with a Wotsity finger. I've always known the pillar of leaves is there. I've squeezed behind it when I've played hide and seek with Zen and I've drawn it on my map. But this is the first time I've noticed what a strange shape it is . . . sort of boxy and *grave*-like.

CHAPTER TWO

Even though I should be going home, I decide to investigate the ivy and I walk into the oldest part of the graveyard.

People round here call this *Pirate Corner* because so many of the headstones have a skull and crossbones engraved on them. Zen's mum is a historian, and she says this was just something people did in the olden days, but Zen and I think there are loads of pirates buried up here.

I stand in front of the clump of ivy. Then, with rain trickling down my neck, I push my hands into the leaves. My fingers brush against cobwebs and tangled stems. There must be spiders in here, but I keep going until my fingers touch something cold and hard. I feel a shiver of excitement. There's definitely something in there!

I rip away the furry stems and glossy leaves until I can

see a patch of stone. It has letters engraved on it – a K and an I – and numbers too. It must be a headstone!

The dark clouds are making it hard to see, but I'm not going anywhere until I know who this grave belongs to. I need to put it on my map.

I tear away more leaves until I've uncovered the whole headstone. It's taller than me and tilting so far to one side that it's almost touching the sea wall. I feel a dip of disappointment when I realise it doesn't have a skull and crossbones engraved on it, but it does have a cherub's face and entwined leaves and faded writing.

I put my finger inside the first letter and I trace the words as I read them out loud.

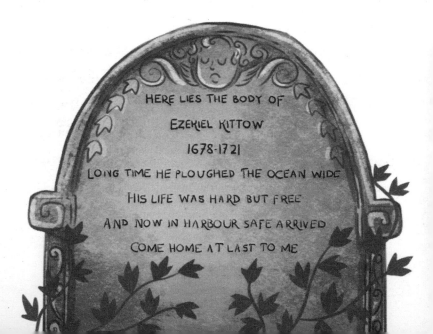

HERE LIES THE BODY OF

EZEKIEL KITTOW

1678-1721

LONG TIME HE PLOUGHED THE OCEAN WIDE

HIS LIFE WAS HARD BUT FREE

AND NOW IN HARBOUR SAFE ARRIVED

COME HOME AT LAST TO ME

It's nice, I think. Like a poem.

I just need to add Ezekiel's grave to my map, then I can go.

My map is my hobby. Some twelve-year-olds collect stickers or play football. Others, like Zen, build axolotl towns on Minecraft. (Actually, it might just be Zen who does this.) But I like to spend my free time making a giant map of Fathom.

I pull a Crunchie out of my rucksack and shove it on top of the grave, then find my pencil case. Next I take my map out of its plastic holder. It starts flapping in the wind so I press it against Ezekiel's grave and find the place where I'm standing right now.

It's as I thought. Where the grave should be, I've drawn a bush!

Before the rain can smudge anything, I rub out the bush and replace it with a headstone half the size of a baked bean. Then, using my brand-new red gel pen, I add the initials EK.

Just as I'm drawing the curly bit at the bottom of the K, lightning explodes from the sky. It lands so close that the hairs on my head stand on end and I get a massive whiff of sparklers.

Definitely time to go.

I put my map in its holder, shove everything back in my bag then run down through the graveyard.

'Bye, Mum!' I shout as I pass her grave.

'Bye, Sid!' I reply on her behalf, which I know is a pretty weird thing to do, but I do what I like in here. I carry on, hurtling past the mausoleum with its ugly gargoyles and clearing the stream with one jump.

But when I reach the gates I skid to a stop.

I've only gone and left my Crunchie on Ezekiel Kittow's grave!

I'm about to go back and get it when I hear a horrible scraping sound. It's like rocks being dragged over more rocks and it's coming from inside the graveyard. I stare as the wind whips the trees backwards and forwards and sheets of rain sweep over the graves, soaking my face and uniform.

Then I hear it again.

Scraaaaaape!

It's coming from the mausoleum. I stare at the funny little building. It's like something from a fairy tale: brambles cover the roof and stone creatures cling to the walls.

Right now the gargoyles are peering at me through smooth, pupilless eyes. Some have tails. Others snouts. All of them hold on to the crumbling walls with long pointed fingers.

Once the mausoleum had a door and a couple of windows, but these were bricked up years ago and now all I can see are pale squares showing where they used to be. Of course, Zen and I have often wondered what's inside: witches, ghosts, trolls . . .

Really, we haven't got a clue.

Scraaaaaape!

With a jolt I realise that a pinprick of light is gleaming on the front of the building. I wonder if someone's in the graveyard with me, shining a torch, but a look over my shoulder tells me I'm alone. And now the light is getting bigger! My heart thuds as I watch it shining in the darkness, stretching until it shows the outline of a door.

But that can't be right. The mausoleum doesn't have a door. It has bricks, and ivy covering those bricks . . . So why can I clearly see a door . . .

A door that's opening!

I make a sound that's halfway between a scream and a sob. A *scob*, I think, as I stumble backwards, tripping over a pot of fake flowers. Still scobbing, I crouch behind a stone angel. Run! hisses the sensible voice inside my head. No, Sid, stay where you are and watch! hisses another, much stupider voice.

Stupid wins. I squeeze my mouth shut and peer around the angel.

A golden mist has begun to roll out of the half-open door. It twists between the graves, licking the feet of cherubs. I hold tight to my angel as the mist comes creeping towards me.

Then, just when I think things can't get any weirder, a huge figure steps into the doorway, blocking the light. It's a man, and he's so tall he has to stoop to avoid hitting his head on the door. He has a bushy beard and he's wearing a long coat. Clutched in his hand is a cutlass.

Pirate, I think, because that's exactly what the man looks like. He's even got one of those triangle-shaped hats – a tricorn – on his head. My heart hammers as I watch him take a great gasping breath of air then turn to look into the graveyard. His dark eyes slide from left to right, then settle on my stone angel.

I don't scob. I scream, and I jump out from my hiding place and go hurtling through the graveyard gates.

CHAPTER THREE

I skid on the wet cobbles as I race down to the harbour, past shops and cafés, then up the lane that leads to the model village. I open the gate, leap over the bucket-sized church and clear the high street in three big steps. Then I throw myself through the kitchen door, slam it shut and lean against it, gasping for air.

Dad looks up from his workbench. My terrified brain just manages to register that he's painting a tiny Dalmatian.

'What's up, Sid? You look like you've seen a ghost!'

'Do I?' I say, then I burst out laughing, and I laugh way too loudly and for much too long.

Dad frowns. 'Sid, are you OK?'

Now this is the moment when I should say, 'No, Dad,

I'm not OK, because I just saw a magic door appear on the side of the mausoleum and then a pirate stepped out of that magic door!' But I don't say any of this, because if I did, I'm sure Dad would never let me play in the graveyard again, and I can't let that happen. I love it there.

You see, I've got a bit of a track record when it comes to seeing ghosts. Well. Smelling them. I've smelt roses in winter and Battenburg cake in the downstairs loo and a year ago I smelt baking bread in a castle where bread hadn't been baked for two hundred years. Dad rolled his eyes when I told him about these things and said I'd inherited Mum's big imagination. But if I tell him I just saw a pirate walk out of the mausoleum, I won't get a smile and an eyeroll. Dad will be seriously worried, and I know he'll blame it on the graveyard.

He's not exactly thrilled that I spend so much time there. Part of him likes me 'visiting Mum', as he calls it, but a bigger part of him wishes I was at the park or beach with all the other Fathom kids.

No. I can't tell him about the pirate, so instead I stuff my trembling hands in my pockets, smile, and say, 'I got caught in the rain. That's all.'

He swirls his paintbrush in water. 'In that case, run upstairs and get changed. Tea's nearly ready.'

Upstairs I move automatically. I hang my uniform over the radiator and pull on my softest pyjamas. My room is warm and cosy. It has a fluffy rug and fairy lights hanging round the window. Usually it makes me feel calm and happy, but right now my heart is pounding so hard it hurts and my fingers shake as I do up my pyjamas.

What Dad said has freaked me out. Because if I'm totally honest, the pirate *did* look like a ghost. He was so big and shadowy, plus there was all that golden mist rolling around.

The thought of seeing a ghost should make me happy. Zen and I have spent hours in the graveyard trying to spot ghosts and playing creepy games, but what just happened wasn't fun like those games. It was terrifying!

For a moment I'm so desperate to talk to someone that I almost ring Zen, but I don't. He'll start going on about restless spirits and demons and I don't want to hear anything like that. I want someone to give me a logical explanation that's going to make me feel better.

Then I remember Marek.

He's the caretaker at the church and he's tall and has a beard. Maybe it was him that I saw? The cutlass could have been a spade and the gold mist . . . some sort of weed killer! I feel a giddy rush of relief. Yes. That has to be it! I bet I mixed up the mausoleum with the shed and turned Marek into a pirate ghost because Zen and I had just had a fight with a ghost and then I found that grave up in Pirate Corner.

My big imagination made up the rest.

Feeling much better, I grab my favourite striped jumper and head downstairs. Dad knits all my jumpers and sometimes he stitches words on to them like **SPOOKY** and **I ♥ THE DARK**. This one simply says **BOO!**

No wonder I just invented a pirate ghost.

CHAPTER FOUR

Hundreds of tiny things watch me as I eat my fish-finger sandwich.

Dad runs Fathomless – *Fathom's To-Scale Model Village, Established 1998!* The model village not only fills our entire back garden, but creeps into the house as well. That's because the kitchen doubles up as Dad's workshop. So right now, I'm surrounded by shelf after shelf of miniature cats, foxes, boats, bats, children, babies, dogs, wheelie bins, grannies, owls, bats and squirrels. There's even a tiny weeny dog poo sitting next to my hot chocolate.

That's Dad's idea of a joke.

He drops a pile of cucumber sticks on my plate, saying, 'There you go, something healthy.'

While I eat, I tell him about finding Ezekiel Kittow's

headstone, missing out everything that happened afterwards.

'I'll take a look next time I visit,' he says, then we both fall quiet.

I'm not sure if Dad's thinking about Mum, but I am. I'm wondering what it would be like if she was in the kitchen with us right now. I can't remember Mum because she died when I was a baby, but Dad's told me loads about her: how she was loud and loved sharks, and never stopped talking or singing or laughing. She was from France and Dad says she only ever spoke to me in French.

Right now, as the wind rattles the window and I sip my hot chocolate, it's hard to imagine a loud, chatty, shark-loving French lady hanging out with us.

Dad breaks the silence by saying, 'How was school, Sid?'

He asks me this every day, and every day I say the same thing. 'Fine.'

And I suppose it was fine. But just thinking about Penrose Academy, with its packed-lunch-box smell, hundreds of students and hundreds of rules makes my sandwich turn into a fishy lump in my stomach. I'm not really a school girl. I'm more of a graveyard girl.

Luckily, I know what will cheer me up.

'Dad,' I say, grabbing an apple, 'can I go and work on my map?'

'Course you can,' he says.

Dad understands that looking after a miniature world is a full-time job.

Up in my room I spread my map across the floor.

It's massive, bigger than my rug, and made up of lots of pieces of paper all Sellotaped together. I started making it in Year Six when our teacher asked us to draw a map of Fathom and since then it's grown and grown.

To begin with I just put the usual map stuff on it, like roads and houses. Then I drew all the wheelie bins, benches and postboxes, but it still didn't feel complete. I wanted my map to show *everything*. So I started adding memories and thoughts and feelings. That's why there's a red thumb hovering over the arcade – to remind me of the time I got my thumb trapped in a slot machine – and a fox running across the beach with an ice-cream cone in its mouth.

As the rain drums against the window, I pick up a pencil and lose myself in Fathom's twisty streets. I rub out, draw and colour in. When I get to the graveyard and the tiny mausoleum the size of an M&M, I wonder if I should add some gold mist and a door, and maybe a dark figure . . .

My rubber hovers over the mausoleum, but I decide to leave it as it is. It was Marek, I tell myself firmly, and I've already got him on my map cleaning the bells in the church tower.

The last thing I look at is Ezekiel Kittow's headstone. It looks a bit messy because it was so wet when I drew it. I decide to rub out the pencil and do it again. But no matter how hard I rub, the line won't budge. I give up before I rub a hole in my map. I guess I must have used a pen by accident.

Later that evening, when I'm getting ready for bed, I open my bedroom window and let the moonlight and seaweedy air wash over me. The storm has blown itself out. Seagulls call from the rooftops and waves swoosh on the distant beach. Everything feels blissfully calm and back to normal.

I think over what happened in the graveyard, only now I don't see a pirate stepping out of the mausoleum. I see Marek coming out of his shed with a spade tucked under one arm.

Leaving the window open, I get into bed and listen to the sea. I count waves like other people count sheep: *one, two, three, four* . . .

I barely notice when Dad comes in. 'Night, Sid,' he says, tucking the duvet around me. He strokes my hair back from my face, then goes out, shutting the door behind him.

A few minutes later I hear something in the lane outside. It sounds like footsteps. They're heavy and clomping and they stop just below my window. Then I hear something else: a faint drip, drip, dripping sound.

Must be the rain, I think, as I drift off to sleep.

CHAPTER FIVE

When I leave the house the next morning, Fathom has a washed-clean feel. The sky is blue and the air is as refreshing as a Polo mint.

I walk down to the harbour, waving at Mrs Ferrari as she puts the chalkboard outside Mermaids Café. Then I wait by her giant fibreglass ice cream for Zen. He's late, as usual, but this gives me a chance to look at what the storm has left behind.

Waves have thrown shells and sand across the cobblestones and there's seaweed draped over the harbour wall. I'm just about to go and pop one of the fat blobby bits when I hear a voice say, 'Hello!'

I turn round, expecting to see Zen, but there's no one there.

Then I hear the voice again – 'Hello! HELLO!' – and I realise it's coming from somewhere above me.

I look up, and there, perched on Mrs Ferrari's fibreglass ice cream, is a parrot. It's massive and it has brilliant blue feathers, a golden chest and a curved black beak.

'Hello,' it says again, tilting its head to one side.

The voice is so human, so *real*, and the parrot is so beautiful, that for a moment all I can do is stare. It puffs up its feathers, sticks out its black tongue and stares right back at me. Then I make the connection: pirates and parrots . . . they go together like fish and chips or Zen being late for the bus. Nervously I watch as the parrot tucks its head under a wing to scratch at some feathers. Could this parrot be anything to do with the pirate I saw last night?

No, it wasn't a pirate. It was Marek the caretaker. It has to be!

'All right, Sid?'

I spin round to see Zen walking towards me holding a mug of tea. As usual, his shirt is untucked and his shoelaces are undone.

'There's a parrot on the ice cream!' I blurt out.

Zen blinks at me. 'What did you say?'

'There's a massive parrot on the ice cream, Zen, and it spoke to me!'

But when I turn round the parrot has gone.

'It was right here,' I insist, walking around the ice cream then looking up at the sky. 'It was blue and it said "hello"!'

'Awesome!' says Zen enthusiastically. 'It could be an escaped pet . . . or maybe a pirate lost it!'

The laugh that bursts out of me sounds more like a strangled gasp.

Zen frowns. 'Are you OK?'

I still don't want to tell him about last night because I know he'll much prefer the pirate ghost explanation to the Marek one. So instead I say, 'You just reminded me of something. Yesterday, after you left the graveyard, I found a grave in Pirate Corner.'

His eyes light up. 'No way!'

This distracts Zen and as we walk to the bus stop we talk about Ezekiel Kittow's grave. Of course, he wants to see it for himself and I agree to show him after school, before we go looking for the parrot.

The parrot is a lost pet and the pirate was Marek, I tell myself as the bus pulls in and Zen hides his mug in a bush, ready to pick up on the way home.

The parrot is a lost pet and the pirate was Marek, I think as we find a seat and the bus starts to chug up the hill.

I repeat the words like they're a spell and by the time we're walking into school, I'm barely thinking about pirates or parrots. This might also be because I'm trying so hard to act normal.

Zen doesn't care whether anyone at school thinks he's normal. As we walk along the corridor he chats away about how we should play a detective game – I can be Shirley Holmes and he'll be Whatsupson and our first case will be solving the mystery of the missing parrot. He talks loudly, occasionally using his Whatsupson voice which is very posh. He yells, 'Good morrow!' to teachers and students and then – for no reason at all – he jumps up and hangs off a pipe until a passing Year Eleven boy knocks him off with his sports bag.

Zen thinks this is hilarious.

Unlike Zen, I can't be myself at school and instead I try to fade into the background, but that's a really hard thing to do when Zennor Moyo is your best friend.

When we get to my form room, Zen says (still using his Whatsupson voice), 'Will I be seeing you at luncheon, Shirley Holmes?'

Some girls already sitting at their desks look up. 'I think I might go to the library,' I say quickly.

Zen shrugs. 'OK. I'll play football.' Then walks off, calling out a final booming, 'See you later, Shirley!'

In the end Zen and I don't go parrot hunting after school because he remembers that he's supposed to be helping his mum stuff a squirrel. This isn't a particularly unusual thing for Zen to do as his mum and dad run Fathom's Museum of Curiosities, which is full of things like stuffed squirrels.

So we say goodbye outside the museum and I carry on up the lane alone.

I'm nearly at home when I notice a line of wet footprints leading towards the gate of the model village. I follow them, putting my feet into each print. They're massive. Whoever made them must be huge. But when I reach the gate they stop abruptly.

I look around, wondering who they belong to, but there's no one nearby.

I glance down, blink, and just like that, the footprints are gone.

And I don't mean faded. I mean they have totally and utterly vanished.

A cool breeze blows up the lane from the sea. It ruffles my hair and sends a crisp packet skipping past. I crouch down and touch the pavement where the footprints were a moment ago. It's bone dry.

I sit back on my heels and look around again, paying special attention to the dark alleyway opposite my house. Someone must have made those footprints and they can't be far away.

The breeze blows a little stronger and a knot of worry twists inside me. First a pirate steps through a brick wall, then a parrot talks to me, and now footsteps are disappearing.

What is going on?

Nothing, I tell myself as I let myself into the model village. I saw Marek in the graveyard, then an escaped parrot. And wet footprints do disappear. It's called evaporation. It's *science*.

CHAPTER SIX

The next morning, I feel nervous leaving the house.

I stand at the gate and look up and down the lane. Then I glance back into the model village. Luckily the only strange thing I see is a grown man on his hands and knees arranging tiny food on a tiny blanket on a fake beach.

'Bye, Dad,' I say.

He looks up, smiles, and waves a miniature éclair at me.

My footsteps ring out as I walk towards the seafront. I keep my eyes fixed on the patch of blue sea at the end of the lane, and I don't look down a single alleyway. It's a relief when I come out on the harbour with its clanking boats and noisy seagulls.

Zen's late (of course) so I sit on the harbour wall and wait for him. There are no parrots around today, but I do see a tiny crab crawling over the cobblestones. 'What are you doing up here?' I ask, then I pick it up and take it down to the beach.

I'm just letting it go when I hear a deep voice singing something about, 'Whisky, whisky, whisky, oh!'

I look up, and what I see makes my Weetabix churn in my stomach.

Lying in a pile of seaweed, with his arms and legs flung out wide, is a pirate. He looks like he's been dumped there by a wave. He has shaggy hair and a huge beard with bits of green tangled in it. A tricorn hat rests on his stomach and his cracked leather coat is spread out like wings.

The reason I feel sick is because he looks *just* like the man I saw stepping out of the mausoleum . . . and nothing at all like Marek.

For a moment I can't move or breathe or even think. All I can do is stare at the pirate as he sings his noisy song. I take in his dirty boots and sunburnt, scarred skin. His clothes are soaking wet and even his beard is dripping with water.

Then I notice something that makes Weetabixy milk rise up my throat.

Even though it's early, the beach is busy. There are dog walkers and joggers, and a couple of swimmers, but not one of them is doing what I'm doing and staring at the large singing pirate.

A lady with a labradoodle passes by, but she doesn't even glance down when the pirate swishes his cutlass past her labradoodle's nose.

Panic rises inside me. Why is no one looking at the pirate except me? It's like they can't see him!

Then the word that I've been trying to banish comes rushing back to me.

Ghost.

Could the pirate possibly be a ghost? I shake my head. It's impossible. Ghosts don't exist, Dad's always telling me that. They're something Zen and I pretend to catch in the graveyard; they're not part of real life.

Then I wonder if everyone *can* see the pirate, but they're ignoring him because he's being so embarrassing. Grownups do that all the time. There's a woman called Petra who

lives in a shed at the allotments and people ignore her too.

The pirate's voice gets louder. 'Whisky, whisky, WHISKY, OH!' he bellows.

If I knew that just *one* other person could see the pirate, I'd feel so much better.

'AHOY THERE!' I turn to see Zen waving from the top of the steps. He's holding a pile of toast and, as usual, his shirt is untucked and his trainers are undone. 'What are you doing down there, Sid? A poo?'

This is a typical Zen greeting. But for once in my life I'm not in the mood for poo jokes.

I run up the stairs. 'Zen!' I grab hold of him, nearly knocking the toast out of his hands. 'Can you see that pirate down on the beach?'

Zen squints into the sunshine, then says, 'Yeah, I can see him.'

I'm so relieved I want to hug him. 'I know this is going to sound crazy, but I thought he might be a ghost!'

Zen laughs, folding a piece of toast in half and shoving it in his mouth. 'He's not a ghost,' he mumbles, but then he ruins everything by adding, 'He's a zombie.'

'What?'

'He's a pirate zombie,' he says seriously. 'Fathom's full of them. It's an infestation. I can see eight of them on the beach right now, and a couple are sitting outside Mermaid's drinking cappuccinos.'

I glance at Mermaid's. Two men are sitting outside, but they aren't pirate zombies. They're Roger and Seb who run the Cod Father fish and chip shop.

I think I might cry. Zen thinks this is one of our games!

I decide to try one last time. 'Zen, listen to me. There *is* a pirate lying on the beach and I want you to look at him and tell me what he's doing.'

'Yoga,' he says, followed by, 'Come on, Sid. If we don't go now we'll miss the bus.'

CHAPTER SEVEN

As usual, the school bus is crowded and noisy.

In a daze, I follow Zen on board then we sit behind three other Year Seven students, Owen Kidd, Kezia and Lara. Straight away Zen starts telling me about his latest addition to his Minecraft town, Lotl-Land – a cheese cave full of cats. I nod and smile, but I don't take anything in. All I can think about is the pirate.

Why was I the only person who could see him? I can just about believe the other people on the beach were ignoring him but his loud singing wouldn't bother Zen.

Zen is quite literally embarrassed by nothing. Once, in Year Two, he accidentally took off his pants when he was getting changed for PE. If I had done that I would have refused to go to school ever again, but Zen thought it was hilarious. In fact he still regularly says to me, 'Hey, Sid, remember when I took my pants off in Year Two?'

No, Zen wouldn't care how embarrassing the pirate was being. If he'd seen him on the beach he'd have marched down to say hello. Then I remember Zen's glasses. He's supposed to wear them every day so he can see the board, but he never does.

'Forgotten your glasses, Zen?' I ask.

'Glasses are for nerds like you, Sid, not for super cool dudes like me,' he says, followed by, 'Yeah. I've lost them. Don't tell my mum.'

I smile as I realise what this means. Perhaps the joggers and dog walkers were ignoring the pirate because he was being embarrassing and Zen really couldn't see him!

This is such a reassuring thought that in lesson one, history, I do something unheard of.

I put my hand up.

I never put my hand up at school because I hate people looking at me, but today it's worth it because Mr Chowdhury is talking about Pirate Day.

'Now as many of you know,' he says, standing in his favourite position with his arms folded and his thumbs tucked into his armpits, 'in three weeks' time, one of our local villages, Fathom, will be celebrating Pirate Day. This is a special day when everyone who lives in Fathom dresses up as a pirate and parades through the streets.'

Well, not quite everyone, I think. I used to love taking part in the parade, but a few years ago, around the same time I stopped putting my hand up in class, I realised I didn't want to dress up any more. So this year, just like last year, I'll be wearing my favourite stripy jumper and helping Dad in the model village.

Mr Chowdhury carries on. 'There's a Yo-Ho-Ho-ing competition, sea shanties and one person is crowned Pirate of the Year. Now, can anyone tell us a bit more about it? Perhaps one of the students who lives in Fathom?' He looks expectantly around the room.

Owen Kidd puts his hand up and tells us that his sister's boyfriend was *nearly* Pirate of the Year, but he was beaten by someone with a real beard. Then Max says that the youngest ever Pirate of the Year was eighteen.

'Anyone else got something to share?' asks Mr Chowdhury, hopefully.

I *totally* have something to share. My mum was Pirate of the Year not once but *three times*, which is a Fathom record. Two of her red sashes hold back the curtains in our living room and the third hangs over my bed. *Laure Benoit-Jones*, it says, *Pirate of the Year 2003*.

My mouth goes dry as my hand leaves my lap and creeps above the level of the desk. I'm going to do this. I'm going to put my hand up and tell the class about my mum, Laure Benoit-Jones, pirate extraordinaire!

'No more Pirate Day facts?' asks Mr Chowdhury.

Boom! My hand is totally up and my face is as red as one of Mum's sashes.

'No?' says Mr Chowdhury, his eyes skipping over my hand. 'OK, in that case please can you all answer the questions on the board.'

He hasn't noticed me! My hand shoots down and I feel a rush of relief, but only for a second. Mum was a legend. I should have jumped to my feet and shouted out, 'I've got something to share, Mr Chowdhury!'

But I didn't. Because I'm a coward.

It's hard to concentrate when you're feeling like a coward, and perhaps that's why my eyes drift to the window. I stare at the empty playground. I watch as a water bottle rolls across the concrete then gets stuck in the fence. Then I see a big blue parrot swoop past the window.

I gasp so loud that Mr Chowdhury looks up. 'What is it, Sid?'

Without thinking, I blurt out, 'I just saw a parrot!' *Again*, I add in my head.

Laughter breaks out across the room, and I feel my cheeks burn.

'All right, that's enough,' says Mr Chowdhury. 'Sid probably saw a parakeet. There are plenty of them in London and I expect one found its way down here.'

'Yeah, *probably*,' says a voice behind me, and I know without turning round that it's Owen Kidd. Ever since I got the same pencil case as Owen in Year Three he's never liked me. 'Weirdo,' he whispers, just loud enough for me to hear.

I stare at my book. A parakeet, that's what Mr Chowdhury said I saw, but I know what parakeets look like. They're small and green, but the parrot I saw was a huge splash of tropical blue and yellow flying across our playground. And it looked *exactly* like the sort of parrot that would belong to a pirate.

CHAPTER EIGHT

When I walk out on to the field at lunchtime, the first thing I see is the parrot sitting on the roof of the tuckshop. Its chest is bright yellow and it's as big as a cat, but no one is looking at it except me.

Sweat prickles my skin as it turns to look at me, then says, 'Hello,' in a soft, croaky voice.

Next it opens its wings and flies towards me. In a panic, I start to run. I head towards the netball pitches, but I'm only halfway across the field when the parrot lands on my shoulder with a great flapping of its wings. I stand there, hunched over. The parrot is big and it's clinging to me with sharp claws. It should feel heavy and painful, but I can't feel a thing. In fact, if I hadn't seen the parrot land, I wouldn't know it was there!

44

The parrot opens its beak and makes a clicking sound with its tongue. 'Hello,' it says again.

'Go away!' I whisper.

Slowly but surely, the parrot shakes its head. So I try to push it off my shoulder . . . and my hand goes straight through it. I can't describe how shocking this is. I'm expecting to feel soft feathers, but instead my fingers touch nothing at all and I'm left with an icy sensation in my hand.

Then the chill spreads through my whole body because not only is no one on the playground looking at the massive parrot on my shoulder, I realise that it's a bit see-through. When I squint I can see two girls doing a TikTok dance on the other side of its plump chest.

'Are you a . . . *ghost?*' I whisper.

The parrot whistles, clicks a few times, then screeches, 'GHOST!'

'No, no, no,' I say, shaking my head.

'No, no, no!' repeats the parrot.

'Shut up,' I hiss.

'*Shut up!*' goes the parrot.

'SHUT UP!' I yell.

And that's when I notice that a boy from my form is

staring at me. This makes sense. I'm hunched over with my arm sticking out and I'm screaming at my shoulder. I stand up quickly. The parrot beats its wings but manages to cling on.

Then, doing my best to act like I *don't* have a ghost parrot sitting on my shoulder, I walk across the playground.

The parrot stays with me for the rest of lunchtime. It watches the other children, grooms its feathers and tries to groom me. When this happens, its entire beak disappears inside my head and it feels like an ice cube has been pressed into my skull.

'Please don't do that,' I whisper.

I try to ignore the parrot, but it's hard because it's just so chatty.

'Hello!' it says, again and again, occasionally adding another word, like 'rum', 'bully' and, strangely, 'bum', although it only says this when it gets carried away and says 'rum' and 'bully' too close together.

In the end it becomes so stressful that I go and look for Zen. I can't keep this to myself any more. I have to tell him what's going on.

I find him playing football on the bottom field, but after a few minutes of watching from the sidelines, I realise I can't say anything to Zen because, just like everyone else, he can't see the parrot. At one point he dribbles the ball right past me, but all he does is shout, 'Hey, Sidalangadingdong!'

Now here's the thing about Zennor Moyo. He might pretend plastic bags are ghosts and forget to tie up his shoelaces, but he's super clever. He's in top set for everything and can remember every sum, spelling and French word he's ever been taught. Once, at Fathom

47

Primary, our teacher asked us what we'd done at the weekend and Zen said he'd built a computer *and* read a book.

If I call him over and *insist* that a parrot is sitting on my shoulder, he'll be really nice about it, but he won't believe me. He'll think there's something wrong with me.

I remember the word Owen whispered to me in history: *weirdo*. I'm not exactly overloaded with friends and I really don't want Zen thinking I'm a weirdo too. So before I do something I regret, I turn away from the football game and walk across the field.

'Bully Sid Rum Bum Bully Sid!' squawks the parrot as I pass the netball pitches. 'Bully Bully Rum Bum!' it says as I sit on the bench in the quiet corner, feeling dizzy with worry and pretending to read a book.

Eventually, lunchtime comes to an end. I walk towards the main building, wondering how I'm going to get through geography, but when I get to the door, the parrot flies away.

I'm so relieved that I walk into geography with a massive smile on my face.

'Someone looks happy today!' says Mr Lawrence.

That's because someone just got rid of her ghost parrot!

CHAPTER NINE

To my relief the parrot stays away for the rest of the day.

If I'm jumpy on the school bus, Zen doesn't notice. Perhaps that's because he's too busy talking about Pirate Day. I force myself to stop looking nervously out of the window for parrots and concentrate on what he's saying.

'Mum's ordered me a beard from Poland,' he says. 'It's made of yak's wool and it's green. Are you sure you don't want to dress up with me, Sid?'

'I can't,' I say. 'Dad needs my help at the model village.' But Zen and I both know that Dad would love to see me take part in the parade, just like I used to.

'Is it because my beard is green?' Zen asks.

'No. I love green.'

But it is. A bit. If I'm standing next to Zen and he's

wearing a green beard then everyone will stare. Zen would love this, but I wouldn't. I know how boring this makes me sound so instead I say, 'Sorry. It's the busiest day of the year. Dad needs me.'

Zen keeps up his beard campaign all the way back to Fathom.

'How about a moustache?' he says as we're getting off the bus. 'Just a little one, or some fluffy sideburns?'

But I'm hardly listening because I've just noticed the parrot is sitting on a lamp post, waiting for me. My heart sinks.

'Sid?' Zen nudges me. 'What are you looking at?'

'Clouds,' I say, tearing my eyes away from the parrot. 'There are a lot in the sky.'

'RUM! BUM! BULLY! BUM!' yells the parrot, making me wince.

'Sid, are you OK?' asks Zen. 'You're acting a bit weird.'

'RUM! BUM! BULLY!' calls the parrot.

I force myself to smile. 'I'm fine,' I say, 'just –'

At that moment the parrot dives off the bus shelter and flies straight towards me. I throw my arms above my head and duck to one side.

When I straighten up, Zen is smiling and frowning at the same time. 'Sid, what *are* you doing?'

'Dancing,' I say, and wave my arms around a bit more, ducking from side to side.

Zen laughs and starts to join in, copying my terrible dance. All this is your fault! I think, glaring at the parrot.

Then Zen says, 'Come on. Let's go to the graveyard. You can show me that grave you found.'

The graveyard? There's no way I can go there! The parrot will follow me, just like at school, and talk to me and stick its beak in my head. I can't ignore all that and play with Zen at the same time. I feel like I might cry. I love the graveyard, but I can't go there because I'm being haunted by a stupid bird!

Desperately I try to think of an excuse, but in the end the parrot saves me the trouble by flying through Zen's head.

It's a bizarre sight and it makes Zen clutch his head, double over and groan. Then he starts shivering. Now it's my turn to ask him if he's all right.

'No, not really,' he says through chattering teeth. 'I don't feel too good, Sid. I'm cold. *Really cold.* Perhaps I should go home.' Still holding his head, he turns and walks towards the seafront, muttering, 'Sorry . . . I'm going to get into my Snuggy and work on Lotl-Land . . . See you tomorrow.'

I wait until he's gone, then I turn to look at the parrot who is now back on the roof of the lamp post, nibbling its foot. I check no one is nearby, then I hiss, 'Well? What do you want?'

'BONES!' it screeches. Then it flies down the lane towards the graveyard.

CHAPTER TEN

Now I might be scared of putting my hand up in lessons, Owen Kidd and parading through the village next to a boy wearing a green beard, but when I see the parrot fly through the graveyard gates I don't hesitate. I follow it, even though I'm almost certain it's leading me to a ghost pirate.

You see, I have questions that need answering. Like, how come I'm the only person who can see him and his parrot? And why won't the parrot leave me alone?

I step cautiously between the graves, my eyes flicking into the darkest corners. When I find myself by Mum's headstump, I give the shark's fin a tighter squeeze than usual, then clear away a few weeds.

'Sorry I didn't visit yesterday,' I say.

Actually, I'm not sorry. Mum's dead. She won't mind.

Really I'm putting off the moment when I have to confront the pirate.

I hear a low squawk and look up to see the parrot sitting on the wall that separates the graveyard from the beach. Nearby, sticking out between two headstones, is a pair of big black boots.

My stomach lurches, but I'm not backing away now. Curling my hands into fists, I force myself to walk forward. The pirate is lying against a large monument belonging to a Willoughby Hawke. I feel for my map under my jumper. I'm going to check that monument is there when I get home. I don't think I can trust anything to be where it's supposed to be any more.

The pirate's chin is tucked against his chest and his hat is tipped forward. He looks like he's asleep. Do ghosts sleep? I wonder as I step closer. I watch as his beard rises and falls. And if he's a ghost, why is he breathing?

From where I'm standing, I can see that the green stuff woven into his black beard is actually seaweed. He's got stones and shells tangled in there too. Just like this morning, his clothes are soaking wet. Scars crisscross his face and his skin is brown from the sun. A single glittering

54

diamond dangles from his right ear. It sparkles like the sea.

I've seen plenty of pirates on TV and walking round Fathom on Pirate Day, but I've never seen one like this, one that looks *real*. I can even smell him. The graveyard usually smells of leaves and the sea, but right now a pong of smoke, wet wool and leather is drifting over me.

The pirate moves, scratching his beard, and for a moment I can see through him, just like I could with the parrot. I watch a blackbird on the other side of his stomach pecking at the grass.

Suddenly the pirate pushes back his hat, fixes me with a pair of dark eyes, and smiles, showing a mouthful of crooked teeth. Then in a voice as deep as the sea, he growls, 'Sid, m'lad, I knew you'd come!'

CHAPTER ELEVEN

I gasp and take a step back. 'You know my name!'

'Of course I know your name,' he says, struggling into a sitting position. 'Don't you think I'd want to find out the name of the person who set me free? You're Sidonie May Jones, my little saviour!'

'I'm your *what*?'

'My saviour, my hero! Now, allow me to introduce myself. The name's Ezekiel Kittow, but ever since I set foot on a ship I've been known as Bones, so you might as well call me that.'

He sticks out a great big paw of a hand and I stare at it. What does he expect me to do? Shake it?

He raises one eyebrow. 'Oh no, that won't work, will it?'

A wave of panic sweeps through me. Ezekiel Kittow

was the name I copied off the headstone, the name of a man who died over *three hundred years ago*!

'You're a pirate,' I manage to say, my eyes darting from his tricorn hat to his diamond earring.

Bones winces. 'Personally I would describe myself as a *privateer*, and for much of my life I worked in the king's navy. But, yes, occasionally, once or twice, when I've had no choice in the matter, I have been known to dabble in the ways of a pirate.'

'And you're . . .' I pause, hardly able to believe what I'm about to say next, ' . . . a *ghost?*'

He nods. 'That's right. I'm dead as a doornail. I was captain of a ship called the *Black Gannet* that went down somewhere over yonder.' He waves in the direction of the sea.

Everyone in Fathom has heard of the *Black Gannet*. It was a ship that was wrecked years ago, with all lives lost.

'Is that why you're so wet?' I say.

Water drips from the corners of his hat and pools around his feet. It squelches as he looks down at himself. 'I suppose it must be. You'd have thought I'd have dried out by now!' He laughs, and the parrot joins in with a shrill, 'Ha ha ha!'

57

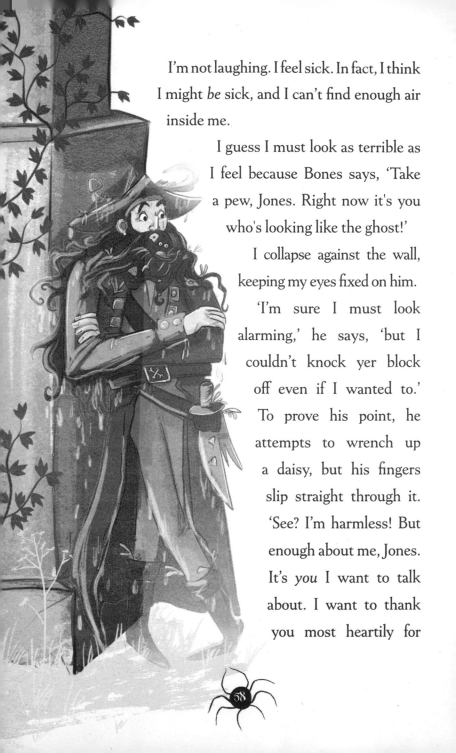

I'm not laughing. I feel sick. In fact, I think I might *be* sick, and I can't find enough air inside me.

I guess I must look as terrible as I feel because Bones says, 'Take a pew, Jones. Right now it's you who's looking like the ghost!'

I collapse against the wall, keeping my eyes fixed on him.

'I'm sure I must look alarming,' he says, 'but I couldn't knock yer block off even if I wanted to.' To prove his point, he attempts to wrench up a daisy, but his fingers slip straight through it. 'See? I'm harmless! But enough about me, Jones. It's *you* I want to talk about. I want to thank you most heartily for setting me free. That was mighty powerful magic you used. What are you? A witch? A sorceress? Some kind of large piskie?'

I haven't got a clue what he's talking about, but there's one thing I need to clear up straight away. 'Look, Mr Kittow, Bones, there's been some sort of mistake. I didn't set you free from anywhere.'

He looks outraged. 'Don't tell lies, girl, I watched you do it with my very own eyes! While the sky was torn asunder with lightning, you placed a gift most precious upon my grave, then wrote my name in *blood*. You broke the spell, Jones. You set me free!'

With a feeling of dread I think back to the moment when lightning flashed down and I used my new red gel pen to write the letters EK on my map. 'I didn't write your name in blood,' I say. 'I used a gel pen, and I definitely didn't give you a gift most precious.'

He splutters. 'Then what would you call that bar of solid gold you left on my headstone?'

'A Crunchie,' I say. 'And it's not solid gold. It's made of chocolate and honeycomb, and I didn't mean to leave it there!'

'Details, Jones, details,' he growls. 'All that matters is that you broke the spell, the door opened and Old Scratch had no choice but to let me walk out of the Halfway House, and for that I am eternally grateful.' He sweeps his hat off his head and shows me the top of his greasy head. 'Thank you, Sid, m'lad.'

'Please,' I say desperately. 'Put your hat back on and stop saying thank you because I didn't mean to set you free from anywhere! You need to go back into that place, whatever it's called –'

'– The Halfway House,' volunteers Bones.

'That's it. Go back in there and tell Old Whatsisname –'

'Scratch.'

'Right, tell Old Scratch that there's been a terrible mistake!'

Bones settles back against the monument, tilts his face to the sky and closes his eyes. If I didn't know better, I'd say he was sunbathing. 'Well, I'm very sorry, Jones, but I cannot do that.'

'Why not?'

He pushes his hat back and fixes me with one beady eye. 'Because I don't want to!'

What I should do?

Most of all I want to run home and tell Dad everything that's happened, but there's no way he'd believe me. I can just imagine his face if I told him that I'd been talking to a pirate ghost *and* his parrot. At first he'd think I was joking, but if I insisted then he'd get seriously worried. He might go and talk to my teachers at school or take me to the doctor's.

No, I'm going to have to sort this out on my own. Somehow I've got to persuade Bones and his parrot to go back into the Halfway House.

'Where exactly is the Halfway House?' I ask, although I've got a feeling I already know.

'That-a-way,' says Bones, jerking a thumb over his shoulder.

For the first time since I set foot in the graveyard, I let myself look at the mausoleum. Instantly the dizzy feeling come sweeping back.

It's changed. It still looks like a witch's house from a fairy tale, but now a lantern flickers over a sturdy wooden door – a door that didn't exist yesterday – and there are windows too. A sign has appeared on the wall with the words 'Halfway House' painted on it in bright gold letters.

'Is it a pub?' I ask.

'Of sorts,' replies Bones. 'It has the appearance of one, but very little ale or good cheer flows there.'

Sweat prickles the back of my neck as I listen to the squeak of the lantern's chain. Then I hear something else . . . A murmur of voices.

Reluctantly, my eyes are drawn to one of the windows. A small pale face is staring back at me. It's a boy with scruffy hair and blue shadows round his eyes. The moment he sees me, his face lights up and he shouts something I can't hear. Suddenly more faces appear at the windows, too many to count, and they are all staring at me with hungry eyes. Then they start pointing and waving, all desperate to get my attention.

Heart thumping, I turn away. 'Those people looking at me,' I say. 'Are they *all* ghosts?'

Bones nods. 'That's right, and they are hoping you will use your wondrous magic to set them free!'

'And that place, the Halfway House. Has it always been there?' I think back to the hours I've spent playing in the graveyard, often next to the mausoleum.

'Of course,' says Bones. 'It been there for ever, but normal folk cannot see it.'

I sneak another glance at the Halfway House. The lantern glows, the writing on the sign gleams, and the faces behind the glass smile back at me. It is frightening and overwhelming . . . but also incredible, like something from a book come to life. *Wondrous magic.*

'So how come I *can* see it?'

Bones gives a throaty chuckle. 'Because you, Sidonie May Jones, are not normal.' Then a second later he adds, 'I believe you might be a witch.'

I feel like I've been hit in the stomach. 'A *witch*?'

He shrugs his big shoulders. 'It is simply a word meaning "magical", and that is what you are.'

I start to back away as panic builds up inside me. 'No,' I say, shaking my head. 'I'm not magical. I'm just a girl. I'm *ordinary*.'

64

He fixes me with his dark eyes. 'And yet here you are, talking to a ghost.'

I bump against a headstone. 'Please, I need you to go away.'

Suddenly Bones loses his smile and looks deadly serious. 'That is my dearest wish, Jones. But to do that, I need your help.'

'I can't help you!'

'Why not?' His words come back, quick as a flash.

'Because you're a *ghost*.'

For a moment, Bones and I stare at each other. His eyes narrow and his smile disappears. 'Fine. But know this, Sidonie Jones. Without your help I am stuck here and I can never go away.'

He pauses and for a moment all is quiet in the graveyard. Even the voices coming from the Halfway House fade away.

'What . . . *never*?' I try to imagine Bones wandering around Fathom for the rest of my life.

'Never, ever,' he says in his gruff voice. 'I will try to keep out of your hair, but Elizabeth here . . .' He nods towards the parrot. 'Well, let's just say she is a bit harder to control.'

On cue Elizabeth flies off the wall and lands on my shoulder. Then she cocks her head to one side and screeches, 'RUM, BUM, BULLY, BUM, RUM, BUM!' in my face.

'She followed me to school,' I whisper.

The grin appears again on Bones's lined face. 'She'll do that. She likes you. She likes all weird folk.' He whispers these last two words, as if they are a secret.

'No,' I say, shaking my head. 'Don't call me that . . .' Elizabeth gives a final squawk and flies into the air. Then, before he can say another word, I turn and hurry out of the graveyard.

CHAPTER TWELVE

Just like yesterday, I run all the way home.

Luckily Dad's still in the kiosk so he doesn't see me burst into the model village, my face pale and sweaty. I let myself into the house and go straight to my bedroom. Then I crawl under the duvet, and I lie there, curled up and trembling as I try to work out what is going on.

If Bones is telling the truth, then I've released him from some sort of ghost pub where he's been held prisoner and now he wants my help. But I don't want to help him. I don't want to see him or have anything to do with him!

Panic races through me as I imagine how I'm going to leave the house tomorrow knowing that, at any moment, Bones or Elizabeth could appear. Then I remember that they are ghosts and they could walk straight through the front door and up the stairs!

And why did Bones say I was a magical? I'm short, I've got brown hair and glasses, and I don't even know my times tables. There is nothing magical about me at all.

I peek out from under my duvet and see my velvet cloak hanging on the back of my bedroom door. I used to wear it when I played in the graveyard with Zen. Looking at it now, I can see that it is a tiny bit witch-like, but I am never putting it on again. Then I see my books about ghosts and my crystal collection and the dreamcatcher I've got hanging by the window.

All kids like things like that, I tell myself, but even so I jump out of bed and stuff the cloak and dreamcatcher under my bed. Then I get changed into my most normal clothes: my skinny jeans and cropped T-shirt with 'Positive Vibes Only' written on it. I look at myself in the mirror and wonder if I should grow my hair long so that I can wear scrunchies, and maybe I should ask Dad if I can get smaller glasses, ones that make me look less owl-like. And as I look at myself, a plan begins to form in my mind.

I will ignore Bones and Elizabeth. If I see them, I will

look the other way. If Elizabeth speaks to me, I will pretend I can't hear her. What Bones doesn't know is that I'm well trained in ignoring people. I've been ignoring Owen Kidd for years!

Without thinking, I find myself getting out my map and adding Bones and Elizabeth to it. I put Bones in the graveyard and Elizabeth on Mrs Ferrari's ice cream, and I colour them in carefully, using my brightest blue pencil for Elizabeth's feathers. As I do all this, I start to feel better. Bones and Elizabeth. They're just a part of Fathom, like Zen and Mrs Ferrari. So what if they're ghosts? Like Bones said, he couldn't knock my block off even if he wanted to.

Soon my map has worked its calming magic and when Dad calls me down to dinner not one bit of me is trembling.

Bring it on, Ezekiel 'Bones' Kittow, I think as I walk downstairs and Dad proudly hands me cheese on toast with cherry tomato eyes and a red pepper smile. Because I am not going to help you!

CHAPTER THIRTEEN

The next morning I'm feeling a little less brave.

When I leave the model village, I scurry down the lane, keeping my eyes glued to the pavement. While I wait for Zen, I stare at my shoes. I'm thinking that if I can't see Bones or Elizabeth, then they can't bother me. But not looking anywhere except at my feet is harder than I thought. Seagulls are flapping past and polystyrene crates of slippery fish are being dumped outside the Admiral Benbow pub. All around me there are intriguing sounds and flashes of movement.

It's a relief when Zen finally turns up and we can set off towards the bus stop. I manage to stare at my feet all the way along the seafront until I hear the jingly jangly music coming from the roundabout. I love the roundabout.

It's run by this man called Roundabout Tommy and it has all these colourful animals on it – horses, zebras, lions – that go galloping around on twisty poles.

'Tommy's got his head inside a hippo,' says Zen.

And of course, straight away I look up. There's Roundabout Tommy, sanding down a hippo's big white teeth, and there's Bones perched on a black swan.

Round and round he goes, up and down. His filthy leather coat flies out behind him and his equally filthy beard blows in the wind. Perched on the swan's head is Elizabeth. I've been dreading seeing Bones, but now that's it's happened it's not so bad. Perhaps that's because he looks so happy. He smiles as he holds on tight to the swan's neck.

Zen nudges me. 'Shall we ask Tommy if we can have a free ride?'

'No way,' I say, pulling him up the hill. 'Come on. The bus is coming.'

All day at school I'm on tenterhooks. When I'm in lessons my eyes keep darting between the door and the windows, looking for any sign of feathers or beards. During break and lunchtime, I hide in the girls' toilets. They're so disgusting I'm guessing that even Bones, a man who's endured life at sea *and* being trapped inside a pub for three hundred years, would avoid them.

Luckily they both stay away all day, and there's no sign of them when Zen and I get off the bus. Even so, I can't bring myself to go inside the graveyard. What if Bones is lying against the monument waiting for me? What if the ghosts are still standing at the windows, waving?

'I think I'm going to go home,' I say to Zen when we reach the gates. 'I've got homework to do.'

He laughs. 'Yeah, right!'

'I've got loads,' I insist. 'Maths and English and French and –'

'Nerd studies?' he suggests, but in the end he accepts that for the first time in my life I want to do homework on a Friday.

On Saturday I spot Bones standing outside the Co-op reading the notices stuck in the window and on Sunday I come across him stepping in and out of the fibreglass ice cream, making his face appear in the swirl of raspberry ripple.

'Sid, m'lad!' he cries when he sees me, and just for a second I think I might laugh because, essentially, an ice cream is talking to me.

72

But I don't. I ignore him and walk straight back to the model village.

Then on Monday Dad sends me to the Co-op to buy potato waffles and I find Bones in the freezer section. Literally. He's standing inside one of the compartments.

He looks down at me. 'Hello!' he says, but he doesn't move or explain what he's doing there. Annoyingly, I want to know, but there's no way I'm going to speak to him. Instead I stick my hand through his boots to grab the potato waffles. Icy cold

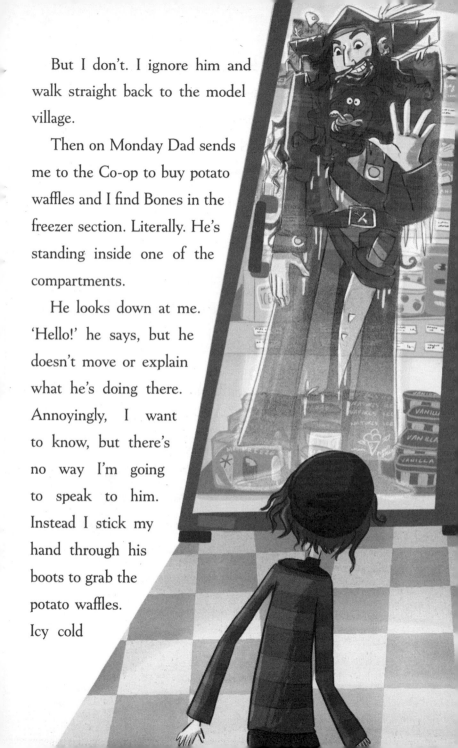

rushes up my arm. I gasp, but I don't let go of the waffles.

'Oooh,' says Bones, eyeing the packet. 'Now what might those be, Jones?'

'Waf–' I start to say, then I remember that I'm trying to be normal and it's not normal to talk to a freezer. Quickly I pay for my potato waffles and get out of there.

That evening I find him in Dad's kiosk.

'Get out!' I say, outraged.

'But it's raining,' he says. 'I'm harming no one in here.'

'I didn't know ghosts could feel the rain.' The words are out of my mouth before I realise what I'm doing. I grab a Twix and go, slamming the door behind me.

After this I see Bones each day on my way to and from the bus stop. Zen's given up asking me to go to the graveyard, but Bones still manages to pop up in the most surprising places: sitting on a bench outside the Benbow pub, bobbing around in the harbour in a rowing boat. He even manages to squeeze himself inside one of the toy-grabbing games at the arcade.

But on Thursday morning, as I walk to the bus stop, I don't see him at all.

To be honest, this makes me feel more nervous than

74

relieved and I sit on the bus next to Zen, wishing the bus would hurry up and leave.

I try to distract myself by tuning into Owen, Lara and Kezia's conversation. They're on the back row, having an argument about who should sit next to the seagull-poo-covered window.

Suddenly Owen calls out, 'Hey, Sid, remember when that seagull pooed on your head and you smelled like a seagull's bum?'

Yes, I do remember. Because even though it happened in Year Three, Owen reminds me about it every few weeks.

'Do you want me to tell him that his face *looks* like a seagull's bum?' asks Zen.

I shake my head. I've learnt that if you want Owen to shut up, it's best to ignore him.

'Hey, Sid!' Owen shouts again. 'Remember when you lost your voice for a whole term?'

I didn't lose my voice. Owen pretended my voice was too quiet to hear. He managed to get the rest of the class to join in, even the supply teacher.

'Hey, Sid!' he shouts, making Zen groan. 'Remember

when I drank out of your water bottle and caught Siditis and became really boring?'

'Stop being so horrible, Owen,' says Lara, coming to my defence. But right now I don't care what Owen Kidd says because I've just seen Bones strolling up the hill towards the waiting bus.

A man with a toddler climbs on board and the doors hiss shut. Go, go, go! I think, but before the bus can pull away Bones has stepped through the closed doors.

I sink down in my seat and watch out of the corner of my eye as Bones tips his hat at the bus driver and strolls down the centre aisle. Then, with a splutter of the engine, the bus starts to rumble up the hill.

'*God's teeth!*' Bones roars as the bus sways from side to side. 'What is happening?' The bus swings round a corner and Bones cries out as he loses his balance and shoves an arm through an old lady's head. 'I beg your pardon, mistress!' he says, bowing deeply.

The old lady shivers and winds her scarf tighter around her neck.

Bones continues staggering down the aisle, pausing to hiss, 'What is this beast we are trapped in, Jones?'

I scowl, and look away, and at that exact moment, the driver hits the brakes and Bones shoots past me. I turn round just in time to see him crash headfirst into Owen Kidd's stomach.

Owen does a dramatic whole-body shudder and yells, 'Cold! Cold!' Meanwhile Bones picks himself up and plonks himself down in an empty seat.

It takes almost a minute for Owen to get himself under control. When he finally stops shivering, he sees me watching him, and says, 'What are you looking at?'

'You, you idiot,' says Kezia. 'Because you just wobbled like a jellyfish and shouted, "Cold! Cold!"'

'Cold! Cold!' goes Lara, imitating Owen's dramatic howl.

'What's going on?' asks Zen.

'Nothing,' I say. 'Owen's cold.'

For the rest of the journey Kezia and Lara yell, 'Cold! Cold!' every few minutes, driving Owen wild and making the driver yell at them to 'Shut up or get off the bus!' And just for a while, perhaps ten minutes or so, I think it's OK being haunted.

But that all changes when Bones follows me into school.

CHAPTER FOURTEEN

The first thing I see when we file into assembly is Bones standing on the stage next to our head teacher, Mrs Drake. They both have their arms folded and matching stern expressions.

As Mrs Drake starts to speak, Bones joins in, muttering, 'Hear, hear!' when he agrees with what she's said and tutting when she mentions a rule that has been broken. He gets particularly angry when she says that some students have been stealing items out of lunchboxes.

'Now, it might have begun as a game,' says Mrs Drake, 'but it needs to stop.'

'Quite right!' Bones bellows. 'Stealing? Whatever next!' Coming from a pirate, this seems a bit hypocritical, until he yells out, 'You never rob from your crew! Never! You hear me?'

'Yesterday,' continues Mrs Drake, 'Violet Vessey had a Penguin *and* a packet of Mini Cheddars taken from her bag. I'd like to remind you that at Penrose Academy, the consequence for stealing is –'

'HANGING!' bellows Jones.

'A one-day internal suspension,' says Mrs Drake.

Bones looks stunned. 'What?'

But Mrs Drake has finished telling us off and is now ushering Jay Beeney on to the stage to play his clarinet.

I'm the only person in the hall who gets to hear Bones's song. I guess it's a sea shanty. He strides around the stage, singing or, rather, shouting at the top of his voice, slapping his thighs and occasionally throwing an arm around Mrs Drake. Each time he does this she shivers and it looks like Jay's clarinet playing is repulsing her.

It is quite shrill.

For the rest of assembly, Bones sits next to me, making me shiver and applauding loudly when the girls' netball team are given a trophy.

Unfortunately, assembly isn't enough school for Bones and he hangs around for the whole day. To begin with, I think he's behaving himself. He doesn't speak to me

79

during science, just sits quietly watching a film about habitats, and during break he drifts around the playground making people cold. But he can't resist saying something in art.

He's looking over my shoulder, watching as I decorate my clay pot, when he whispers, 'That looks like the nose that belonged to a sailor we called Grog Blossom Jim, and that is not a compliment, Sid, m'lad.'

'I'm a girl!' I shout at the top of my voice.

It's only when the whole room falls silent that I realise what I've done. My cheeks burn as everyone turns to look at me. The silence is broken when Miss Haines whoops and starts to clap, saying, 'Say it loud and say it proud, Sid. Good for you!'

CHAPTER FIFTEEN

It's been a stressful day, but the worst is yet to come.

Dad has made an apple crumble for tea, and he's just putting a scoop of ice cream into my bowl when Bones runs through the door (literally).

'Jones!' he cries, skidding to a halt in the middle of the kitchen. 'There you are. I have the most urgent enquiry!'

This is the first time I've ever seen Bones in my house and it's a disturbing sight. He's so tall that his head almost touches the ceiling and the delicious smell of crumble has been overwhelmed by his smoky, leathery pong. Water drips off him, only to land on the floorboards and vanish a moment later. I glare at him, willing him to get the message and go away.

'Everything all right, Sid?' asks Dad.

'Yeah . . . great!' I say, pulling my eyes away from Bones and picking up my spoon.

Bones plonks himself on the bench next to Dad, looking like he's come to tea.

'Now listen close, Jones,' he says, leaning over the table and putting his elbow in my pudding. 'What manner of food is being sold at Curry Magic? The smells drifting from inside are mouth-watering. I believe some sort of banquet is being prepared and I am most curious about it. I have never smelled anything so heavenly in my life!' He looks at me expectantly.

Obviously I can't reply so instead I mouth, 'Go away.'

'What was that, Sid?' says Dad. 'Speak up!'

'Indeed,' says Bones. 'I never could stand a wiffle waffler.'

'Oh . . .' I say, not sure who to look at. 'I was just thinking that we should go away somewhere.'

Dad laughs. 'Well . . . maybe. What's brought this on?'

I shoot a glance at Bones. 'I don't know. All of a sudden I'd like to GO AWAY, that's all.'

Dad ignores the weird way I'm talking and seriously considers the question. 'Well, it's hard to leave the model village, but why not? I've always fancied Scotland . . . Or maybe we should visit your nan and grandad in France.'

Bones doesn't budge. 'Out with it, Jones,' he says. 'What the devil is happening at Curry Magic?'

He's obviously not going to go anywhere until I tell him, so I jump to my feet and say, 'Dad, can I go and see Zen?'

'Aren't you going to eat your pudding first?'

'I'll have it later,' I say, then I grab my coat and walk out of the house with Bones following me like a big dark shadow.

Once we're out on the lane, he strides along next to me, his hands shoved deep in his pockets. 'Now where might we be going, Jones? For a stroll along the Cockle? To the Benbow for a tot of rum? Along to Curry Magic to join in the feast?'

I look around to check no one is nearby, then I hiss, 'No! I'm taking you to a place where no one ever goes.'

'Righto!' he says cheerfully, then he does a quick whistle and Elizabeth flies out of an alleyway and lands on his shoulder.

I try to hurry Bones along as we walk through Fathom's winding streets, but it's hard because he keeps getting distracted.

'Now what might they be?' he says when a car drives past the end of the lane. 'I've seen many of them around these past few days.'

'They're cars,' I say quickly.

'Caaaarrrrs.' Bones rolls the word around in his mouth, savouring it. 'Yes, I've heard mention of *caaars* in the Halfway House, but I imagined them less shiny, more carriage-like in appearance. Was that a big car we were riding in today?'

'No, it was a bus,' I mutter.

'*Bussssss*,' he says, delighted. Suddenly he stops and stares into the window of a cottage. 'And I am mighty curious about these. What do you call them, Sid?'

He's gazing at a TV. Bright images of cartoon trains light up the room. Bones steps closer and closer to the window until his head vanishes through the glass. I desperately want to grab hold of him and pull him out, but I can't do that because my hands will go straight through him.

'Bones, get out of there!'

He reappears with a smile on his face. 'It's like magic! A picture made up of hundreds of other pictures, and all moving so fast I can hardly make sense of them . . . and the colours!'

'It's not magic, it's a TV,' I say, 'and you were watching *Thomas the Tank Engine*. Now, please, can we hurry up?'

'*Thomas the Tank Engine* . . .' he marvels. 'Is he a bus?'

I refuse to answer. Instead I march ahead, leading Bones and Elizabeth to a line of fishing huts at the end of the seafront. When we reach the last hut, I take a key out from under a stone. It's been so long since Dad or I visited that I have to give the door a kick to get it open.

Bones and Elizabeth follow me inside the gloomy room. The only light comes from the window facing the sea. Coils of rope and netting hang from the ceiling and in the middle of the hut lies a peeling fishing boat. Elizabeth settles on a rafter and Bones takes a big sniff of the air then sighs happily. I know why. The hut smells amazing: of the sea and fish and of the layers of gooey stuff Grandad used to paint all over the boat.

'This belonged to my grandad,' I say, 'but he moved to Spain with his girlfriend so now it's ours.'

'It's grand.' Bones settles himself on an upturned crate, then nods towards the window and says, 'Open that for me, Jones.'

I'm not sure why Bones can sit on things but can't open windows, but I do what he asks. Rain and sea air blow in and Bones shuts his eyes, letting it drift over his face. 'Lovely,' he says with a sigh. 'I could be standing on the deck of the *Black Gannet*!'

'Listen,' I say, before he can get too comfy. 'You've been annoying me all week, but now you've gone too far. You can't just walk into my house! Do you think that if you bother me enough, I'll give in and help you?'

A cunning smile spreads across his face. 'You're here, aren't you? Talking to me?'

'Yes, but only so I can tell you to go away!'

'I want to go away, Jones. That is my dearest wish. But I cannot do so without your help.'

I groan. 'Can't someone else help you?'

'No one else can see me, Jones. You're the only one.'

For a few moments we stare at each other. My gaze is

narrowed; Bones's is wide and unblinking. And perhaps it's the fact that a pirate is doing puppy-dog eyes at me that makes me blurt out, 'What do you even need my help with?'

'Just a tiny bit of unfinished business,' he says. 'That is all.'

'What's *unfinished business*?'

'It is the reason me and all those other poor folk are trapped inside the Halfway House.' Then he adds, 'How much do you know about life and death and whatnot, Jones?'

'I know a bit,' I say, thinking about Mum's headstump, and the photos of her that fill our house, and the way Dad gets sad on certain days of the year. 'My mum died when I was a baby.'

Bones takes in this information, then says, 'I am sorry to hear that. Did she lead a happy life?'

For a moment I don't know what to say. Usually when grown-ups find out about Mum they look desperately sorry for me, like they might cry, then they change the subject.

'I think so,' I say. 'She was ill, even when she was a little girl, but Dad says that didn't stop her from travelling and moving abroad and having me.'

'A woman of courage!' says Bones. 'And when she passed over she would have known her littl'un was safe with her daddy. He's a kindly man, is he not?'

'He's lovely.'

'There! Your mother would have had peace in her heart and been free to leave this world and cross over to a wondrous place. But I could not leave, Sid, and neither could the other poor souls trapped inside the Halfway House. You see, we all had unfinished business and so found ourselves tied to this world as surely as a ship is held by an anchor.'

'Couldn't you have just sorted out your unfinished business?' I ask.

'Perhaps,' he says, 'only we made the terrible mistake of stepping inside the Halfway House and then we could not get out again.'

'But you're free now so why can't you sort it out on your own?' I ask. 'You see, I'm quite busy. I've got school and I help Dad at the model village on Saturdays and I've got homework –'

89

Bones cuts me off. 'Jones, the Halfway House has done terrible things to my memory. Believe me when I say, I need your help.'

'And if I do help you – I'm not saying I will – what will happen then?'

He clicks his meaty fingers in front of my nose. 'Then the anchor tying me to this world will be cut loose and I will go!'

'Really? It's that simple? I help you sort out your unfinished business and you'll go away?'

He smiles, showing all his teeth. Outside, waves tumble on the beach. It's getting dark and even the seagulls have fallen quiet. 'Faster than Elizabeth can crack a nut, Sid, m'lad!'

'I'm a girl,' I say.

'Course you are, Sid.'

Suddenly I feel a glimmer of hope. Tomorrow is Friday. If I help Bones after school then he might be gone by tea time!

'Fine,' I say. 'I'll help you. Just tell me what your unfinished business is.'

Bones cackles. Then, after looking over his shoulder

and peering into every corner of the fishing hut, he holds out his fist and slowly uncurls his fingers.

Lying in his scarred palm is a folded piece of paper.

'What's that?' I ask.

'That,' says Bones, 'is a map. Help me find my lost treasure, Jones!'

CHAPTER SIXTEEN

Zen's not on the bus the next morning because he's got the dentist. I'm not sure I'd be able to talk to him even if he was sitting next to me because I can't stop thinking about Bones's map.

I've always loved maps. According to Dad I drew my first map of Fathom – a wobbly blob filled with fingerprint houses – when I was two. Then, when I was six, I made a map of the model village that you can still buy at the kiosk for 20p. I collect maps too and of course I've got my own map of Fathom that's sitting in its holder under my jumper right now. But yesterday was the first time I've ever seen a *real* treasure map.

During morning lessons, a jumble of thoughts about ghosts, maps and treasure fills my mind, and when

Elizabeth turns up at lunchtime it doesn't seem like that big a deal. She lands on my shoulder while I'm sitting on the field eating my egg sandwich and I only realise she's there when I feel a chill and a cheerful voice squawks, 'Hello!'

I try to shake her off, but she clings on. 'Fine. Stay there,' I say. 'Just . . . please keep quiet.'

Clearly Elizabeth is rubbish at following instructions because as I wander around school she chatters away, mainly using her top four words. At one point I come dangerously close to Zen and nearly get dragged into one of his games. He's standing on the steps by the science block and he's got some twigs lined up next to him.

He starts grabbing the sticks and plunging them into hedges – no, sorry, *pirate zombies* – saying stuff like, 'Go back to the grave, ankle biter!' and 'I'm gonna take you to DEATH school!'

I actually find myself whispering to Elizabeth, 'He doesn't mean it. It's just a game.'

I must linger for a moment too long because Zen spots me and runs over.

'Sid!' he says, prodding me with the stick. 'Pretend you're a zombie!' Then he starts making squelching noises.

If I was in the graveyard I'd join in with the squelching noises and throw myself on the ground and start thrashing around. But I'm not in the graveyard. I'm at school. And some boys from our year are watching us with baffled expressions.

I push the stick away and say, 'How was the dentist?'

He frowns. 'Who cares? Listen, last night I came round to show you something important, but your dad said you'd gone to see me! I covered for you, said we must have missed each other, but where were you?'

I say the first thing that pops into my head. 'I went on a walk. I wanted a bit of fresh air.'

'You "wanted a bit of fresh air"? Sid, are you twelve or forty?'

'Rum, bum, Billy, bum!' says Elizabeth.

I glare at her. I'd almost forgotten she was sitting there.

'Sid!' says Zen, waving his hand in front of my face to get my attention. 'Don't you want to know why I came round?' He doesn't wait for me to answer. 'I went out to explore the shipwreck and I found something *amazing*!'

The shipwreck. Last summer, when Zen and I were on the beach, we found a bit of black wood sticking out of the sand and Zen insisted that it was the remains of the *Black Gannet*. I never actually believed it was the shipwreck, but right now a ghost parrot is biting my ear and anything seems possible.

'What did you find?' I ask.

'A Spanish doubloon!' he says, then he thrusts a rusty disk under my nose.

I take it and rub my fingers over the surface. Orange flakes fall to the ground and I see a lady with curly hair.

'Zen, why is Queen Elizabeth on a Spanish doubloon?'

'OK, it's a penny from nineteen eighty-three,' he admits, 'but that's not the amazing thing. Sid, you've got to visit the wreck with me. The storm has moved the sand and there's tons more wood sticking up!'

I bet there isn't. Zen would say anything to get me out there. A few weeks ago he told me he'd found a pirate's tankard, but it turned out to be a Starbucks cup with 'Jasmine' written on the side.

'Please, Sid,' he says. 'We might find some treasure!'

'Treasure!' cries Elizabeth, making me jump. 'Treasure! TREASURE!'

'I can't,' I say, backing away. 'I'm busy.'

'More homework?' he asks, one eyebrow raised.

'That's right,' I say.

Then I turn and hurry across the playground with Elizabeth clinging to my shoulder. I only stop when I reach a lonely, litter-strewn corner. I stare at Elizabeth and she stares back at me.

'I'm going to find Bones's treasure,' I say, wagging my finger at her, 'and then you are going to go away and leave me alone!'

She replies by biting my finger. 'OW!' I say, even though all I feel is an icy shiver.

CHAPTER SEVENTEEN

When the bus pulls into Fathom, Zen doesn't even bother asking if I want to go to the graveyard so I can go straight to the fishing hut. I tell myself that I'm walking fast because I want to get rid of Bones, but there is another reason.

I can't wait to see his map.

Yesterday all I got was a glimpse of thick damp paper before Bones curled his fingers round it, hiding it from view. I'm planning to get a proper look at it today, but first I have to find Bones.

The fishing hut is empty. I'm not surprised – Bones doesn't seem like a man used to following orders – but this does mean I have to look for him all over Fathom. He's not in any of his usual places, so in the end I decide to try the graveyard.

I stand outside the half-open gates. I've not set foot inside since I first spoke to Bones. I've been too scared about seeing the pale faces at the window of the Halfway House. But if I want to find Bones, I'm going to have to go in there.

Before I can change my mind, I walk through the gates and go straight to Mum's grave. I grab hold of the shark's fin, very aware of a low babble of voices coming from somewhere behind me.

'Sorry about that, Mum,' I whisper. 'I didn't mean to make a ghost pub appear in the graveyard.'

'*C'est bon, Sid,*' she replies, in my head.

Then I hear something else. A strange squeaking sound. It's faint at first, then it gets louder. It sounds like something is being rubbed against glass.

Slowly, I look over my shoulder.

The lantern flickers over the doorway to the Halfway House and the gargoyles grin at me. A girl is standing at the window with her finger pressed against the glass. She looks about my age. She has a cloud of red hair and freckles. When she sees that I've spotted her, she grins, showing yellow teeth, then points at the window. That's when I see the letters written in the dust. An H and an E.

I watch, frozen to the spot, as the girl closes her eyes, then carries on writing. One by one letters appear until they spell, 'HELP US'. Then she adds a smiley face emoji. How does she know about emojis? She's wearing a shawl and she has an ancient-looking bonnet on her head! The girl opens her eyes, beams, and then a small fluffy animal with horns appears by her side and blinks its yellow eyes at me.

'Jonesy! Over here!'

I turn to see Bones by the sea wall. I run over and see that, once again, he's resting against Willoughby Hawke's monument.

'This stone has a most pleasing slant,' he says when he sees me, 'and it offers a fine view of the sea.'

'How come you don't fall through it?'

He shrugs. ''Cause us ghosts are like ships on the ocean: we float, Jones!'

'Listen, some girl with red hair just wrote a message to me on the window of the Halfway House!'

'Ha!' he says. 'That would be Peg Tiddy.'

'Who's Peg Tiddy?'

'She's a witch.'

'A what?'

'Oh, don't look like that. She's a harmless one. Her familiar, a goat who goes by the name Radulfus, causes more trouble than her.'

I look back towards the Halfway House. The girl is still watching me. She waves and automatically my fingers wiggle back at her.

'If I find your treasure and you go away, will the Halfway House go back to normal?' I ask, really hoping he'll say yes. How can I come and play here with Zen if ghosts are watching everything I do and possibly writing me messages?

Bones shrugs his big shoulders. 'I don't know. But there is no need to worry about Peg Tiddy or Radulfus. They can't get out of that place unless you let them out, can they?'

The thought of a witch and her familiar loose in Fathom isn't good so I push it away. 'Listen, if I'm going to help you find your treasure then I need to see your map again.'

'Shhhh!' he hisses, peering over his shoulder. 'Don't mention *that* here, Jones. It's not safe. There's many who would like to get their hands on my map!'

'Fine,' I say. 'Then let's talk about your treasure. What is it?'

He smiles sheepishly. 'Ah . . . well. My mind is a *little* vague when it comes to my treasure. You see, Jones, just like the planks on the *Black Gannet*, my memory has holes in it, lots of them. Being in the Halfway House does that to you. The longer you're there, the more you forget. I can't even remember the name of my own father!'

'But you said that finding your treasure was your unfinished business, so you must know what it is.'

He raises his eyebrows. 'Ho ho! You'd think so, wouldn't you? But it's not as simple as that. I was drowned, Jones. There's no pretty way to put it. I was returning home to Fathom and we were within spitting distance of home when the *Gannet* went down. I know that I was returning to find my treasure, only – and here's the sticking point – I don't know exactly what my treasure was.'

My heart sinks as I realise there's no way I'm going to be able to get rid of Bones by teatime. 'You must remember something,' I say. 'Think!'

So Bones screws up his face and does a good impression of someone thinking.

'Hmmmmm . . .' he goes.

'Well?'

His eyes light up. 'I'm seeing gold, Jones, pure gold . . . and emeralds, real whoppers, that shone as green as the ocean after a storm!'

At least we have something to go on.

'So your treasure was made of gold and it had emeralds on it. Was it a crown? Or a necklace? Was it one of those cup thingies – a chalice – all studded with jewels?'

Bones shakes his head. 'I'm sorry, Jones. That's all I can remember about the *look* of it, but I can tell you how it made me feel.'

'And how was that?'

'Like I had to guard it with my life! My treasure was the most precious thing I ever laid eyes on, and bear in mind that I saw some mighty fine booty in my day – barrels stuffed full of Portuguese coin, Venetian silk, rubies as big as hens' eggs, wine so fine men would cut throats for it!' He mimes pulling a blade across his own throat. The action is horribly realistic.

I swallow and carry on. 'So what you're saying is that your treasure was valuable?'

He splutters. 'Valuable, Jones? It was priceless!'

'But if you don't know what it was, how do you even know it's in Fathom?'

He snarls with frustration. 'Because I was sailing home to claim it when the *Gannet* went down and I was *so close!*' Bones is a big man. He has shoulders like a bear and hands the size of dinner plates, but when he says this his voice trembles. 'I have to find my treasure, Jones. It is most precious to me.'

'I can see why you couldn't pass on to the other side.'

'Unfinished business,' he growls, curling his hands into fists.

I wince, thinking about the poor map being squashed in his palm. 'But maybe,' I say, reaching towards him, 'if you show me your map, then I can help you finish it.'

He thinks for a moment. Then, after turning and staring hard at the Halfway House, he opens his palm. The map is still there, a crumpled square. Carefully, he unfolds it.

I reach forward to take it from him, but my fingers slip straight through it. The map is a ghost, just like Bones. I'm about to ask Bones to hold the map closer to me when

I hear a great bellow of rage coming from the Halfway House, followed by the smashing of glass.

Bones flinches and hides his map.

The crashing and yelling continues. It sounds like a fight is taking place.

'Bones, what's going on?' I ask.

'That is Old Scratch,' he says. 'Come on. He is clearly in a terrible mood, and when he is like that, he is best avoided.'

He jumps to his feet and walks towards the gates.

I run after him. There's something I should have asked the day I found out about the Halfway House. 'Bones, who exactly is Old Scratch?'

Behind us there is another crash, followed by the sound of splintering wood. Bones glances back with a wild look in his eyes then says, 'He is the innkeeper of the Halfway House, and he is a devil of a man.'

CHAPTER EIGHTEEN

Ten minutes later Bones and I are sitting at the end of the Cockle with our legs dangling over the sea. We've come here because it's quiet and we can see if anyone is coming towards us. Bones wants to keep an eye out for any 'scoundrels' who might want to see his map.

'What, like Old Scratch?' I ask.

Bones shudders. 'He does not want my map. He wants *me*, the filthy, lousy, scurvy cur. He wants me back in the Halfway House!'

'But why?'

'That is something me and the other ghosts have spent much time discussing, but we do not know, Jones. He trapped us all there and now he is mighty furious that I have got out, but enough about him.' He opens his map and holds it in front of my face. 'We need to find my treasure!'

It feels like Bones is changing the subject, but I can't resist looking at the map.

It's a square of cream-coloured parchment, and someone, presumably Bones, has drawn a few things on it. I can see a heart-shaped blob of land, a hill, some trees, a lot of sheep, one enormous pig, flowers, a field of corn, a mermaid waving in the sea, and, slap bang in the middle of it, a black cross . . . and that's it. Oh, except for a flag that's fluttering in the top left corner.

'Are you *sure* your treasure is buried in Fathom?' I say. 'Because this map could be of anywhere. In fact, I'm not even sure it is a map.'

I reach into my jumper and take my map of Fathom out of its case. It's about ten times bigger than Bones's and has hundreds more things drawn on it.

'*This* is a map,' I say, unfolding it. 'Look, here's the Cockle and the Benbow. They were both built before you were alive, so how come you haven't put them on your map?'

Bones takes one look at the patchwork of paper flapping in my hands and says, '*That*, Jones, is a fool's map!'

I hold my map a little closer, not sure if Bones deserves to see it. 'You should know that this is the most detailed map of Fathom in existence and it's much better than your . . .' I look at his map, trying to find the best word to describe it, '. . . *doodles!*'

He raises one eyebrow. 'Ah, well maybe I did doodles on purpose. If you've hidden something precious then you don't want to go telling people exactly where you've put it, do you? No. You need a *mysterious* and *cunning* map, one that shows round abouts where it's hidden, but not exactly, see?

Then, when you return to the place, you use your map to show you where you buried it.' He points at the middle of his map where hundreds of years ago he drew a big black cross. 'X marks the spot! I made this map simply to give the old memory a nudge in the right direction.'

'And has it given the old memory a nudge in the right direction?' I ask.

He studies his map, tugging on his beard. 'I must confess it has not.'

I fold up my map and put it away. 'Does it even tell you *round abouts* where your treasure is hidden?'

Bones frowns. 'Again, I would have to say no.'

'So how can you be so certain that you hid your treasure in Fathom?'

'Because I *knows* it, Jones. The moment I set foot outside the Halfway House, I had a powerful strong notion that I was close. We just need to find that spot.' He jabs his finger so hard at the black cross that his hand goes right through it.

I stare at his map. I thought it would make it easy to find Bones's treasure – whatever it is – but this map doesn't even tell us where to start looking. In fact, it's hard to see how his picture of hills, trees and pigs (and one mermaid) can lead us to anything.

'I suppose we could walk around the village and see if anything matches up with the things on your map,' I say.

In a flash, Bones leaps to his feet. 'That, Jones, is a first-rate plan!' He slaps me on the back so hard that an icy chill swooshes through me and I think I might topple into the sea.

'Please don't do that,' I say through chattering teeth.

But he's already striding back towards Fathom, bellowing, 'Hurry up, Jones! We have treasure to find!'

CHAPTER NINETEEN

For the next hour, Bones and I roam the streets of Fathom.

As we walk, Bones bombards me with questions, but there are so many people around that all I can do is nod or shake my head, otherwise I'd look like I was talking to myself. Soon Bones realises that he can only ask me 'yes' or 'no' questions.

'What might that be, Jones? Some form of trinket box?'

I shake my head. We're going past the Cod Father fish and chip shop and Seb is standing outside, tapping on his phone.

'A talisman?'

Shake.

'A relic?'

Shake.

'Oh! Might they be *teevees*, like in the houses, only these are in a snuffbox?'

'Kind of,' I say. Now we're halfway down an alleyway behind the Benbow and it's safe to speak. 'They're mobile phones.'

'Mobile what nows?'

'It doesn't matter. Look, save up your questions until we're back at the fishing hut. Right now you should be *quietly* trying to remember where you hid your treasure.' I point at a wooden door that's all boarded up. 'This place used to be a Victorian swimming pool, but when you were alive it was a coaching inn and it had tunnels in the cellars that were used for smuggling!' This is one of the coolest things I know about Fathom, but Bones seems more interested in a cat walking along a wall. 'Bones, there are tunnels under the Benbow too. I've even drawn them on the back of my map, see?'

But he barely glances at it. Instead he says, 'Bad luck, cats.'

I shake my map. 'Right, but don't you think you might have hidden your treasure in one of the smugglers' tunnels?'

He looks offended. 'I would never have put my treasure in no tunnel belonging to a *smuggler*!'

'Fine,' I say. 'We'll keep looking. Just stop asking me questions because I can't reply.'

'My lips are sealed,' he says.

They really aren't. As we wander up and down Fathom's lanes, Bones chatters away in his deep voice telling me about the time he got barred from the Benbow (for bringing in a live salmon hidden in his britches) and listing the many things he considers bad luck on board ship (cats of all colours, bananas, twins, women, whistling, whistling women, Fridays, men with ginger beards, whistling men with ginger beards).

Every now and then I get him to open his map and I whisper something like, 'Try to imagine the public toilets aren't there,' or, 'Remember, before the Co-op was built, that was a chapel.'

Each time Bones frowns, looks hard at his map, looks around, then announces, 'I am sorry, Jones, but my treasure isn't here.'

In a way I'm relieved. I don't know what I'd do if the Co-op had been built on top of his gold. Before we carry on,

I get my pencil case out of my bag and copy Bones's map on to a ripped-out page from the back of my English book. I make sure I get everything right, even drawing the mermaid with wobbly lines and making the sheep far too big. Now I won't have to keep asking him to hold his ghost map up.

After another half hour of looking, we end up back on the seafront.

'I need to go and have my tea now,' I say.

Bones frowns and his hairy eyebrows almost hide his eyes. 'Right you are, Sid, m'lad.'

He looks so despondent that I want to cheer him up. 'Listen, tomorrow's Saturday so we can search for your treasure all day.'

He throws his arms out wide. One goes through the window of Mermaid's Café and the other straight into a post box. 'Where's left to look, Jones?'

Just then I spot Fathom's Museum of Curiosities. Zen's mum and dad run it, and right now Zen is standing outside with his little sister, Skye. It looks like Zen's simultaneously trying to polish *and* try on the suit of armour that holds the 'OPEN' sign. Skye is sitting on his metal-encased foot.

I remember what Zen said about his shipwreck. Could it really be the wreck of the *Black Gannet*?

'Bones, if you could see your ship again – I mean, what's left of it – do you think it might jog your memory and remind you where hid your treasure?'

His face lights up. 'What, set eyes on the *Black Gannet*? Why, I believe it might, Jones! I spent much of my life on that ship, working my way up from bosun to captain. But is it possible that I can see it again? Don't get a poor sailor's hopes up for nothing.'

I look across at the museum. Zen has put on the helmet of the suit of armour and is banging his head against the wall, shouting, 'Take that! *Ow!* Take that! *Ow!*' Skye is giggling like mad.

'There's a tiny chance,' I say.

CHAPTER TWENTY

Early the next morning, Bones and I set off across the beach.

When I left the house I told Dad I was going to work on my map and all he said was, 'Wrap up warm and take a banana.' So right now I'm wearing an anorak, I've got my map in its case around my neck, and I'm eating a banana.

Bones eyes it suspiciously. 'I'm not sure I should let you go anywhere near the *Black Gannet* with that yellow abomination.'

I shove the last bit in my mouth. 'A banana can't bring bad luck to a ship that's already sunk, can it?'

'I s'pose not,' he mutters. Then without warning, he throws his arms up in the air and roars, 'YAARRGHHH!'

I jump and so does Elizabeth, who's sitting on my

shoulder. 'Why did you do that?'

He grins. 'The wind, Jonesy, the waves, the endless blue . . . Doesn't it make you feel alive?'

I suppose my heart *is* thudding hard, but that's because Bones just shouted in my ear. Also, I'm feeling guilty. The wreck – if it really is a wreck – is hidden away at a place Zen and I call the *secret beach*. Zen loves the *secret beach*, but I couldn't invite him along today because then I wouldn't have been able to talk to Bones.

And this morning Bones is very chatty. While I scramble over patches of slippery weed and haul myself over rocks, he simply walks straight through them, telling me about skirmishes he's had and his many close encounters with mermaids and sea serpents.

'A serpent once tried to swallow our ship whole, and that is not a lie, Jones,' he says as I lead him into a cave. 'It had *hundreds* of arms, white as can be, and big bulgin' eyes!'

'Are you sure it wasn't a giant squid?' I ask.

He gives this some thought, then says, 'No. It was a serpent.'

The cave curves round and then we're walking back out into sunshine.

'The wreck is somewhere on this beach,' I say.

As usual, the *secret beach* is deserted. A huge stretch of wet sand stretches to the horizon where frothy waves tumble over each other. The best rockpools are here, deep and filled with brightly coloured weed and scuttling crabs.

Bones and I walk out across the sand, picking our way between the rockpools, until I spot a piece of wood sticking up. 'Over there!' I shout, running forwards, but when I reach it I come to an abrupt stop.

I'm surrounded by weed-covered timbers that rise out of the sand like snapped bones. Zen was telling the truth! 'It never used to look like this,' I say, staring. 'Last time I was here there was only one bit of wood.'

'Storms do that,' says Bones, striding to the front of the wreck. 'I've seen the ruins of a village appear out of the sea only to disappear again the next day.'

'It's amazing!' I say.

'I'd say it was a sorry sight,' says Bones with a shake of his head. 'To think the *Black Gannet* used to strike fear into the hearts of bold men!'

'Are you sure it's the *Gannet*?'

'I have a feeling she might be,' he says as he picks his way between the timbers.

I crouch down to look at a curved piece of wood that's hidden below some seaweed. It has barnacles and rust on the front, but when I scrape these away I see a piece of metal that looks like a lock with holes punched into it.

'Bones, look at this,' I say. He comes and peers over my shoulder. 'This thing has letters written on it: an A and an S.' I smile up at him. 'Shame they're not B and G for B*lack Gannet*!'

He lets out a bark of laughter. 'Why, they're just as good. I had a lass in my crew who went by the name of Anne Spargo – although when she first came aboard she told me her name was James – and I believe this lump of wood belonged to her. It was her trunk, perhaps?' He gives me an icy clap on the shoulder and turns in a circle. 'This is all the proof I need, Jones. I am sure this is the *Black Gannet*!'

I feel a tingle of excitement. Has Zen been right all along?

'The bowsprit rose here,' says Bones, striding to one end of the wreck, 'and this was the main deck.' He turns to face me. 'The guns were below deck, and you are standing where the foremast was.' He sighs deeply. 'You should have seen her when the wind was in her sails. She looked like an angel flying over the waves – a pretty sturdy, heavily armed angel, mind.'

'Is this helping you remember?' I ask hopefully. 'Because if we're going to find your treasure, it would really help if we knew what it was.'

His face darkens. 'It is helping me remember *that* night.'

'When the ship sank?'

He nods and stares across the sand, back towards Fathom. 'We were but a few miles from harbour when the wind became wild. I could see lights twinkling in the distance, but I said we must drop anchor and wait it out. My crew urged me on. They knew how I hungered for home and my treasure. We struck rocks. We were sunk. The last sounds I heard were the cries of my men. Elizabeth was shut up in my cabin.' He shakes his head. 'And all because I had to have my treasure.'

It seems wrong to push him now, but I have to ask. 'But what was your treasure, Bones?'

'I do not know, but that night it shone so bright in my

mind that I thought nothing of my men and only of what was waiting for me.'

'*Where* was it waiting for you?'

'That is a question I have been asking myself night and day for the past three hundred years.' He's staring at his hands now, turning them this way and that. Perhaps it's the bright sunshine that's shining down on us, or the white of the waves that are creeping closer, but his hands suddenly seem more see-through than usual. And I notice something else. A trace of golden dust is rising from his palms like two thin trails of smoke.

'What's that?' I ask, trying to catch hold of it. Glitter coats my fingers, then fades in front of my eyes.

'It is of no importance,' he says, stuffing his hands into his pockets. 'We should go. The tide is about to turn.'

We leave the wreck and trudge back across the sand in silence. Elizabeth flies over our heads. I think she can tell Bones is in a thoughtful mood because for once she doesn't squawk or chatter.

Suddenly Bones stops walking.

'*No . . .*' he whispers.

I follow his gaze. There, half hidden in the shadows at

the bottom of the cliff is a man. He is tall, pale and he has a domed forehead and straggly grey hair. His clothes – an embroidered waistcoat and long coat – are as pale and faded as his skin. He's staring directly at us.

He looks like a moth, I think, as his yellowing coat whips around him, the tattered ends fluttering in the wind. 'Can he see you?' I whisper.

'Oh, he can see me all right,' says Bones. 'For *that* is Old Scratch.'

So this is the innkeeper of the Halfway House. He's standing completely still, a smile hovering on his cracked white lips.

'Is he a ghost?' I ask, because he certainly looks like one.

Bones shakes his head. 'I don't know what manner of creature Old Scratch is. Every now and then he comes into the Halfway House, tramping up from the cellar. He can hold tools in his hands, drink, eat. In that way he is like you or any other living person, but he has not changed a jot since the first day I set eyes on him.'

'But . . . how can that be?' A shiver runs through me. If what Bones is saying is true, then Old Scratch is over three hundred years old, but even with his grey hair he looks younger than my dad.

'No one knows,' says Bones. 'But look, the sea is coming. We must get out of here.'

'If we're going to go through the cave, we'll have to walk right past him,' I say. 'He won't do anything to us, will he?'

Bones looks at Old Scratch with a grim expression. 'I cannot say. You heard the cacophony in the Halfway House. The man has a terrible temper and uncommon strength, and you . . .' He takes in my thin anorak and yellow wellies, '. . . well, you are but a child.'

I feel a squirm of fear in my stomach, but there is no time to feel afraid. Old Scratch has started to walk towards us.

'I know another way off this beach,' I say. 'Come on.' Then I lead Bones towards the huge pile of rocks that separates the *secret beach* from the one next door.

Old Scratch continues to follow us. Each time I glance back I see him striding forward, his hands hanging heavily by his sides. My heart speeds up. I want to run, but I don't want him to know that I'm scared.

We've nearly reached the rocks when he shouts,

'Ezekiel Kittow!' in a dry rasping voice. 'Do you think you can run away from me? Do you think you can run away from time itself?'

Bones ignores him and we hurry forward. The sea has started to foam around our feet. 'Where are we heading, Jones? Remember, I can walk through these boulders, but you cannot!'

'It's here,' I say, and I drop to my knees and lift up a huge piece of seaweed. Over the years the sea has hollowed out a tunnel under rocks. Zen and I found it years ago and sometimes, when we don't mind getting wet, we use it to get in and out of the *secret beach*.

Bones eyes the gap. 'You reckon you can fit through there, do you?'

'Yes . . . probably,' I say, but a glance over my shoulder tells me I have to. Old Scratch is metres away from us and his eyes are fixed on me. This close I can see how solid he looks – different to Bones and Elizabeth – and the expression on his face.

Another bubbling wave foams around my knees as I duck my head down and wriggle into the tunnel. Icy water seeps through my leggings and inside my anorak. I really hope my map is safe in its holder! I keep wriggling until the gap gets wider and I can pull myself out on the other side of the rocks.

It's like I've stepped into a different world. I'm on a busy, noisy beach and I can see surfers and children running barefoot across the sand. Fathom's shops and cafés line the harbour. Best of all, Old Scratch is nowhere to be seen. The panic I felt a moment ago fades away.

Bones steps straight through the rock, gives himself a shake, then says, 'We must go!'

I have to run to keep up with him as strides across the beach towards the stone steps. His hands are clenched and his face is twisted in a scowl. All his happiness from the sunny day and being by the sea has vanished.

'Bones, stop!' I whisper, aware that there are people around me. 'What's the matter?'

He leads me to the bottom of the harbour wall, well away from the people on the beach.

'I have lied to you, Jones. I told you that if you didn't help me find my treasure, then you'd be stuck with me for ever. That was not the truth. I'll be here, somewhere, but I won't look like this.' He holds his hands in front of me, then slowly turns them from left to right. Once again the shimmering dust rises from them. It glitters in the sun before vanishing. Then I realise that I can see straight through his hands to the steps beyond.

'You're fading,' I say. And when Elizabeth flaps her wings, I see that she's fading too. The feathers under her wings have become a dull buttery yellow.

Bones nods. 'Like Old Scratch said, my time is running out.'

'What will happen then?'

A dark look passes across his face. At first I think he's furious, but then I see his hands trembling. He's scared. 'There is a word for what I will become . . .'

'What is it?'

'*Wraith*,' he says with a shudder.

'What's a wraith?'

'I think it might be better if I show you,' he says. 'Come on. Old Scratch rarely visits the Halfway House during the day. You should meet Emma.'

'Who's she?'

'It is more a question of *what* is she,' he replies, and then he starts trudging up the steps.

I throw a final glance back at the beach. Sun sparkles on the sea and Old Scratch is nowhere to be seen.

CHAPTER TWENTY-ONE

As we walk towards the graveyard, Bones has second thoughts about taking me to meet Emma.

'This is a foolish idea,' he says. 'You saw Old Scratch. He is an angry fellow. Perhaps it is best if you stay away from the Halfway House.'

I shake my head stubbornly. Now that I've seen Old Scratch I understand why the ghosts have been staring so desperately from the window and writing me messages. No wonder they want to get out if they are stuck in there with him! I want to understand everything about the place.

When we are in a quiet bit of the lane, I say, 'Bones,

how did you all end up trapped in the Halfway House? If I saw Old Scratch I'd run in the other direction!'

'Because we were tricked, Jones. The night I stepped into that miserable tavern is one I remember clearly. After the Gannet had sunk, me and my buckos found ourselves wandering the streets of Fathom. We were cold, wet, confused, and all of us were trying to find my treasure.'

'Wait,' I say, interrupting him. 'Why were your crew with you if it was your unfinished business? Shouldn't they have been able to leave this world straight away?''

'They should, but we had sworn an oath never to leave each other's side. Through storms and doldrums we stuck together, and when the ship sank they kept their oath in death and my unfinished business became their unfinished business. Straight away we could feel it, Jones, time slipping away.' He pauses to stare at his fading hands.

'What happened next?' I ask.

'We were feeling desperate and scared when we saw a light flickering in the graveyard. Suddenly this fellow steps out of the shadows – Old Scratch – although we did not know his name then. "Good evening, gentlemen," he says, ever so polite. "Won't you step inside my establishment and warm yourselves by the fire? Inside my tavern you shall have all the time you need. All I ask is that you sign your names in my book." Then he held out this great big book. So, naturally, we wrote our marks and rushed inside. The door closed behind us and Old Scratch had us trapped!'

We've reached the graveyard now, and I can see the lantern glowing through the trees, just like it did the night Bones walked into the Halfway House. Suddenly I'm not feeling so confident about walking up to the door.

'Could I get trapped in there?' I ask.

Bones shakes his head and drops of water scatter and fade. 'No. Only lost souls can be trapped in the Halfway House.'

'And you're sure Old Scratch won't turn up?'

'I cannot be certain,' he admits. 'But if he does pay a visit, we always have fair warning.' He points towards the sturdy wooden door. 'You see, he rarely uses that door. Instead he clomps up and down from the cellar.'

'But how does he get in and out of there?'

Bones shrugs his big shoulders. 'That we do not know.'

There seems to be an awful lot they don't know about Old Scratch.

We take a few steps closer to the mausoleum, or the Halfway House as I've now started to think of it. The gargoyles stare at us and the pub sign swings. The usual babble of voices drifts from inside. I hang back, looking and listening for any sign of Old Scratch.

'Scared, are you?' says Bones. 'I don't blame you. Let us forget this caper and find somewhere to look at my map.'

I shake my head. I am scared, but I'm curious too. This is my chance to see inside a pub full of ghosts. 'How will I know who Emma is?' I ask.

Bones chuckles. 'Oh, you'll know all right.'

We step closer and closer to the building. Bones is being cautious now, creeping slowly. When we reach the door, he puts a finger to his lips and listens carefully.

This is the closest I've been to the mausoleum since its transformation. The writing on the sign gleams as if it was painted yesterday and orange light spills from the lantern. This time there are no faces watching me from the windows.

'PSSST!' goes Bones. The voices inside fall quiet. Bones puts his face close to the door and whispers, 'It's me. Is he in there?'

A moment later a gruff voice says, 'All clear, Captain!'

'It's safe,' says Bones. 'Open the door.'

'Why can't you?' The bravery I felt a moment ago is slipping away.

Bones holds his big hands up. 'I can't open nothing, can I?'

So I reach forward and that's when I notice the words carved on the mossy doorstep:

LOST SOUL,
step forth into this
timeless tavern

I'm not sure if this is an invitation or a command.

Bones prods me with an icy finger. 'Well, go on, Jones. If you are going to do it, get on with it!'

I reach forward and turn the heavy doorknob. The door opens with a loud creak and Bones steps back, leaving me alone.

CHAPTER TWENTY-TWO

A rush of cold air sweeps over me and I understand why there were no faces at the window. A crowd of people – no, *ghosts* – are gathered just inside the door, waiting for me.

'Why don't they just walk out?' I whisper to Bones.

'Oh, you'll see,' he says.

Suddenly there is a collective gasp and then they all start talking at once.

'Sid! Sid!'

'There she is!'

'Will you look at her? She's almost as small as Little Will!'

'Ye gads! She looks like a mouse!'

Then they begin pushing and shoving and, because they're ghosts, this means heads and hands and arms and legs start appearing all over the place. Smiling faces pop out of stomachs and people disappear only to be replaced by someone entirely different a second later.

It's like a magic trick at a fancy-dress party, and it's happening so fast my eyes can hardly keep up. One moment a man with long curling hair is standing in front of me, but I only see his foxy smile for a second before a woman wearing goggles and a leather flying hat walks straight through him. She looks at me, wrinkles her nose and says loudly, 'Is that *her*?'

'Uh huh,' says a plump man dressed as Elvis.

Then I hear a rumble of voices coming from the back of the crowd and I see a lurking group of sailors, all soaking wet, just like Bones. This must be Bones's crew.

And then one by one, the ghosts fall quiet and for a few awkward moments we just stare at each other. Bones is still standing behind me, keeping away from the door. The ghosts are keeping their distance from it too.

'Hello, Sid!' These words are spoken by a boy so small

that I've only just noticed him. He's got tufty hair and he looks as bony and fragile as a bird. His clothes are rags held together by more rags and he's twisting a cap in his hands.

'Little Will?' I ask and his pinched face lights up with a smile. Suddenly he runs towards me with his arms outstretched, but when he reaches the doorway he slams into some invisible barrier, then shoots back, landing on his bottom.

He looks up at me with the biggest, roundest eyes I've ever seen, then grins and says, 'I forgot about that!'

So this is why the ghosts can't walk free. The door might be standing open, but they can't step through it.

'How do, Cap'n?' growls a bald man at the back of the crowd. He has a scar running from his eyebrow to his lip. 'Found yer treasure yet?'

'Getting close,' replies Bones. 'Sid here is helping me.'

'I say, Sid!' A pretty woman steps forward. She's wearing blue dungarees and she has a red scarf knotted in her black hair. 'The name's Olive Buckmore and I'm ever so pleased to meet you.' She gives me such

135

a lovely smile that I find myself beaming back at her. 'Here's an idea. Once you've seen to Mr Kittow's unfinished business, how about you do your magic trick again and get me and my pal, Peg, out next? We'd be ever so grateful!'

A chorus of protests ring out from the ghosts.

'It should be me next! I'm the oldest!'

'No, me. I've been here longest!'

'Shut up, boy. It should be me. I've been here the shortest!' protests Elvis.

Suddenly a red-haired girl elbows through Elvis and stands next to Olive, grinning. It's Peg Tiddy, the witch. With her threadbare dress and shapeless shoes she makes a strange contrast to her 'pal' Olive.

'I reckon it should be Olive, then me,' she says. ''Cause we're the best.'

A small furry face appears in the middle of her apron and bleats at me. I guess this is her goat, Radulfus. He bleats again, louder this time, looking up at his mistress.

'I know she doesn't look it,' Peg says to him. 'But I reckon she must be cleverer than she seems. She's probably gawpin' because she's stuffed so full of magic she can't shut her gob.'

That's when I realise my mouth is hanging open. I shut it and take a step back, walking into Bones. Cold washes through me, making my body shake.

'Don't be afeard, Jones,' he says. 'They might look strange, but they're a kindly bunch when you get to know them.'

Suddenly a high-pitched wail echoes from the depths of the pub. I jump, but the ghosts don't seem bothered by it at all.

'Oh gawd,' says Peg. 'There she goes again.'

The wailing gets louder and the ghosts shuffle apart. Next a screeching blob of white shoots towards me going, 'WIIIIIIINE!' Then the blob splats against the invisible barrier as if it's hit glass. I see holes where eyes and a mouth should be, then the wailing thing slides to the floor, lifts back up in the air and shoots around the pub in a zigzagging pattern.

'You should be honoured,' says Olive. 'Emma's doing her best impression of an air-raid siren for you.'

The blob zips back through the ghosts, then hovers in

front of me, still wailing and gazing at me with her empty black eyes.

'Emma?' I say.

'WIIIIIIINE!' she replies.

So *this* is a wraith.

CHAPTER
TWENTY-THREE

'Where are our manners? Won't you step inside, Sid?' Olive Buckmore smiles brightly and makes a sweeping gesture as if she's inviting me into her lovely home.

'Really?' I say, looking back at Bones. 'We can go in?'

He shrugs. 'Well, you can, but there's no way I'm setting foot in the place. I'll stay out here enjoying the sea air.'

'*Pleeease* come in, Sid,' says Peg. 'If you don't, I'll curse you with a thousand crusty warts!' She starts cackling, and I'm not one hundred per cent sure if she's joking.

I look beyond the ghosts into the Halfway House. I'm tempted. How often does a person get the opportunity to walk inside a pub full of ghosts? It's obviously cold in there, but beyond the shifting bodies, I can see tantalising glimpses of silvery cobwebs and strange contraptions attached to the walls.

'Yes, please come in,' says Will. 'You can have my stool!'

I take one last look at Bones. He's heaved himself up on to a stone memorial and is scratching his nose. 'Keep your ears open for Old Scratch!' he shouts, and then I step inside the Halfway House.

In a flash, the sunshine and birdsong are replaced by darkness and a bitter cold. It takes a moment for my eyes to adjust, but when they do, I look beyond the shifting bodies of the ghosts and stare in amazement.

From the outside, the Halfway House is the size of a garage, but the room I'm standing in is big, and it has nooks and crannies leading off in all directions. The ceiling is low and blackened with soot, and stubs of candles flicker on wonky tables. There's a fire in a huge brick grate, but the glowing coals don't seem to give off any heat.

I step further into the room and the ghosts shuffle after me.

One wall is taken up with a bar, filled with dusty rows of bottles and glasses. There is dust drifting all over the place, and it's golden and sparkly, just like the dust I saw coming off Bones.

But the strangest thing about this pub has got to be the clocks. They're everywhere. There are carved cuckoo clocks, clocks with pendulums, golden clocks with their cogs on display and even a station clock with a face as big as a wheel hanging from the low ceiling.

I look from these clocks to the ghosts, who are still staring at me. More gold dust floats through the air. The silence is filled by a never-ending cacophony of ticks and tocks.

'Well, what are you thinking, oh magical one?' The sarcastic words are spoken by a young man lounging on a bench. He's wearing a spotless three-piece suit and his gleaming hair is brushed back from his narrow brown face.

'Clocks,' I say, stupidly.

'We're doomed!' he says with a roll of his eyes.

'Give her a chance,' says Peg. 'I knows powerful magic when I'm close to it. It makes my stomach go wriggly and right now, lookin' at Sid here, I feel like I've got a nest of

141

vipers in my guts!' She beams cheerfully.

'Yeah, leave her alone, Holkar!' says Will, then he points at a stool. 'Sit here, Sid, next to me.'

I sit down and once again the ghosts crowd around me, although I notice the pirates and the woman wearing the goggles have slunk off to sit at a table at the back.

Peg and Olive take the bench opposite me. Emma floats backwards and over our heads, occasionally dropping down to hover in front of my face and let out a mournful and very smelly, '*WIIIIINNNNE!*'

'So what do you think of our prison?' asks Olive, one eyebrow raised.

I run my fingers through the sparkling dust that's floating through the air. 'I like it. It's dark and pretty.'

Olive laughs with surprise. 'I promise the novelty wears off after a while. Now tell us how you did it, Sid.'

I blink at her. 'How I did what?'

'How you broke the spell keeping Bones trapped in here? We were all watching at the window when it happened. I saw you leave the gift –'

'That's right,' interrupts Peg, 'but it was me who saw you write his name in blood!'

'It was red gel pen,' I say, but no one is listening. They've all begun to relive the moment I performed my 'sorcery' and set Bones free.

'You had an ancient scroll,' says Holkar, the smartly dressed man, 'and a zipped purse full of talismans.'

I shake my head. 'No, that was my map and pencil case.'

'Oh! Oh!' says Will, jumping in his seat, keen to get everyone's attention. 'You had those stuffed beasts attached to your bag, remember? With bulging wicked eyes!'

'*What?*' I say. 'I don't have any stuffed beasts attached to my bag!' But then I realise that I do. Nine of them, in fact. 'Those aren't beasts,' I say. 'They're Beanie Boo keyrings.'

'*Beanie Boo keyrings,*' whispers Peg, in awe. 'That is high magic, to be sure!'

Holkar coughs then says in a clipped voice, 'There was lightning. I know that for certain. It struck four times.'

'And don't forget the magic dance you did with the boy,' pipes up Will.

'What magic dance?' I say.

'This one,' says Will and he jumps up and starts leaping around the pub, reaching his arms up to snatch at the air.

145

'We weren't dancing. We were trying to get a plastic bag out of a tree.'

But the ghosts aren't interested in my version of events – *the truth*. They're too busy laughing at Will who is, admittedly, doing a very funny dance.

'Yes!' cries Peg. 'That dance must have created a magical charm that Sid used to defeat Old Scratch's dark magic!'

'I didn't do anything at all!' I must shout these words because instantly the ghosts fall quiet. 'I'm sorry to disappoint you, but I can't do high magic or any kind of magic and I didn't do anything to set Bones free.'

Olive puts her icy hand on top of mine. 'Yes, you did,' she says with calm certainty.

A bang rings out somewhere below the pub, followed by a heavy thump.

The ghosts' eyes dart around anxiously, first to each other and then to a door that's tucked away at the back of the pub.

'Old Scratch!' hisses Will.

''Tis the innkeeper,' says Peg. 'You must go, Sid!'

Footsteps start to thump up a hidden staircase.

'Go, Sid, *go*!' cries Olive.

I jump up and run through the pub. I dodge round Emma and just as I hear the squeak of hinges, I slip through the door and out into warm bright air.

Bones is where I left him. I'm about to slam the door shut when he shakes his head. Just in time I realise that if I do, Old Scratch will know someone's been inside.

I force myself to close the door slowly. Through the narrow gap, I catch a glimpse of Old Scratch as he steps into the pub. He strides into the middle of the room and stands very still, his long coat flowing around him. Then I hear a low growl and a dog pokes its nose round the folds of his coat. The dog has treacle-coloured fur and bulging shoulder muscles. As Old Scratch glares at the ghosts, the dog snarls, showing its teeth and red gums. Saliva drips from its gaping mouth.

Old Scratch is showing his teeth too. They gleam in the candlelight as he stares into each corner of the pub. His eyes move towards the door and that's when the dog barks and hurls itself forward.

I don't wait another second. I pull the door and it shuts with a click.

'*Jones!*' Bones is beckoning to me from behind a

147

monument. 'Let's get out of here!'

The dog's barks fade away as I run after Bones, following him down a pathway and out of the graveyard.

CHAPTER
TWENTY-FOUR

Bones and I walk towards the model village.

My arms and legs are trembling and Bones seems jittery too.

He talks at lightning speed, throwing his arms into the faces of tourists who shiver and button up their coats. 'Turned up and surprised us, didn't he? But, like I said, we had fair warning.' He stomps his boots on the cobblestones. 'Clomp, clomp, clomp, that's a sound I learned to dread, the rotten old stampcrab! And he had Snout with him too? That was a surprise. I've not seen Snout for many a year.'

We cut through an alleyway, which gives me the chance to ask, 'Is Snout hundreds of years old, like him?'

'She's ancient, all right, but she's not like Old Scratch. She's a ghost.'

I look at Bones in horror. Old Scratch has a ghost dog? 'Can she bite?'

Bones gives this some thought, then says, 'In an icy sort of way. So, you got a good look at Emma?'

'What was she screaming about?'

We've reached the end of the alleyway and I can see the open door leading to the model village, but we don't go any further.

'For many a year we thought she was crying out "wine",' says Bones. 'Then Olive Buckmore took the trouble to try to talk to her and discovered that she's actually shouting "*Wayne*". We don't know why, but we presume this Wayne character is her unfinished business.'

'And Emma's a wraith?'

'Very nearly. She stepped into the Halfway House in the nick of time. A few minutes later and she'd have had no voice at all.'

'And that's what you will become?'

Bones lets out a deep breath and for a moment I can see right through him, all the way to Dad's kiosk.

'Yes, I'm fading and turning into a wraith. It began the moment I stepped out of the Halfway House and it will only stop if I find my treasure. I'm disappearing, hour by hour, minute by minute.'

Elizabeth is sitting on his shoulder. He rubs his big fingers through her feathers and a dusting of gold rises up in the air. I'm not sure if either of them can feel anything, but it seems to make them happy.

'And if we find your treasure?' I say.

Bones smiles. 'Then I will become whole again, my crew will step out of the Halfway House, and, together, we will sail away from this world.'

'We've got your map,' I say and my hands feel for my own map under my jumper. 'Maps are amazing things. If you have lost something, they help you find it. We can find your treasure, Bones.'

He smiles. 'With your help, perhaps I can, Jones.'

CHAPTER TWENTY-FIVE

Saturdays are the day I help Dad at the model village. So all afternoon, I pull up weeds, rearrange tiny tourists on the beach and clear the blockages that are stopping water from flowing around Gull Island.

Visitors come and go, hardly noticing me as I do my jobs. I work quietly, snipping leaves and wiping tiny windows clean, but my mind isn't quiet. It's buzzing with thoughts about Bones and his treasure, and the strange, dark place called the Halfway House. And of course, I think about Bones's map.

Dad's busy in the kiosk, which means I decide to use the model village to try to make sense of it. Fathomless is accurate. The curve of the harbour matches up perfectly with the real one down the road, and all the roads and buildings are in the right place too. But no matter which way I turn my copy of Bones's map, I can't make it match up with anywhere in Fathom. Perhaps the coast has changed beyond recognition. Or perhaps Bones is really rubbish at drawing maps.

Eventually I give up and sit on the normal-sized bench behind the tiny cricket pitch. I daydream about what Bones's treasure might be. My thoughts of bracelets and tiaras are interrupted when I hear a voice shout out, 'Sid, look at me. I'm a giant!'

Zen is stomping along Fathomless's narrow seafront. Suddenly he starts roaring and clawing at the sky. 'What am I now?'

'A tyrannosaurus rex?'

He picks up Mrs Ferrari from outside the miniature Mermaid's Café and lowers her towards his mouth. 'Nope. Godzilla.'

'Do not eat her,' I say, jumping up and snatching Mrs Ferrari out of his hands. 'She's Dad's favourite.'

I put Mrs Ferrari back in the doorway of her café. It's a

bit strange having Zen here. We used to go to each other's houses all the time, but just before we started secondary school something changed. I started to feel shyer about being best friends, especially after Owen Kidd saw me coming out of the museum and shouted, 'Been visiting your boyfriend!' Since then I've stuck to playing with Zen in the graveyard, a place that's so quiet no one ever bothers us.

Suddenly Zen looks up and says, 'I've found out something outrageous, Sid.' For a moment I think he's talking about me going to the beach without him, but then he adds, 'Fathomless is ranking higher than the Museum of Curiosities on TripAdvisor. That's why I'm here. I've come to check out the competition.'

'Oh . . . OK,' I say. 'So, what do you think?'

Zen looks around. He crouches down by the fish and chip shop and sniffs deeply. 'Has your dad added smells?'

I smile. 'Yes! So far he's done three. Mermaid's smells of chocolate ice cream and the church smells of dusty books.'

Zen nods appreciatively. 'Nice.' Then he crawls round on his hands and knees sniffing the ice-cream parlour and the church.

'Hey, this is new!' He's noticed that Dad's changed the roundabout. It's always turned, but last summer Dad took it apart and rebuilt it so that each animal goes up and down as well. 'Very cool,' he says. 'Very cool indeed!'

I feel a rush of pride. Zen's right. Fathomless is very cool indeed. Dad's done a good job.

For a few seconds Zen and I stand in front of the roundabout in an awkward silence. I have this sudden urge to tell him everything that's happened. But what would he say if I told him that a few hours ago I was sitting in a ghost pub chatting to a load of ghosts? It's almost impossible for me to believe I was there. Then I realise there is something I can tell him.

'Hey, Zen,' I say, 'I know you'd have liked to come, but I went to the *secret beach* this morning, and I think you're right. There's loads more wood sticking out of the sand. It could be a shipwreck.'

He looks disappointed for a second, then his eyes light up. 'It's amazing, isn't it? I know I should tell Mum, but if I do she'll go and look at it and then it won't be our shipwreck any more, or even our *secret beach.*'

Zen's mum, Abigail, is a historian. She once found a three-thousand-year-old pie in an Egyptian tomb and accidentally broke the finger off a bog girl. Suddenly I realise that I've missed hearing her stories.

'I definitely think it's the wreck of the *Black Gannet*,' Zen says. 'Did you know that loads of stuff from the ship washed up in Fathom after it sank? Mum's put some of it in a display at the museum. You should come and see it . . .' Another awkward silence falls over us then Zen notices something over my shoulder and blurts out, 'Hang on . . . are those waves?'

We watch as little waves roll up the pretend beach, washing around the feet of the tourists.

'Dad made a wave machine,' I say. 'He wants everything to be as realistic as possible.'

'If that's what he's aiming for, he's done it a bit small,' says Zen. Then he nudges me and grins. 'That was a joke.'

'I know,' I say. 'You didn't give me time to laugh.'

'Sorry,' he says, then he lies flat on his stomach so he can have a good sniff of Mermaid's. 'Hey, Sid!' he calls from the ground. 'Have you changed your mind about Pirate Day? My beard's arrived. It's immense.'

I glance at Dad, who right now is hiding in his kiosk, a woolly hat pulled low on his head. Last night Dad asked me if I was going to dress up. He thinks Mum's things will fit me, but I've seen pictures of her wearing her costume and she looked like she'd stepped off the set of *Pirates of the Caribbean*. The thought of me walking around Fathom dressed like that makes me feel slightly sick.

'I've got to help Dad,' I insist.

After a lot more crashing around, and being told by Dad

157

that no, he's still not allowed in the sea, even with his shoes and socks off, Zen goes home.

'Come back soon!' Dad calls after him. Then he looks at me, clearly delighted that Zen called round.

'What?' I say.

'It's good to see Zen visiting again, just like he used to.'

'Dad, we still hang out together, just . . . not all the time.'

'Fine. It's nice, that's all,' he says, and then we start packing up for the day.

It's fun. Like putting the village to sleep. We drain the sea and wipe the seabed dry to stop algae growing. We put the figures who aren't stuck down into plastic boxes and turn off the smells and sounds. Dad leaves me to tidy the kiosk, which means I also get to choose my payment: one chocolate bar or packet of crisps or ice cream per hour.

I've done four hours' work, so I go for my usual two packets of Wotsits (because I'm addicted to them), one Crunchie and a Magnum Gold.

I'm just locking the kiosk when I smell something familiar: Bones.

His body might be fading, but his smell isn't. I look up to see him standing in the empty seabed. Elizabeth is sitting on the Cockle looking like a giant prehistoric bird.

'Jones!' he roars. 'A nipper sitting outside the Benbow was drinking some sort of potion. Rainbow-coloured it were, and thick as snow.'

'That sounds like a slushie,' I say. 'But listen, we've got more important things to think about than slushies. I know where we can go next to look for your treasure.'

His eyes light up. 'Where, Jones?'

I tell him all about the Museum of Curiosities and the new display. 'My friend says it's full of things that were washed up from the *Black Gannet*. Perhaps something will jog your memory. We can go tomorrow, first thing.'

He claps his hands together, then strides backwards and forwards across the empty seabed, stopping in the middle of Gull Island. He grins at me. 'We're getting close, Jones. I can feel it!'

'Sid?' Dad's voice makes me jump. 'Who are you talking to?'

I look from Dad, who is standing at the back door, to Bones, who is triumphantly swishing his cutlass through one of Dad's precious bonsai trees.

'A ghost pirate,' I say.

'Well, I'm afraid it's time to stop playing and come inside. Your jacket potato is ready. And guess what?' He doesn't wait for me to reply. He's too excited. 'I've put chips on it!'

CHAPTER TWENTY-SIX

The next morning, Bones and I are the first customers to walk through the doors of Fathom's Museum of Curiosities.

Zen's mum is standing behind the counter. When she sees me, she beams and clasps her hands to her chest. 'Sid! How lovely to see you!'

'Hi, Abigail,' I say, and suddenly I'm embarrassed that it's been so long since I visited.

For a moment Abigail doesn't speak. She just gazes at me as if I'm her long-lost daughter. She's got a round face and big black eyes like the ones you see painted on a sarcophagus. I know this because there's a sarcophagus standing behind her. Today, just like every day, she's wearing bright pink lipstick, and her hair is cut even shorter than mine, so all I can see is her beaming face.

'Zennor told me that you might be coming,' she says, then she turns and bellows up the stairs. 'Zennor, Sid is here!'

While Abigail continues to smile at me, Bones walks through a wall into a room labelled 'Strange and Stuffed'.

Zen clatters down the stairs wearing his pyjamas. 'Have you come to see the things from the *Black Gannet*?' he says. 'Mum, can we show her?'

The words '*Black Gannet*' make Bones drift back into the room.

Trying to ignore him, I keep my eyes fixed on Abigail. 'I'd love to see the exhibition. I can pay to get in.'

'Don't be ridiculous,' she says, waving my money away. 'When does a friend pay to visit another friend? Follow me. We've got a whole new room to show you: Fathom's Murky Past!'

The Museum of Curiosities is in an old house with the rooms all knocked into each other. I follow Abigail and Zen past circus posters, toys, gas masks, insects and jars of old sweets. Everything is random and higgledy-piggledy.

We pass a mannequin wearing a bear costume and a glass case containing stuffed squirrels. They're all arranged as if they're at a wedding. The squirrel bride even has a bunch of dried flowers clutched in her claws.

'Ah, here we are,' says Abigail, ushering us into a room with 'Fathom's Murky Past' written over the door. 'This is where we've put everything connected to Fathom's infamous pirates, smugglers, witches and ghosts. All the stuff you and Zen love.'

The room is full of intriguing objects. There's a model of a headless horseman in one corner and what looks like a skeleton peering out from behind a curtain. A collection of crystal balls are arranged on the windowsill and I can see a wand in a display case.

'Is that a *real* wand?' I ask.

Abigail laughs. 'Well, it's *real* as in, it belonged to a woman who claimed she was a witch. Sally from the Black Spot Cat Café brought it in. It was her grandmother's.'

Bones strides around the room. I'm still trying to ignore him, but he's so noisy and he smells so strongly that it's difficult. Elizabeth, thank goodness, has decided to stay outside.

163

'Here's all the *Black Gannet* stuff,' says Zen, pulling me towards a display case.

Bones joins us, not caring that his elbow is poking into Zen's head.

'Mum, it's freezing in here!' Zen complains.

All the objects in the case are brown and misshapen. I can just about make out leather and wood, but it's hard to tell what anything is. To be honest, I'm disappointed. I'm not sure what I was expecting to see – gold rings and strings of pearls cascading out of a treasure chest?

'Well, well, well,' says Bones, pointing at a very small and thin spoon. 'I do believe that is my earscoop! There are not many things finer in life than sitting on the deck of your own ship and cleaning out your lugholes!'

Abigail joins us and, along with Bones, starts telling me what I'm looking at. 'That green object is a brass button and next to it is a bilge strainer. Ah, look, that's my favourite exhibit.' She points at a foot-shaped piece of leather. 'It's the base of a shoe. Imagine the size of the man who wore that, Sid!'

Bones's laughter fills the room. 'You can easily do that, Jones, for he is standing right next to you. That shoe was

166

mine! No other fellow on the *Black Gannet* could match me for height. And that's no bilge strainer,' he says, talking over Abigail as she tells me about weevils. 'It's what the cook, Davy Wicket, used to get the brine off pickles.'

But I've stopped listening to Bones. Instead I'm staring at a portrait hanging over the case. It shows a fragile-looking woman wearing a blue dress. Clasped in her hands is a dazzling gold cross studded with big, fat emeralds.

CHAPTER TWENTY-SEVEN

My heart beats fast as I stare at the woman and the gold cross. 'Who's that?' I ask.

'A Spanish infanta,' says Abigail, 'Isabella of Castile.'

'And why's her picture above this case?' I'm really hoping this isn't one of the more random exhibits in the museum.

Abigail's eyes light up. 'The Castile Cross was a marriage gift given to the infanta in 1716. It was almost certainly made from gold stolen from the Incas and it was part of a haul of treasure lost when a Spanish ship was taken by pirates.' Abigail points at the cross. 'Legend has it that each of those emeralds was the size of a musket ball.'

'Musket balls are the size of blueberries,' Zen adds, helpfully.

'Can you imagine how much that cross would be worth today, Sid?' asks Abigail.

I gaze at the beautiful cross. 'It would be priceless . . . but where is it now?'

'It's a lost treasure. It hasn't been seen for over three hundred years.'

I'm so excited that I have to force myself to speak calmly. 'Why have you put a picture of it above these things from the *Black Gannet*?'

Abigail's eyes glitter. 'This is the thrilling part. No one knows exactly who the *Black Gannet* belonged to – ships used to change hands quite regularly –'

'It belonged to ME!' Bones cries, outraged.

'But one theory is that when it sank it belonged to a local man named Ezekiel Kittow.'

'Thank you,' says Bones.

Abigail carries on, totally unaware that she's having a conversation with a ghost. 'Now, Ezekiel was once in the infamous pirate Blackbeard's crew –'

'For a matter of weeks and only because I would have

been dead otherwise,' Bones mutters.

Abigail carries on. 'You'll have heard of Blackbeard, of course. Well, a very unreliable book of piratical history published in 1738 claims that Ezekiel was given the Castile Cross after taking a bullet for Blackbeard, so just maybe Ezekiel brought the cross home and hid it somewhere in Fathom.'

I look at Bones and I don't have to hide my excitement now because Zen is as thrilled as me.

'Hidden treasure!' he says, grabbing my shoulders and giving me a shake. 'Sid, maybe it's buried somewhere near the wreck!'

'What wreck?' asks Abigail, quick as a flash.

'Nothing,' says Zen. 'It's just a game.'

'Come on,' says Abigail, pulling Zen away and leading him towards the stairs. 'Now you go and get dressed, then you can show Sid the rest of the new exhibits.'

The second they're gone, Bones bursts out, 'I never took no bullet for Blackbeard! The scoundrel used me as a human shield and I got a musket ball in the leg. When I lived to tell the tale, he gave me the cross to shut me up then left me for dead in Nassau.' He bursts out laughing.

'The jewels on that cross were so mighty, he assumed they were tourmalines. If he'd known they were emeralds, he would never have given it to me!'

I stare at him. He's really missing the point. 'Bones, don't you see? You said your treasure was "pure gold" and that it had emeralds on it that were "whoppers". The Castile Cross *must* be your treasure!'

'Well now . . .' He frowns and gazes at the picture of the infanta cradling the cross. 'I s'pose you could be right.'

'Of course I'm right! Your treasure was so famous, someone put it in a book.'

Bones gives this some thought. 'Perhaps. But your friend was wrong about something. My treasure wasn't on the *Gannet*. It is in Fathom. I'm sure of it.'

'Perhaps you hid it in Fathom, then went back to sea.'

He starts to nod. 'Yes. I'd never cart something that valuable around with me, would I? I'd put it somewhere safe . . . somewhere I knew well.'

'Like Fathom.'

'And then I'd mark the place on a map!' He looks at me and grins. 'Come on, Jones. Let's find somewhere where we can hunker down and look at my map. We need to discover exactly where I hid that cross!'

He turns and strides out of the room. He's going so fast that he's vanished by the time I reach the exit.

Abigail is standing by an open cabinet, polishing silver spoons. 'Off already?' she says, frowning. 'Zen will be disappointed.'

'I know, and please will you tell him I'm sorry? I've got to go and –'

Suddenly Bones's head shoots through the wall behind Abigail. 'Hurry up, Jones!' he thunders. 'I'm fading, remember?'

Abigail frowns. She's probably wondering why I'm staring open-mouthed at a wall. 'What have you got to do, Sid?'

I look back at her. She's turning one of the silver spoons round and round as she polishes it with the cloth. It's very pretty and engraved with entwined leaves. 'I've got to go and eat something!'

'You've always loved Zen's dad's cherry scones,' she says. 'He baked some this morning. If you go along to the museum café, I'll send Zen to join you.'

I can't tell her that this is an emergency and that I've

got to free a tormented ghost from this world before he disappears, so instead I blurt out, 'I'm allergic to cherries!' Then I dash out of the museum.

CHAPTER TWENTY-EIGHT

Bones and I walk along the seafront, side by side. I'm desperate to talk about our discovery, but the village is crowded with tourists. In a way, I'm pleased it's busy. I don't think Old Scratch will come looking for Bones with so many people around.

'What say we pop into the Benbow?' says Bones, veering towards the pub. 'It might help me think if I were surrounded by smoke and ale and merry folk.'

'Smoking is banned in pubs,' I whisper, 'and so are eleven-year-old children who are on their own.'

'Heavens above!' he says, taking in this shocking news. 'Well, we've got to go somewhere and I'm not sure I fancy the graveyard or the fishing hut right now.'

I know what he means. There's a fine mizzle falling and a breeze whipping in from the sea. If we're going to examine the map, we need somewhere warm and dry.

Just then I see Owen, Kezia and Lara walking towards us. They're holding matching bags and cups from the Yo Ho Ho Shake Shack.

'Oh no,' I whisper. I briefly consider turning round and going back the way we've just come, but they're too close.

'What is the matter?' asks Bones.

I don't reply. Owen would love to see me talking to myself. Instead I step into a doorway and pretend to study a menu. Bones stays exactly where he is, blocking the lane.

Kezia shivers dramatically as she walks through him. Then she notices me standing in the doorway. 'Hi, Sid,' she says. 'We've been buying stuff for Pirate Day.' She waves her bag around. 'We got matching socks!'

I really wish she hadn't seen me because now Owen is going to have to say something. He always does.

'Nice jumper,' he says, and then he goes, 'BOO!' right in my face and I smell his strawberry milkshake breath. Straight away Kezia and Lara start laughing, but Bones isn't laughing. He's glaring at Owen and making a growling sound. He sounds a bit like Old Scratch's dog, Snout.

'So what *are* you doing?' asks Kezia.

'Just . . .' I glance behind me and see the words 'Black Spot Cat Café' written on the door. '. . . going in here.'

'Makes sense,' says Owen, taking a slurp of his milkshake. 'Sally's as mad as you are.' Then he turns and walks off.

Bones stares at me. 'Are you going to accept the scoundrel speaking like that, Jones?'

'Yes!' I hiss. 'Trust me, it's the best thing to do with Owen.'

I hear Kezia shriek, 'You are so *mean*, Owen!' But she still follows him up the lane and so does Lara. As they turn the corner, Owen looks back at me and grins. It's not a friendly grin. Just like Kezia said, it's mean.

To get away, I push open the door to the café and step inside. Immediately I'm hit by a blast of hot air that smells strongly of coffee and cats.

'Welcome!' says Sally from behind the counter, and I feel warm, purring bodies twist around my ankles. 'You're Jim's daughter, aren't you? From the model village?

Now what can I get you, my love? Tea? Coffee? Orange squash? Spaghetti on toast? A bowl of Angel Delight with a Ginger Nut pushed in it?'

I feel in my pocket for my purse. 'Just an orange squash, please.'

'Take a seat. I'll bring it over.'

I sit at a table behind a display of pot plants, crystals and candles, and Bones joins me. He looks ridiculously big sitting on the spindly chair, but the table I've chosen is perfect. We're hidden away and the radio is on which means we can talk.

'It's quiet,' says Bones.

He's not exaggerating. Except for Sally and her seven cats, we're the only people in here.

I peer between the plants and watch as Sally bustles behind her counter. My heart is still thumping from what Owen just said. Sally has got a long white plait that hangs over her shoulder and earrings that look like small cats have been squeezed through each earlobe. Her face is almost as tanned and lined as Bones's and she's wearing a pink sweatshirt with

176

'Feminist. Witch. Cat Lady.' printed across the chest.

She sees me watching her and gives me a wink.
Suddenly I feel better. Owen can go and shove his face in
his milkshake. I hope I *am* like Sally!

'So who are those ruffians?' asks Bones.

'They go to my school and really it's just
Owen who's the ruffian. He doesn't like me.'

'Why?' says Bones. 'What did you
do to him? Put a snake
in his bunk? Stole his
cash? Pinched his
baccy?'

Something tells
me these are all
things Bones
has done. I
think back
to the time
when Owen
started
noticing

everything I did and commenting on it. 'It began in Year Three,' I say, 'when Dad got me a Danger Mouse pencil case. Owen had exactly the same one, but then he lost it and said I'd stolen his. Anyway, he never liked me after that.'

Bones nods. 'Something similar happened to me.'

'What? Someone said you stole their pencil case?'

'No, but I had a gang after me – the Fiddlesticks – and they were led by a fellow named Billy Clark. Just like your Owen, he accused me of pinchin' from him.'

Sally brings over my squash and I notice there's a Haribo sitting at the bottom of my glass. She strokes my head like she's stroking one of her cats, then goes back behind her counter.

'Anyway,' says Bones, 'Billy Clark said I'd stolen his rum, then bit this off me to get me to talk.' Bones pulls back his long hair to reveal a bite-sized chunk missing from his earlobe.

'But that's terrible!'

Bones grins. 'Not really. You see, I *did* steal his rum, and all I had to pay for it was one useless bit of ear!' He throws his head back and laughs heartily. When he does this I notice that his diamond earring has vanished.

'Well I never!' he says, when I point this out. 'I reckon we should get a move on, Jones.'

'How much time do you have?' I ask.

He shrugs his big shoulders. 'Old Scratch once told us that lost souls had less than one cycle of the moon to finish their business, but who knows if that was true.'

'One cycle of the moon? What does that mean?'

He tuts loudly. 'Don't they teach you anything at that school of yours? It means twenty-nine days, round abouts.'

I do a quick calculation and realise that if Old Scratch was telling the truth, Bones has nearly used up half of his time. 'We mustn't waste another minute,' I say, and while Sally arranges cakes, Bones unfolds his ghost map and we study it carefully.

'It looks like it's been drawn by a child,' I say with frustration. 'You've added a giant pig and a waving mermaid, but you haven't bothered with a compass. And look, even your skull and crossbones is all wrong: you've used leaves and a shell instead of bones and a skull!'

Bones jabs a finger at the flag. 'That's my Jolly Roger, my flag, and those aren't any old *leaves*. They're branches from the willow tree. I came up with the idea myself. See how the stems of the willow branches are twisted together? That means the crew of the *Gannet* stick together. And bless them, they have stayed by my side even in death.'

Then Bones launches into a lecture about the different flags flown on ships in the Caribbean. 'It was quite the fashion to create your own Jolly Roger,' he says. 'Now Blackbeard had a horrible one, a devilish skeleton pointing a spear at a heart. I liked Jack Rackham's. He took away the bones from the Jolly Roger and replaced them with cutlasses. Most distinguished. That's what gave me the notion to use willow leaves.'

'But why? Willow leaves aren't going to strike fear into your enemy, are they?'

He tuts loudly. 'I wasn't trying to strike fear into my enemy, Jones. Mostly I was trading wine like an honest man . . . well, as honest as any a man was in those days. I believe I made my flag to remind me of home. No matter which lonely spot on the ocean I might be floating on, I only had to look up and see my willow leaves fluttering and I'd be home.'

I point out of the window. 'Bones, I don't know if you've noticed, but Fathom isn't exactly famous for its willow trees. I understand the shell – there are plenty of those – but if you really wanted to remember home, you should have put a couple of mackerel on your flag.'

Bones bangs his fist down on the table and it goes straight through a vase of flowers. 'God's hat!' he cries. 'I was getting cheek for my jack three hundred years ago, and I'm getting it still!'

I glance at Sally, sure she must have heard his bellowing, but she's still standing behind her counter, gazing into space as she polishes a glass. I watch as her hands go round and round with the tea towel. What she's doing reminds me of something I've seen recently, something I'm sure is important . . .

I stare at her turning hands and slowly the dots in my brain join up. 'Spoons!' I cry.

Sally looks up. 'What's that, dear?'

'Nothing, just looking for . . .' I grab a teaspoon. '. . . this!'

Sally smiles and goes back to her polishing.

'Bones,' I whisper, 'think carefully. Did you ever put your flag on a spoon?'

'A spoon?' he splutters. 'I was a sailor, Jones. I ate with

181

this,' he pulls a sharp ghostly knife out of his belt, 'and these!' He wriggles his fingers.

'Are you sure? Because just now, when we were in the museum, I saw Zen's mum polishing a silver spoon and I'm *sure* your flag was engraved on it.'

Bones's eyes narrow. 'Someone put my Jolly Roger on a *spoon*? Show me, Jones!'

CHAPTER TWENTY-NINE

The lobby of the Museum of Curiosities is empty. I can hear Zen's mum talking in the next room, but Bones and I are alone in the reception area.

'Where is this spoon?' says Bones.

I lead him to the display cabinet next to the till. Inside we can see several silver spoons spilling out of a Quality Street tin. A hand-written label next to them reads: 'Look at the treasures Helen Barker found in her mother's shed!'

Bones pushes his face inside the cabinet, but he can't see the spoons properly because a silk scarf is draped over them. His big fingers try to grab one, but of course they slip right through it.

He pulls his head out of the cabinet. 'Get me one, Jones!'

'What?'

'You heard me. Don't just stand there, gawping. Grab me a spoon!'

I understand why he's so keen to see it. If the engraving on those spoons matches the flag on his map, then we've finally found something that links his map to Fathom. But I'm not about to start opening cases and helping myself to silver spoons.

'No way,' I say. 'What if Zen's mum comes back?'

He gives me a hurt look. 'I'm not asking you to pinch it, Jones. I just want to take a peek.'

'No,' I say. 'Bones, I obey the one-way system at school, I tuck my shirt in and I have never dropped a piece of litter in my life. I am not going to open that cabinet!'

He crouches down so his weed-tangled beard is directly in front of my face. 'Listen,' he hisses. 'You and me, Jones, we're shipmates, right? We've embarked on this caper together, and I've got your back and you've got mine. That's what mates do for each other.' He narrows his beetle-black eyes and his smoky-scented chill rolls over me. 'Now, what say I keep watch while you reach into that case and grab me one of those spoons?'

I raise my chin. 'It's probably locked.'

'Try it,' he growls.

So I reach forward and tug at the door and, of course, it swings open.

He grins. 'It's not stealin' if someone's left a door open!'

I'm pretty certain he's wrong about that, but after glancing over my shoulder one last time, I reach into the case and grab a spoon from under the scarf. I hold it next to Bones's map.

With a shiver I realise that the pictures are identical. The willow branches are crossed in the same way and the shell curls in on itself. I smile, but before I can say a word to Bones I feel something pressing into my back.

'Drop the spoon and no one gets hurt,' drawls a dodgy American accent.

I spin round to see Zen standing there armed with a baguette.

'Got ya!' he says.

I yelp, throw the spoon in the air, and for the second time that day I leg it out of the museum.

'So what do we do now?' asks Bones.

We're squeezed into Dad's kiosk because the second I stepped into the model village, Dad asked me to take over. Now I'm trapped in here with Bones, feeling guilty about what just happened and extremely cold because Bones is too big to avoid.

'*We* are not doing anything!' I say. 'Zen thought I was stealing. What if he tells his mum? What if she comes round here and tells Dad? Or the police? This caper has gone too far, Bones. Arghhh!' I put my head in my hands. 'I'm using the word caper . . . and saying "arghhh".' For a moment I consider helping myself to a Fab to cheer myself up, but then I realise that's *exactly* what a thieving pirate would do.

'You need to calm yourself,' says Bones. 'Right now you are fearful: your heart is beating like a drum, you are both hot and cold, and your brain is crashing like the sea during a storm. Am I right?'

I nod, because that's exactly how I feel.

'Now, you might find this surprising, Jones, but when I first went to sea I often felt fearful. In fact, it was such a common occurrence that I devised a solution. Would you like to hear it?'

186

Even though Bones has got me into this situation, I feel so awful right now that I'll accept any advice. I nod.

Bones perches on Dad's stool and says, 'I simply ask myself: what would Margery do?'

'Who is Margery?'

'My sister,' says Bones. 'You see, she didn't have a scared bone in her body. When there was talk of a ghost haunting the Benbow she spent a night in the cellars. When a fierce dog got into the village, she marched up to it, threw a rope around its neck and caught it. When Mother said she would beat us if we ate the apple pie that was cooling on the table, what did Margery do?'

'Ate the apple pie?'

He grins. 'That's right! You see, she was a wild girl, Jones, who kept a frog in her pocket and could whistle louder than any fellow.'

'Did the dog bite her?' I ask.

'Oh yes,' says Bones, 'and she got bitten by weasels, cats and a fox too.' He laughs and shakes his head. 'Poor Margery . . . She died of the sweating sickness when she was but thirteen years of age.'

'That's so sad,' I say. 'Why would I want to be like her?'

'Because I often think, what a blessing it was that Margery never wasted a moment of her precious thirteen years sunk in worries or unhappiness. She may have got bitten and bruised and bellowed at, but she had more adventures than many have in a lifetime. There now, you are smiling!'

He's right. I am. 'Margery sounds like a good sister to have.'

'She was dear to me. She had curling hair, not dissimilar to yours, and her eyes were the colour of the sea before a storm.'

'It's a shame you can't remember your treasure as well as you can remember Margery.'

Bones laughs. 'Never was a truer word spoken, Sid, m'lad, but unfortunately my memory is like a monk.'

I think for a moment, then say, 'Holey?'

'Exactly! Hello, your father has returned.'

I look up to see Dad walking towards the kiosk with a mug in one hand and a sandwich in the other.

'If the caper is still on, Jones, you know where to find me,' says Bones. 'And remember, when you get the collywobbles, just ask yourself: what would Margery do?'

As Dad walks into the hut, Bones steps through the freezer cabinet and into the model village. He whistles for Elizabeth and then the two of them vanish through the wall.

'I was going to ask if you want an ice cream,' says Dad, 'but it's as cold as the North Pole in here!'

CHAPTER THIRTY

Despite Bones's advice, when I wake up the next morning I've got the collywobbles big time. I deliberately leave the house late so I don't have to meet Zen by the fibreglass ice cream, and then I walk towards the bus stop with my head down and my stomach churning. I don't know if I'm more nervous about seeing Zen, or Old Scratch and his terrifying dog.

Of course, Zen is waiting for me on the bus.

My cheeks go bright red when I see him and I remember the moment he caught me holding the spoon. I'm about to sit at the front, next to an old lady, when I remember what Bones said.

Hardly believing what I'm doing, I ask myself: what would Margery do?

If she wasn't scared of being bitten by a wild dog she wouldn't run away from an awkward conversation. I take a deep breath, walk up the aisle of the bus then sit next to Zen. 'Look,' I say. 'About the sp–'

'Spoon!' he cries, pulling one of the silver spoons out of his blazer pocket. 'Here, I asked Mum if you could borrow it.'

I take the spoon. It's dented and spotted with black marks, but the engraved willow branches and shell are still clear. 'But . . . isn't it valuable?'

Zen shrugs. 'Mum says it's worth about forty pounds. She trusts you.'

I take a deep breath. 'I'm sorry I opened the cabinet. I should have asked first.'

Zen laughs. 'No, you shouldn't. Mum thinks you should touch things from history and that spoon was supposed to be picked up. That's why it was in the Touchy-Feely Cabinet. Didn't you see the sign?'

I shake my head as relief rushes through me.

'Mum's not stupid,' says Zen. 'She locks up all the precious stuff.' Suddenly he looks sheepish. 'She also says that I shouldn't have held you up with a baguette. Sorry about that. I've never seen you move so fast!'

I run my fingers over the silver spoon. It feels surprisingly heavy in my hands. This spoon is a clue that might set Bones free, once and for all, but it means more than that. It's a present from someone who has stayed my friend, even though I've stopped going round to his house and playing with him at school.

'Thank you,' I say, holding it tight. 'Tell your mum I'll look after it.'

'So how come you're so interested in that old spoon?' says Zen. 'I mean, each to their own, but we've got a jar of pickled moles in the Strange and Stuffed room. Why didn't you take that?'

Just as I'm about tell him that I've developed a sudden interest in antique silverware, I realise that I don't need to lie. I *can* tell Zen all about Bones and the treasure hunt. I just need to make him think it's a game.

So I take a deep breath, smile, and then say as breezily as possible, 'It's a long story, but basically I've become friends with that pirate we saw on the beach.'

Straight away, Zen says, 'The one doing yoga?'

'That's him! He's a ghost and his name is Ezekiel

192

"Bones" Kittow – your mum mentioned him yesterday – and he's three hundred years old.' I'm gabbling now, but I can't help it. I'm so happy to finally be able to talk to Zen about all this. 'He's lost some treasure and I've promised to help him find it.'

Zen doesn't look at me like I'm weirder than a jar of pickled moles, he just smiles and says, 'The Castile Cross?'

'That's right!'

Zen looks as happy as me. I never usually play games like this on the bus, but here I am talking about ghosts and treasure – two of his favourite things.

'So what's all this got to do with Mum's spoon?' he asks.

'I don't really know where to start looking for it because the pirate's memory is a bit dodgy –'

'Because he's three hundred years old,' says Zen.

'Exactly, but he's got this map that shows where he hid it.'

Zen's eyes light up. 'A treasure map! That's brilliant!'

'You'd think, but the map is rubbish. I can't make it match up with anything in Fathom. In fact, I was ready to give up, but then I realised that a flag drawn on the map is exactly the same as the engraving the spoon.' I show Zen the twisting willow leaves and shell.

195

'Can I see the map?' asks Zen.

I take my copy out of my pocket. 'Careful,' I say as he opens it up. 'Remember it's three hundred years old.'

It's clearly not three hundred years old. I've used a red biro to draw it and my spellings are written on the other side.

Zen takes the map, studies the flag I drew, looks at the spoon, then says seriously, 'You're right. They're identical. There *must* be a connection.'

'I know! But *what's* the connection? I was hoping this spoon would lead me to a spot in Fathom where I could start digging.' I laugh. 'I guess it was a stupid idea. What can a spoon tell me?'

Zen looks at me solemnly. 'All objects have stories to tell, Sid. You have to listen to them carefully if you want to learn their secrets . . . at least that's what Mum says.' Then he takes the spoon and says, 'Hello, spoon? Where did Sid's ghost hide his treasure?' He puts the spoon to his ear and starts nodding and going, 'Uh huh . . . right . . . OK, I'll tell her.' He looks at me. 'Sorry, Sid, the spoon hasn't got a clue. Apparently my mum was talking rubbish.'

I start laughing and Zen joins in.

'What a couple of losers,' Owen says from the seat behind us.

'You've put *what* down your troosers?' replies Zen, which is stupid and doesn't properly rhyme, but now I'm laughing so hard that this time it's me the bus driver is yelling at to 'Shut up or get off the bus!'

Elizabeth and Bones stay away from school today, but at lunchtime Zen comes to find me instead.

'Hey, Sid,' he says, sitting next to me on the field. 'Do you want to play pirate ghosts?'

Usually, if Zen asked me this at school, I'd make up an excuse about needing to change my book in the library or finish my homework, but not today.

'Definitely,' I say. 'I need your help.'

Unlike me, Zen's got a phone, so we use it to try and match the coastline on Bones's map with the real one in Fathom. But we can't, no matter which way we turn it. Still, it's fun looking, and we end up walking into school together and sitting next to each other in geography.

Mr Lawrence starts talking about a trip we're going on

this Friday, reminding us that we'll need sensible shoes because we're going to walk along the cliff path from Fathom to the Hidden Gardens of Trendeen. To be honest, I've been so distracted by Bones and his treasure that I'd forgotten all about the trip.

Suddenly, Zen nudges me and says, 'Look!'

Mr Lawrence has put an old photograph on the interactive whiteboard. It shows a thatched cottage with a horse and cart standing in front of it. 'This was Trendeen's original farmhouse,' he says. 'It's a ruin now, but if you look closely at the photo you might be able to spot the Hawke family crest displayed over the door. That's the name of the family who owned the Trendeen farm and estate.'

I stare at the board and a shiver runs through me. I can see the crest. It shows two knotted willow branches cupping a shell . . . It looks exactly like Bones's flag!

Zen nudges me and whispers, 'The spoon has spoken!'

CHAPTER THIRTY-ONE

After school, I want to tell Bones what I've discovered, but Zen is keen to go to the graveyard.

'Come on,' he says, when we get off the bus. 'Surely you can't have more homework? We can go up to Pirate Corner and see if we can find any more ghosts!'

Despite my worries about seeing Old Scratch and the Halfway House, I know that I can't stay away from the graveyard forever, so I find myself following Zen through the rusty gates.

At first I'm tense. The ghosts inside the Halfway House are being extra noisy today, and the lantern is shining brightly, but as we walk past, Zen doesn't give the building a second glance. Presumably all he can see is the neglected mausoleum with its bricked-up windows and door. Also, he's busy telling me how to make a Wotsit wand.

'What you do is suck one end of a Wotsit then stick it to another one. Yesterday, I made a wand that was *six Wotsits long*!'

'Sounds good,' I say, but I'm barely listening. Peg and Will are waving like mad from the Halfway House. Peg, I see, has drawn another emoji on the window. This time it's a poo. I'm just wondering how Peg could possibly know about smiley face and poo emojis when I realise Zen's got them all over his rucksack.

I flash them a quick smile then run after Zen.

Once I'm away from the Halfway House, I start to enjoy myself. I know I should be telling Bones about our spoon discovery, but it's good to be here with Zen doing something normal for once . . . If making Wotsit wands then having sword fights with them could ever be described as normal.

Eventually Zen eats his wand and decides to go home for more food.

'Coming?' he asks.

'I think I'll stay for a bit longer,' I reply.

There's something I want to do. Something that's making me feel scared and excited all at the same time.

As soon as I've waved goodbye to Zen, I walk towards the Halfway House. I do this carefully, running from grave to grave then creeping up to peer in at the window.

The darkness of the inn is pierced with dots of candlelight. I can see the ghosts gathered around tables, chatting and laughing. Light shines on the bottles behind the bar. Will and Peg are still by the window, giggling about something, and the pirates are sitting at the back. Old Scratch is nowhere to be seen.

I look at my watch. It's five fifteen, ages until tea. This is the perfect opportunity to go inside and talk to the pirates. Bones said that his unfinished business had become their unfinished business, so surely one of them will remember something about his treasure?

I go to the door. Then, before I can change my mind, I turn the brass doorknob and step into the freezing room. My breath puffs in front of my face and Will cries out, 'Sid's back!'

The ghosts are thrilled to see me. Even the pirates jump

up from their benches and gather around, bombarding me with questions.

'How's Captain?'

'Are these your familiars?'

'Why are you dressed like a lad?'

Quickly I explain that Bones is fine – as far as I know – that the familiars are still Beanie Boo keyrings and that I'm not dressed like a lad, I'm wearing school uniform.

'I never went to school,' says Will. I'm about to say, 'Lucky you,' when he adds, ''Cause when I was six, I started working at the mine with my sisters, smashin' up

stones.' He mimes bringing a sledgehammer down on an invisible stone. 'I was ever so strong.'

Will's arms are like twigs. It's hard to imagine him smashing up a biscuit.

'Why are you here, Sid?' asks Olive, resting her hand on my arm.

The cold that washes through me is shocking, but I try not to shudder. I turn to the pirates and say, 'I was wondering if you can remember anything about Bones's treasure? We're sure it was a gold cross, but we don't know where he hid it.' For a moment, I think about showing

them the map, but then I remember how secretive Bones was about it.

The pirates glance at each other, shifting uneasily. Then a man wearing a leather waistcoat steps forward.

'Peter Byron, quartermaster,' he says, nodding. 'You should know, Mistress Jones, that we don't like to prattle about another fellow's business.'

'I know,' I say quickly. 'But Bones's business is yours too, isn't it? It's why you're trapped here.'

'That it is,' he agrees. 'We took an oath to follow each other to the ends of the earth and we will not leave until Captain has his treasure.' The other pirates murmur their agreement.

A woman gives me a fierce glare, then raises her cutlass and pokes it into my chest. It feels like a spike of ice under my skin, but I refuse to step back. 'Captain saved my life and that of most of these men. We don't tell his secrets!'

I guess this is Anne Spargo.

'Listen, he's fading. If we don't find his treasure soon then he's going to become a wraith, and that means you will all be stuck in here forever with no chance of ever escaping!' The pirates shoot alarmed looks at each other.

'Please, if you can remember where he hid it you need to tell me.'

The pirates form a huddle and start whispering among themselves.

I feel an icy prod on my arm and realise Will is tugging at my sleeve. 'Tell us what school is like,' he says, patting the stool next to him.

'Yes, do tell,' says Olive, flashing one of her big smiles. 'Do you play lacrosse? I *adored* lacrosse!'

'Is school where you learned all your magic?' asks Peg.

The pirates are still talking animatedly, so I sit down and tell Will, Peg and Olive all about Penrose Academy. I tell them about different lessons and about the pasta station in the canteen and our Chrome books. Of course, they want to see mine, so I take it out of my bag, but I guess electronic devices don't work in the Halfway House, because it won't even turn on.

I try not to get too distracted. I listen carefully for Old Scratch. As the ghosts bombard me with questions and ask me to bring back pictures of all the things they've heard about, but never seen (the Eiffel Tower, elephants, sharks, rockets, the real Elvis Presley), But it all seems quiet behind the door that leads to the cellar.

'What does he do down there?' I ask.

Olive shrugs. 'We haven't got a clue. Mends his clocks? Dusts?'

'He *dusts*?' This seems like a strange hobby for a man like Old Scratch.

'He's always dustin',' says Peg.

'Which is a shame, because us ghosts are dusty!' says Will, then he wriggles his body and one or two glittering dust motes rise off him.

'I should go,' I say, glancing at the pirates to see if they have any information, but they are still arguing among themselves. 'I need to find Bones and tell him about the school trip I'm going on. Not that I really want to go on the school trip.'

Quick as a flash, Olive says, 'Why not? A trip sounds like a fine thing to do!'

'Because we're going to have to walk along the cliff path in pairs, and I've got no one to walk with.'

'What about that fellow we just saw you with?' says Peg. 'The boy with poos on his bag. Your sweetheart!'

'Zen's not my sweetheart!' I say, horrified.

'You'll be married soon, no doubt,' she says, giving me a cold nudge in the ribs.

'I really won't. I'm twelve.'

'I was married when I was fourteen,' she says. 'His name was Avery . . . Or was it Robert?'

'Avery was your chicken,' says Olive.

Before they go too off-topic, I need to set them straight about something. 'Listen, the law has changed and you can't get married when you're fourteen any more. And even if you could, I'd never marry Zen because he's my friend!'

'In that case, why can't you walk along the cliff path with him?' asks Will, innocently.

I sigh. I'm not sure the ghosts will understand, but I decide to try to explain it anyway.

'Because I don't like it when people look and stare at me. It didn't use to bother me, but I guess I've changed and now I hate standing out, and Zen's the sort of person who always stands out. He's the opposite of me. He doesn't care if people think he's strange, which is good because he's always doing such strange things.' The ghosts gaze at me, listening intently, so I carry on. 'He kept a pebble in his pocket for two years that he called "Bam Bam", and you must have noticed how often he falls over on purpose and seen the waistcoats and hats he wears. They come from his mum and dad's museum. Once he wore a top hat to school!'

Olive tilts her head to one side and raises as eyebrow.

'What?' I say.

'You used to wear a fine velvet cloak, if I remember correctly.'

'But I don't now, do I?'

'And you used to carry that wrinkly old man around on your back,' says Will. I have not got a clue what he's talking about until he adds, 'He was green.'

'That wasn't an old man. It was my Yoda rucksack!' I don't add that I stopped wearing Yoda after Owen said he made me look 'super freaky'.

'And you're always taking your shoes and socks off,' says Olive.

'I like how it feels,' I protest.

'And you squeeze trees,' says Will.

'I hug trees,' I say. 'There's a difference.'

'Most strange,' says Peg, shaking her head.

'That's not fair,' I say. 'You talk to a goat!'

This makes Olive hoot with laughter and then Will and Peg join in too. Ghosts, I'm starting to realise, find a lot of things funny.

''Scuse me, Mistress Jones.' Peter Byron is back. 'We've had a talk and none of us knows where his treasure is hidden.'

'Seriously?' I say. 'It took you half an hour to realise you know nothing?'

He looks slightly offended. 'We gave it proper consideration. Pollard, here,' he nods towards a stocky man with curly hair, 'is sure he saw Captain putting a cross in a secret place, inside a chest, but that isn't exactly helpful, is it?'

'Not unless you know where he put the chest?' I say. The pirates shake their heads. 'So none of you remember him burying a gold cross anywhere in Fathom?'

The pirate's booming laughter fills the inn. 'Buryin' gold? Why would anyone ever do that?'

'I buried a cheese,' says Peg.

And that's when I realise my visit hasn't helped at all . . . but it has been good fun.

I tell the ghosts that I've got to go, and they see me to the door.

'Come back soon!' they call as I leave.

'And bring your sweetheart next time!' adds Peg with a wild giggle.

As I hurry towards the gates, I glance at my watch. I've been in the Halfway House for ages. Dad will be wondering where I am. But then I stop and stare. My watch still says it's quarter past five . . . exactly the same time that I walked inside the pub.

Could my watch have stopped? But the clock on the church tower says that it's quarter past five too. I've been in the Halfway House for at least an hour, but not a single minute has passed. Then I remember the words engraved on the doorstep:

LOST SOUL,
step forth into this
timeless tavern

Time stops inside the tavern. That's why the ghosts inside aren't fading away like Bones. Feeling like I've just been given the gift of an hour, I decide to go and find Bones. Now I can tell him about the spoon!

CHAPTER THIRTY-TWO

Bones is in the fishing hut and he's thrilled to hear that I've spotted his flag carved over the doorway of the farmhouse at Trendeen.

'The spoon must have come from Trendeen too,' I say. 'For some reason the Hawke family used your Jolly Roger as their family crest.'

'We need to explore this Trendeen place!' he says.

'That's the best bit. I'm going there on a school trip this Friday. The farmhouse is a ruin now, but we might be able to find it. There has to be a connection between you and the Hawke Family. The man who first farmed the land was called Jonah Hawke. Do you remember him?'

'Jonah Hawke?' says Bones, tugging his beard. 'I can't say I recognise the name, but no matter. This is an excellent clue, Jones, and you're right: there must be a reason why this Hawke fellow put my Jolly Roger all over his house and spoons. We'll have to keep our wits about us when we visit. I've a feeling we're getting close!'

'*We?*' I say.

'Well, I'm coming on this school trip too. I might have buried my treasure there. Do you think you should take a spade, just in case?'

'I don't think Mr Lawrence will let me,' I say, trying to imagine walking along the coast path to Trendeen, clutching a spade and with Bones walking by my side. 'And it might be better if you stay here. I'm going to have to fill in worksheets and do surveys and stuff.'

'Worksheets, Jones? *Surveys?*' He jumps to his feet. 'Perhaps you haven't noticed, but I'm disappearing. It's not just my earring that's gone. Two buttons vanished this morning.'

I look at his big chest. Where his two buttons should be there is a trace of the glittering dust that I noticed floating in the Halfway House.

'Fine. You can come, but you've got to promise to keep quiet. I can't talk to you when other people are around.'

'My word is my honour, Sid, m'lad.' Then he mimes locking his lips with a key.

The rest of the week passes quickly. Bones and I pore over the map, and I even manage a couple of quick trips to the Halfway House.

The first time I take a *National Geographic* magazine and I amaze the ghosts with photos of whales, crocodiles and puffer fish. The second time I show them my map and they all gather round to look at it, even the pirates. Olive tells me it's 'absolutely super' and Will says it's 'bloomin' snap', which apparently is a good thing, and even though I'm standing in a freezing pub surrounded by icy ghosts, I feel a warm happy glow inside me.

On my last visit I take in the whoopie cushion Zen got me for my birthday. Of course, Will loves it and gets me to sit on it again and again. 'Leave it on Old Scratch's stool!' he begs when it's time for me to go, but there's no way I'm leaving anything behind in the Halfway House.

Old Scratch hasn't got a clue I've been visiting and I want to keep it that way.

On Friday, the day of the school trip, I get dressed quickly, making sure I put my copy of Bones's map in my pocket. Then I rush out of the house feeling half-nervous, half-excited.

As usual, I'm worried about Owen laughing at me (and Zen giving him something to laugh at), but at the same time, I can't wait to study Bones's map at Trendeen. Like Bones keeps saying, I'm sure we're getting close.

Zen is waiting for me by the ice cream. I'm pleased to see that he isn't wearing his top hat. He does have a tweed waistcoat buttoned up over his hoody, but seeing as my map is hanging in its case round my neck, I can't complain.

'Are we going to find your ghost's treasure today?' he asks.

'That's the plan,' I say.

All week we've studied the map at school, and Zen has come up with outlandish ideas about where the treasure might be hidden. I've gone along with it all, but I haven't told him anything about the Halfway House or Old Scratch.

The last thing I want is for Zen to start knocking on the walls of the mausoleum and calling out to Old Scratch.

'Listen, Zen,' I say, as we walk to meet the others. 'Mr Lawrence is going to try to get us to spot leaves and insects, but the only thing we need to find is Bones's treasure, got it?'

'Absolutely. All I'm going to be looking for are some giant pig and a mermaid with a sausage for a tail.'

'The imp!' says Bones, walking through the wall of the Benbow and joining us. 'My mermaid's tail is as delicate as they come. I think it must be the way you drew it, Jones.'

I scowl at him, giving him a *shut up* look, and then I try to focus on Zen. Bones promised he wouldn't talk to me today.

'Look for this coastline,' I say, pointing at Bones's map. 'It's unusual. I bet we can find it.'

'Don't worry, Sid,' Zen says. 'With my detective skills we'll find your pirate ghost's treasure.' Then he draws a banner in the air. 'We can be *Sid and Zen, Detectives for the Dead!*'

After we've met up with our class, Mr Lawrence gives us a safety talk. Then we set off along the cliff path. Fathom is behind us, the cliffs are ahead of us, and the sea is still and pale. It's a perfect day and as the sun warms my back, I feel myself relax.

One thing that isn't relaxing is the constant chattering of Zen, Bones and Elizabeth. They talk so much that in the end I let their voices wash over me, along with the sound of the waves breaking at the bottom of the cliffs.

'What a grand day!' cries Bones.

'Rum! Bully! Rum!' goes Elizabeth.

Meanwhile, Zen comes up with slogans for our Detective Society. 'How about, We solve the *ghost* crimes? Or, You can *spectre* good service? No, I've got it! We're *dead* good detectives!'

'I like that one,' I say.

'Very witty,' adds Bones.

The cliff dips down and Mr Lawrence lets us stop for a rest by the entrance to Orlig House.

It's the grandest house for miles around and it belongs to a woman called Molly Noon who, according to Kezia, is 'massively famous' and 'stunning' and 'a trillionaire'.

'What's she famous for?' I ask Zen as we sip our water.

'Something to do with yoga and YouTube and herbs,'

214

he says. 'Or maybe it's herby soap . . . or herby tea . . . I don't know.'

I gaze up at the mansion's many windows. I'd love to take my map out of its case and check that I've drawn Orlig House correctly, but Owen is nearby, and I don't want him to see my map.

'That is a fine building,' says Bones.

I'm about to reply, when I remember I can't talk to him so instead I nod. It is fine. It's ancient and made of honey-coloured stone. But it's not all old. I can see a brand-new Audi parked on the driveway and the gates set into the wall are electric and have cameras moving around on them.

'Hey, Sid,' whispers Zen. 'Don't freak out, but someone in Orlig House is watching us.'

I follow his gaze. Looking out of one of the windows in a tower is a girl with dyed red hair. She looks young, our age, and she's wearing a fluffy white hoodie. Before I can get a better look at her, she disappears behind a curtain.

'She's probably a ghost,' says Zen. 'We should get some business cards made up and pop one through the door.'

'She's no ghost,' says Bones in my other ear. 'Ghosts don't hide.'

CHAPTER THIRTY-THREE

'I don't want to see a single person on those rowing boats until you've finished your worksheets,' says Mr Lawrence as he hands round clipboards.

'Look at them boats, Jones.' The words are hissed in my ear by an excited Bones. 'We'll have to have a go on them!'

'Boat,' says Elizabeth. 'Boat. Rum. *BOAT!*'

'Later,' I whisper. 'First we go down to the beach.'

The Hidden Gardens of Trendeen might look like a modern tourist attraction, with a boating lake and gift shop, but it also has a garden tucked away in a valley and this garden leads to a beach. It's this beach that I want to explore.

'Right, off you go,' says Mr Lawrence. 'Stick in your

pairs and happy plant hunting!'

Everyone disappears down winding paths and Zen turns to me and grins. 'OK, so how about we find a bench, randomly write some stuff on the worksheet, then get an ice cream and get lost in the maze?'

'No,' I say. 'First we go to the beach. We're looking for hidden treasure, remember?'

He shrugs. 'OK, but my brain needs to be cold to detect things effectively. I need an ice cream.'

Once Zen has got a Cornetto and a packet of Oreos we set off into the valley and soon ferns and palm trees tower over us. It's like walking through a jungle.

'Bit creepy, isn't it?' says Zen cheerfully.

It is a bit, but I'm not enjoying it quite as much as Zen. Perhaps it's the wind whispering in the trees, or the shifting shadows, or the creaks and rustles coming from the dense shrubbery, but I start to feel like we're not alone.

'Did you hear that?' I ask, when a twig snaps somewhere in the bamboo grove.

I stop walking.

'Hear what?' asks Zen.

'Yes, what?' adds Bones.

'Shh,' I say.

Then I hear it again, another snap followed by a panting sound. 'I'm sure I can hear breathing,' I say. I stare into the shifting leaves, but they form a wall I can't see through.

'OK, I admit it,' says Zen, holding his hands up. 'I'm breathing.'

'Zen, I'm not joking.' Sweat prickles my skin.

'What's the matter?' asks Bones. 'Do you think it's Old Scratch? I'll go and look.' And before I can say anything he's plunged into the leaves, leaving me and Zen alone.

It's strange how lost I suddenly feel. I know that Bones can't actually do anything to protect me from Old Scratch – like he said, he couldn't knock my block off even if he wanted to – but having his big smoky presence nearby makes me feel safe.

Zen and I walk on towards the sea that we can just see glinting between the trees. While Zen talks about Oreos, and the best way to eat them, I keep glancing into the bushes.

Then something happens that's so sudden, I don't have time to react.

There is an explosion of noise behind me. I hear leaves

crunching, and panting, and I turn just in time to see a shape hurl itself towards me. It has powerful shoulders and lips pulled back over terrifyingly sharp teeth.

'Snout,' I whisper, backing away and bumping into Zen.

'What are you doing?' he says, laughing.

That's when I remember that Zen can't see Snout.

The dog leaps forward, sinking its gnashing teeth into my ankle. I feel a biting, tearing cold and I scream and try to push the dog off. My hands don't do anything; the cold just spreads to my fingers and rushes up my wrists. I kick my leg, smashing it up and down, and still the dog won't let go, and the longer it bites the weaker I feel.

I sink to the ground, and Zen crouches next to me.

'Sid, what's the matter?' He's worried now.

I can't speak. The cold is too intense.

Then Bones comes running out of the bushes. 'Get out of here!' he bellows. Snout lets go of my leg and disappears up the path with Bones chasing after him. The whole incident has lasted less than a minute, but I'm left shaking with fear and shock. That wasn't like the chilly tingle I feel when I touch Elizabeth. It hurt!

The cold fades away and I look up to see Zen staring

down at me, his eyes wide with concern. 'Are you all right?' he asks.

'Sorry,' I say, as I get to my feet. 'It was a spider. It freaked me out.'

He starts laughing. 'It must have been a big one because you've never been scared of spiders before. You acted like you were being attacked by a tiger!' He hands me an Oreo.

'Eat this. You need some sugar to help you to recover from the deadly spider attack.'

We carry on towards the sea. I'm jumpy and I can't stop looking around me. It doesn't help that Zen keeps shrieking, 'Watch out! Spider!' and throwing acorns and leaves in my face.

Bones catches up with us just as we reach the beach.

'I saw him off,' he says. 'There was no sign of Old Scratch, but he must be around somewhere. You know that was a message, don't you, Sid?' I can't say anything so he carries on. 'He wants me back in the Halfway House and he was warning you off. Telling you to forget about finding my treasure, and perhaps he is right!'

'Hey, Sid,' says Zen, who's just ahead of me. 'Shall we forget about playing pirate ghosts? I really want a go in the maze.'

I stride past Bones and Zen, out onto the beach. I'm surrounded by sea and sunshine and rocky coves. Palm trees wave in the breeze and the sand is so fine it's almost white. Just off the coast is Gull Island. If I was a pirate, this is exactly where I would hide my treasure.

'No way,' I say. 'We're not giving up now.'

CHAPTER THIRTY-FOUR

Zen and I walk along the beach, looking from the map to the coastline around us. The land Bones drew is distinctive – a heart-shaped blob that sticks out into the sea. Only Zen doesn't think it looks like a heart. 'Nah, it's more of a chicken,' he says, peering over my shoulder. 'See, that's its beak and there's its feathery bum.'

We've been up and down the beach twice now and, whether it's a chicken or a heart, there's nothing here that looks anything like it. I'm so disappointed that I plonk myself down in the sand and absentmindedly rub my ankle. It's warmed up again now, but the memory of those ice-cold teeth hasn't gone away. Bones takes himself off to wade around in the surf, muttering and grumbling, and calling things out like, 'God's hat, it makes no sense, Jones. I am sure we are close!'

As he strides through a wave, I realise I can see straight through him to Gull Island. I don't have to concentrate to do this, or squint. He wavers in and out of my vision for a few seconds.

The sight makes panic bubble up inside me and I think how strange this is. Two weeks ago I was desperate to get rid of Bones, but now I hate seeing him disappear.

'Time to go on the boats?' asks Zen.

'I guess so,' I say, and we walk back the way we've just come, ticking off plants and trees as we go. Of course, I'm jumpy in the darkest part of the valley, where the shadows seem to wrap around us, but I don't see any sign of Old Scratch or Snout.

'Come on. Let's go up here,' I say, leading Zen towards a large pond. I feel better in the sunshine and we quickly find an oak tree, some wood sorrel and even a yellow-bellied newt. I pretend to be excited about this. I can't let Zen know how disappointed I feel about the map. After all, he still thinks it's a game.

Back at the lake we put on lifejackets and climb aboard a blue rowing boat called the *Saucy Frida*.

'Room for one more?' bellows Bones, then he jumps into the boat and plonks himself opposite us with a smile on his face. 'Now don't that feel good, Jones? I do believe I have already forgotten about that scoundrel and his hound!'

We start to row and after a few minutes I understand why Bones is so happy. It does feel good floating around on the *Saucy Frida*. The lake might not be the sea, but it's big and sunlight sparkles on the surface and the sky is a deep blue.

'We could be in the Caribbean,' says Bones, lifting his face to the sun.

Unfortunately, Zen and I discover that we're hopeless at rowing, and after we've gone in three circles Bones starts captaining us.

'Pull down harder, Jones, that's right. Now get your pal to ease up a little. He's pulling the blade too hard. And glance behind you, for mercy's sake!' He's obviously desperate to have a go himself but has to make do with us 'useless lubberworts' instead.

Bones's instructions help and soon we're confidently

making our way across the lake. 'Where did you learn this stuff?' asks Zen, after I tell him that he needs to 'strengthen his length and go easy on the pitch'.

'A friend,' I say. 'He used to be a sailor.'

'Well, say thanks to your friend,' he says, 'because we are good at this . . . Unlike Owen!'

Owen, Kezia and Lara are in a boat called the *Mad Rat*. It looks like Owen has insisted on taking the oars and now they're stuck in an over-hanging tree.

'Owen, you're doing it wrong!' shouts Lara. 'We're going backwards and I've literally got a tree in my hair!'

Zen and I find ourselves rowing past just as she says this, and I make the mistake of laughing. I can't help it. Lara really does have a tree stuck in her hair!

Owen looks up and stares hard at me. His cheeks are flushed and he's sweating from the effort of rowing. 'What are you laughing at?' he says, before adding a muttered, 'Weirdo.'

What happens next could be an accident, but I'm almost certain it's deliberate. Owen flicks his oar into the air, sending water showering down on us.

'Ye gads!' roars Bones, who is even wetter than usual.

'That scurvy imp insulted your honour, Jones, and you are sitting there and accepting it. For shame! Take your revenge, girl!'

For a moment I forget that there are only two of us sitting in this boat and not three. '*Revenge?*' I say, horrified at the thought of doing anything that might annoy Owen.

'Good idea,' says Zen. 'Let's get him!' And before I can

say another word he's slapped his oar down into the lake, soaking Owen.

'Ha ha!' cackles Bones. 'A strike! Follow it up, Jones. Now's your chance, quick, before the villain can reach for his weapon.'

Without stopping to think, I shove hard on my oar and a wave of lake muck crashes over the *Mad Rat*.

'Urghh!' says Owen, pulling weed out of his hair and flinging it back at me.

'What did you do that for?' yells Lara, grabbing the oar off Owen and splashing water at us.

'Get them again, Jones!' shouts Bones. 'Now is not the time for mercy!'

And like a good sailor following her captain's orders, I do exactly what he says. *SLAM!* My oar goes down into the lake and water pours down on Lara. *SLAP! SLAM!* Now Kezia and Owen are soaked too.

And then I go into a frenzy.

Perhaps I'm finally getting Owen back for years of teasing and weirdo comments, or maybe it's the stress of looking after Bones and being attacked by Snout . . . Whatever the reason, something makes me start roaring and pumping my oar in and out of the water.

'Blimey, Sid!' laughs Zen, but he joins in too and soon it's hard to even see the *Mad Rat* under the barrage of water we're sending its way.

I don't really want to get the girls wet. Their only crime is hanging out with an idiot like Owen. But seeing as he's cowering behind them, I have little choice. Plus, they're leaning over the side of their boat and shovelling water at us, so I don't feel too bad about it.

For the next few minutes, the *Saucy Frida* and the *Mad Rat* are locked in combat.

Owen chucks more weed, a tree branch and even a sandwich at us while the girls continue to splash us with their hands. Zen and I stick with using our oars as water slappers and I guess this, along with being captained by a pirate, gives us the upper hand.

'SHOW NO MERCY!' bellows Bones. 'Turn the *Saucy Frida* about. That's right! Now aim for the bow. We'll have her sunk in no time!'

'What on earth do you lot think you are doing?' The cry comes from the muddy bank where Mr Lawrence is standing. Judging by the state of his clothes he's had to scramble over a few bushes to get there. And I might have accidentally splashed him.

We lower our oars and our rocking boats come to a standstill.

Kezia, Lara and Owen are soaked while Zen and I are only damp. This doesn't work in our favour.

'Right, you two, out!' says Mr Lawrence, pointing at me

and Zen. 'You're going to spend the rest of the day with me.'

'But Owen started it, sir!' protests Zen.

'Get your friend to hush his tongue!' cries Bones, horrified. 'You must take your vessel to shore and accept your punishment like a true sailor!'

'Come on,' I say to Zen. 'Let's go.'

For a few minutes we row in silence. Then Zen looks at me and grins. 'We got him, didn't we, Sid?'

'We got him so good,' I say, and then we both start laughing.

'I don't know what you two are laughing about,' says Bones, arms folded. 'You're two of the most undisciplined sailors I have ever laid eyes on. If you were on my crew, I'd have had you on bread and water rations for a week.'

CHAPTER THIRTY-FIVE

'They didn't have tea or cake in the prison in Nassau,' says Bones. 'Or views like this!'

Mr Lawrence has made Zen and me sit at opposite ends of Trendeen's tea garden. He's giving Zen a talking to and it's my turn next. Getting into trouble is something I dread, but now that it's happened, I feel strangely calm. After all, my punishment isn't so bad. Mr Lawrence let us buy snacks and right now I'm eating a coconut flapjack and staring at the sea. I'm not even on my own. Bones is keeping me company and telling me about his days locked up in prison at Nassau in the Bahamas.

'What did you do?' I ask.

'Not much. I ran up a debt fitting out the *Black Gannet* and got hauled inside until a pal paid it off. My memory lets me down again for I cannot remember who that kind fellow was, but I do remember my prison mate. A knave who went by the name of Edward No-Thumb, on account of the fact that an eel had bitten off his thumb.'

As Bones rambles on about No-Thumb's various bad habits (picking his teeth with fish bones and eating grubs), I get out his map. The tea garden is on a hill, and from here I've got a great view of the coast.

My eyes flick from the map to the beach. Just when I'm about to give up and go back to my flapjack, something catches my eye. A tall tree rises up on Gull Island, and there's something about the way it leans to the left that reminds me of the tree on the map. I turn the piece of paper a fraction and, just like that, everything falls into place. The cove that Zen said was 'sitting under the chicken's bum' is there, and so is the hill and every single tree drawn on Bones's map. It all matches!

I laugh out loud. 'Look at this!' I whisper to Bones, shoving the map under his nose. 'I think I know where you hid your treasure!'

Suddenly Mr Lawrence plonks himself down next to me, sloshing coffee on the table. 'Well I never,' he says, plucking the map out of my hands. 'Where did you get this, Sid? Gull Island hasn't looked like this for over two hundred years.'

Bones sucks in an outraged breath and snatches at the map. Of course, his hands go straight through it. 'The thieving varmint!' he cries.

'I drew it,' I say quickly. 'I copied an old map that I found in a book.'

He laughs. 'And no doubt you added a mermaid while you were at it! You see that narrow piece of land?' He taps the map, making Bones suck in his breath. 'That is what we geographers call a "spit". Over the years it was worn down until a big storm washed it away completely. Overnight, Gull Head became Gull *Island*.'

Suddenly Bones throws his arms up in the air and roars, 'GULL HEAD! I remember that place, Sid, truly I do. It was very dear to me!'

Of course, I can't say anything – Mr Lawrence is still sitting next to me – so instead I smile at Bones and hope he understands how happy I am that we've finally found the place where, round abouts, his treasure is hidden.

'My goodness,' says Mr Lawrence, seeing my grinning face. 'If you're that interested in Gull Island, you should visit. Look.' He points at the sea directly in front of the island. The tide is on its way out, and as the waves wash back I see granite rocks below the surface of the water. 'There's a causeway that appears at low tide. You need to watch the tides closely, of course, but plenty of people explore Gull Island.'

'Thank you, Mr Lawrence,' I say. 'That's amazing!'

'Oh!' His cheeks go pink. 'You're welcome, Sid. It makes a refreshing change to meet a student who's so passionate about maps and coastal erosion. Now, about the incident on the boating lake –'

'Are you going to tell my dad?' I say. 'Or Zen's parents?'

After a moment Mr Lawrence says, 'No, I don't think I will. You two don't usually fool around.' Then he adds, 'Have you heard of *Camden's Britannia*?'

Of course I have. Anyone who loves maps knows about the *Britannia*: it's the finest collection of county maps ever made. But I don't tell Mr Lawrence this. I've got the feeling that if I let him tell me all about *Camden's Britannia* then

Zen and I won't get in trouble, and that seems totally fair to me.

While Mr Lawrence talks about Roman Britain and fine engravings, I keep glancing at the causeway to Gull Island. With each rolling back of the waves, a few more rocks are revealed. I'm desperate to get on to the island to start exploring, and so is Bones.

'It's there, Jones!' he cries, striding through a lady about to sink her teeth into a cream-laden scone. She coughs, spluttering jam and cream everywhere. 'My treasure has to be there!'

CHAPTER THIRTY-SIX

Bones, Zen and I practically bounce along the cliff path back to Fathom.

Zen is overjoyed that my interest in maps has got us out of trouble and Bones is happier than I've seen him in days. He strides along, arms swinging, whistling and singing. Every now and then he turns to look back at Gull Island. Now he's found it, he doesn't seem to want to leave it behind.

And me? I feel happy in a way that's hard to describe. Like I've climbed a mountain and now I'm running down the other side with my arms windmilling round and round. In just one day I've survived a ghost dog attack and being told off, I've had a fight with Owen (and won) AND I've solved the mystery of Bones's map. Tomorrow is Saturday, so Bones and I can go back to Gull Island. And this time I'm taking a spade.

Soon we're walking down the slope that leads into Fathom. As we go past the graveyard, Bones nudges me. 'Sid, what say you and I take a little trip to the Halfway House and tell the gang our good news?'

Through the trees I can just see the light from the lantern hanging over the door. I think how overjoyed the pirates will be to hear we're getting close to finding Bones's treasure. Perhaps the information will help them remember something? I can't reply – Zen's walking alongside me – so instead I grin and do the tiniest of nods.

'How come you're so happy?' says Zen.

'Just remembering when I knocked Owen's sandwich back and it hit him in the face.'

'Soggy tuna mayonnaise . . . that can't have been good. Hey, do you want to come back to the museum? I've made a racetrack on Minecraft and I'm going to use it to race axolotls and cats.'

Bones tuts. 'There's no time for cat-racing, Jones. We've got to see my crew, then go back to the fishing hut to plan our trip to Gull Island.'

I've got so used to lying to Zen that the next words fly out of my mouth. 'Sorry, Zen, I can't. I've got to go home and help Dad.'

Zen narrows his eyes, just slightly, and I get the feeling he knows that I'm lying. Then he says, 'Sid, I've been thinking about your map. Where did it really come from?'

I pause. I could tell him the truth. I could say, 'Zen, you're not going to believe this, but just like I said, the map belongs to a pirate ghost called Bones. He's walking next to you right now. In fact, a few minutes ago, when you said you were cold, that was because his ghost parrot did a ghost poo on your head.'

But I don't. I couldn't stand it if he gave me the look that Owen gives me all the time. The *Sid's a freak* look. Because no matter how good a friend Zen is, how could he possibly believe everything that's happened to me? So instead I tell yet another lie.

'You've got me!' I say, forcing out a laugh. 'It doesn't really belong to a pirate. I drew it in English when we were watching a film. I made the whole thing up.'

He looks at me for a moment longer, then says, 'The thing is, it doesn't *look* like you drew it. You're amazing at art, but the sheep on your map look like hippos, and it hasn't got a compass. You're always telling me that a map without a compass is useless.' He's not smiling like he usually is. He looks more . . . fed up.

'You're right,' I say quickly. 'I should add one.'

We've reached the graveyard and Mr Lawrence says that if we live in Fathom we're free to go.

'See you on Monday,' I say to Zen. Then, before he can give me any more of his suspicious looks, I turn and leg it down the lane towards the seafront.

Bones jogs along after me, his cutlass and pistol clinking against each other.

'What is a hippo, Jones?'

'I'll show you a picture later,' I say. 'Come on. We need to get back to the graveyard without Zen seeing.'

I lead Bones down an alleyway, then we wait behind a bin until Zen goes past. We give it a couple of minutes, then run back up the lane and into the graveyard. Using the headstones as cover, we creep up to the window of the Halfway House.

This time Will spots us straight away. 'Come in!' he shouts. 'He's not here. It's safe!'

Just like first time we visited, Bones stands clear of the door, saying, 'I'm telling you, Sid. I will not put so much as a toe inside that place.'

Instead the pirates gather close to the doorway, and while Bones tells them the good news, I go inside.

Once again the cold takes my breath away and the tick-tocking of the clocks rings in my ears. I sit down with Will, Peg and Olive, and the other ghosts gather round. 'Something brilliant has happened!' I say, then I tell them what we discovered at Trendeen. By the time I've finished, I've stopped shivering and the ticking has faded into the background. I'm starting to get used to the Halfway House.

'Now you know where to look, you will find Bones's treasure,' says Peg firmly. 'I know it.' Then a glittering tear runs down her cheek. Radulfus appears from nowhere and nuzzles his nose against her face. 'Don't worry about me, yer daft demon. I am just happy for Bones and his crew, that is all. Soon they will be free!'

'And perhaps we will be too,' says Olive, resting her hand on top of Peg's. Their fingers merge together.

This is all too gloomy for Will. 'Tell us more about school, Sid. I love hearing about school.'

'Honestly, I prefer it here,' I say.

'What? Why?' Will is dumbstruck.

'Well, for one thing, at school we get homework and it takes ages and ruins your weekends.'

Olive knows what homework is, but Will and Peg don't so I show them my homework diary that's at the bottom of my rucksack.

'See, I've got French and English to finish before Monday, but all I want to do is look for Bones's treasure!'

'But we can help you,' says Olive. 'Mr Holkar!' she calls across the gentleman with the slicked-back hair. 'You can speak French, can't you?'

'*Bien sûr*,' he says with a shrug. '*Je suis un génie!*'

'What?' says Peg, wrinkling her nose.

He rolls his eyes. 'I am informing you that I am a genius.'

'Yeah?' says Peg, unimpressed. 'Well, I can turn a cow's milk sour just by givin' her a funny look, so shove that in your pie hole!'

'And Beau Fiddler believes he has a way with words,' says Olive.

A man I've barely spoken to steps up to the table. He has rosy red lips and cheeks and long curly hair that is almost certainly a wig. He flashes me a grin before twisting a hand in the air and bowing deeply. From upside down he says, 'It is a delight to meet you, m'lady Sidonie.' Then he lifts his head up, stares at me, and adds, 'Has anyone ever told you that your eyes are as blue and clear as sapphires?'

'They're brown,' I say.

He shrugs and drops down on a stool. 'No matter. I am a highwayman, ma'am, but fear not –'

'I'm not scared.'

He carries on as if I haven't spoken. '– for my deadliest weapon is my tongue not my sword.' Then he smiles, showing me all of his very white teeth.

'So, about my homework . . .' I say.

Because time doesn't pass inside the Halfway House, I don't actually waste a second of my life doing my homework. All the ghosts make suggestions for the description of an old man that I have to write for English, and Holkar helps me complete a French verb table.

'What a blessed relief that was,' he says as I put my things away. 'It has been ninety years since I had such mental stimulation.'

'He's saying we're thick as hens,' says Peg, which makes Will collapse into giggles.

And perhaps that's why I don't hear the footsteps . . .

'Hide!' snaps Holkar, but already the cellar door is being kicked open.

I slide under the table, pulling my rucksack down with me. I don't have time to feel scared. I sit there curled up with Will's dirty feet dangling in front of my nose. The door slams shut, then all is quiet.

'Why is that door open?' Old Scratch's voice is dry and crackly, like dead leaves.

I watch as a pair of boots march across the pub to the open door, and I feel a small rush of relief as I realise Snout isn't with her master. If the dog was here, she would sniff me out in seconds.

Again, everything is silent as Old Scratch stands at the open door. Bones must be hiding, because after a moment, the door is yanked shut. I hadn't thought that the Halfway House could get any darker, but now it's become a shadowy cave, filled with the sound of a hundred clocks and my heavy breathing.

Sweat prickles the back of my neck as Old Scratch

starts to pace around the room. He goes from table to table. The ghosts are utterly quiet.

'I said, *why is that door open?* Did Bones come back? Was that girl with him?'

Tick tock, tick tock, go the clocks.

'I hoped you enjoyed that little glimpse of freedom,' hisses Scratch. 'Because it's all you are ever getting.'

'That's not true!' Will's voice rings out. 'Sid Jones will get us out of here too!'

'*SHH!*' says Olive.

But it's too late. Scratch is on his way over. He stops by our table, the toes of his boots almost touching my trainers.

'Sid Jones . . . how helpful to learn her name.' He pauses and another of the silences fills the pub. Pressed close to me are the ghosts' legs and the tiny, glittery bits of dust. My nose twitches. No . . . I can't let myself sneeze!

I screw up my face as Old Scratch starts to talk again. 'Tell me, William Buckle, do you truly believe that girl, that scrap of a thing, actually broke the dark magic keeping Bones here?'

The tickle in my nose becomes painful.

'Yes, I do!' Will says.

Scratch's laugh makes the pub feel even colder. 'Idiot boy. That girl, that *mouse*, who scurries about in the shadows could not have done it. No, some other trickery was used by Kittow, and when I find out what it was –'

The sound I make is tiny, the smallest of squeaks as I try to keep the sneeze tucked inside me, but Old Scratch hears it.

'What was that?'

Now I need to sneeze so badly that my eyes are watering.

Suddenly a deep voice rings out. It's one of the pirates, and he's singing the song I first heard Bones sing on the beach, the one about whisky. He stands up and his voice gets louder.

'Shut up!' snarls Scratch. '*Shut up*, I said!'

But he doesn't shut up, and when he gets to the chorus, the other pirates get to their feet and join in too. Their voices are so loud and deep that I can feel the song inside me. It even drowns out the sound of the clocks.

Old Scratch crashes over to them and slams his fist on the table. 'Be quiet, I tell you!'

But they get louder, and they start to stamp their feet.

Will's grubby face appears under the table. 'He's not looking, Sid. Go!'

I don't want to come out from my hiding place, but I've got to get out of here.

Keeping low to the floor I poke my head out from under the table. Old Scratch's back is turned. He's going from pirate to pirate, shouting into their faces, yelling, 'Shut up, I say! SHUT UP! Do you want me to board up those windows so you never see the light of day?'

I crawl as fast as I can. When I reach the door, I put my hand on the knob. I know the door squeaks. How can I get out without Old Scratch hearing me?

The pirates must realise my dilemma because at that moment their voices rise to a mighty crescendo.

I twist the door knob and slip out of the pub. There's no time to close the door behind me. I run.

'Jones, over here!' Bones waves to me from behind a headstone. I dart towards him and throw myself behind the stone slab just as the door to the Halfway House is pushed wide open.

'Shouldn't we make a run for it?' I whisper to Bones.

'No! Old Scratch is angry and he knows magic, and

you do not want your back turned to a man like that. Keep quiet and still.'

I press against the sun-warmed stone, but it does nothing to stop my arms and legs from trembling.

'Where are you, Sid Jones?' Old Scratch shouts.

Silence. Then I hear footsteps crunching on gravel.

Suddenly a dry voice rings out. 'You should have run when you had the chance!'

CHAPTER THIRTY-SEVEN

I cover my mouth to stop myself from squealing and look at Bones. He's crouched next to me, but unlike me, he seems calm. He fixes me with a grim look and raises one finger to his lips.

I hear more footsteps and see a shadow flit over a grave. Old Scratch is just behind the headstone!

'You're here too, aren't you, Bones?' His voice crackles. 'But you couldn't have opened the door, so it must have been the girl.'

I widen my eyes at Bones, desperately hoping that he'll tell me what to do. If we move, Old Scratch will see us, but we can't stay here. He's so close I can hear each breath he takes.

248

'Has it started yet, Kittow? Have you started to fall apart? How long have you got, I wonder? If you want time to stand still, you know you are welcome back in the Halfway House.'

'Bones!' The voice rings out from somewhere in the trees. It sounds just like me calling Bones's name, only I haven't said a word. 'Bones!' comes the voice again. It's Elizabeth, and she's imitating my voice!

Old Scratch moves away from us.

I peer around the side of the headstone. I can see him standing by a stone angel, staring up at the trees. He could be a statue himself. His clothes are the colour of yellowing bone and he's so close that I can see the veins on his forehead and the wind blowing the frayed edges of his coat.

'Bones!' calls Elizabeth and then she adds one of her cackles of laughter.

Old Scratch snarls then stomps towards the trees.

This is our chance!

I beckon to Bones, then creep out from behind the monument and take the winding path that leads to the top of the graveyard. There's no gate up here, but I've got a plan. Bones follows me. For such a big man, he moves quietly. He's obviously used to sneaking around.

'BONES!' screams Elizabeth, only this time she doesn't bother imitating my voice, and then she cries, 'Rum! RUM!'

'The game is up,' hisses Bones. 'You must hide.'

We're at the top of the graveyard now, surrounded by a wall that's too high to climb. If Old Scratch glances this way he'll almost certainly see us, but I'm not hiding. I've been hanging out in this graveyard for years and I know all its secrets.

'Follow me,' I say and I run towards the elm tree that grows close to Bones's grave.

'What are you doing?' Bones hisses. 'You've led us to a dead end, Jones. I can go anywhere I choose, but you're trapped and I cannot leave you alone with that man!'

A flash of a cream coat and fast approaching footsteps tells me that Old Scratch is climbing the path that leads to exactly where we are standing.

'This isn't a dead end,' I say. Then I drop down and squeeze inside a crack at the bottom of the tree. I pull myself inside the tree, into a hollowed out space that's full of dead leaves and presumably lots of insects. I sit there for

a second, catching my breath. I'd love to stay here, curled up, but I've got to keep moving. I can just imagine Old Scratch's white hand reaching into the tree and grabbing hold of me.

I look up. There's a hole higher up the hollowed tree trunk and light is pouring through it. When Zen and I were younger and played zombies in the graveyard, this was our escape route.

Quickly I push myself up through the middle of the tree. I've done this loads of times before, but I must have grown since the last time because it's a tight squeeze. My trainer catches on something sharp and for a moment I'm stuck. Panic sweeps through me, but I kick and kick until I hear a snap and pull my foot free.

I heave myself up and stick my head out of the hole. Ahead lies the sea but below me there are sand dunes. I wriggle forwards until I can tumble into the sand.

Bones has simply walked through the wall and is crouched down, waiting for me.

'I know you're both up here!' shouts Old Scratch from the other side of the wall. 'I've got a message for you, Sid Jones. Children who play in graveyards and go snooping in places they don't belong get nasty surprises!'

I don't wait to hear any more. Side by side, Bones and I creep along the graveyard wall. And when we reach the lane that leads into Fathom, we run.

CHAPTER THIRTY-EIGHT

We fall inside the fishing hut.

'We should be safe here,' I say. 'Old Scratch doesn't know about this place.'

We throw ourselves down on the crates and Bones looks at me with wild eyes. 'That was quite the adventure,' he says with a grin.

'You said I'd hear his footsteps on the stairs, but I didn't hear a thing! I was so scared I nearly sicked up my flapjack!'

Bones cackles. 'Once Blackbeard decided to use me for target practice. He put a pineapple on my head and levelled his pistol. I was so fearful I fainted clean away. When I came round he was eating pineapple and I'd been forgotten!'

'How can you laugh about that?' I say. 'It sounds terrifying!'

'Oh, it was,' he says, still chuckling. 'What a day, eh, Sid? We got chased by the innkeeper, we found Gull Head and we had a sea battle with those scallywags!'

Bones jumps up and starts pacing around the hut, occasionally walking through a wall and disappearing for a moment. He can't stop talking about Gull Island. 'Did you see the tree, Jones? All tilted to one side, and the creek and the stack of rocks? The sight of that place filled my heart!' He almost shouts these last words. 'I felt like I had arrived home. For so many years I have had this ache in me.' He thumps hard on his chest. 'The thought of my lost treasure hurts more than any wound I ever received, but when my eyes settled on that island . . .' He sighs deeply. 'The pain went, just for a moment.'

'Your treasure has to be there,' I say. 'First thing tomorrow we'll go back. You might remember where it is. We probably won't even need the map!'

It happens so suddenly that I don't even have time to stand up. There's an almighty thud and the door to the hut comes crashing open.

CHAPTER THIRTY-NINE

'HA!'

Zen is standing in the doorway with his T-shirt untucked, his waistcoat flapping.

'I knew it,' he says. 'I thought we were back to being proper friends, Sidonie Jones. We hang out together all day, we find a newt, I share my Oreos with you, we even destroy Owen *and* get his precious Nike top wet, and how do you repay me? I ask you to come and see my cat versus axolotl racing track and you make up a lie and come and hang out with someone else!'

'But . . .' I glance at Bones, who is watching Zen with interest. 'I'm not hanging out with anyone else.'

'Yes, you are,' says Zen. 'I heard you talking to someone and laughing and I know you didn't draw that map!' But then he steps into the gloomy hut, looks around, blinks, looks around again and realises that, except for me, the hut is empty.

'See?' I say. 'There's no one here.'

'Oh . . .' He looks embarrassed and backs towards the door. 'Sorry, Sid. I guess I made a mistake.'

But then he stops looking embarrassed and stands a bit taller. 'Actually, I'm not sorry. The thing is, Sid, we've been friends for years, but recently you've changed. Most of the time you ignore me at school and you hardly ever come round to my house. I liked finding a newt with you today, but at the back of my mind I was thinking, if I found this newt at school, would I be able to show it to Sid? You see, sometimes you're not friendly at school, Sid, and that sucks, because if I did find a newt at school I'd want to show you, because that's what friends do. They show each other newts even if they are at school!'

He shakes his head and reaches for the door. 'Sorry. I'm going now. I can't stop talking about newts.'

Something tells me that if I let Zen walk out now then

I will lose the only non-ghost friend that I have. I jump to my feet. No matter what Zen thinks of me, I have to tell him the truth.

'Don't go,' I blurt out. 'You're right to be suspicious. I've told you loads of lies and there is someone here.'

'Where?' says Zen, looking all around.

I feel hot all over. Will Zen believe what I'm about to tell him? I guess there's only one way to find out.

'He's sitting over there,' I say, and I point at the crate under the window where Bones is now sitting, arms folded, legs set wide apart.

Zen eyes the crate. 'Um . . . OK.'

'I'm not making this up, Zen, and it isn't a game, I promise. A pirate, sorry, a privateer, is sitting on that crate right now, watching you. He's big and he's got seaweed in his beard and more scars than I've ever seen on one person. He was the captain of the *Black Gannet* and he was sailing back from Nassau when his ship went down.'

'Don't forget my bird,' says Bones.

'And he's got a parrot. Right now she's perched on his shoulder picking her beak with her claw.'

Zen's eyes narrow. 'Your pirate has a parrot too?'

I nod. 'She's a macaw and she's called Elizabeth and she can talk.'

'If they are here in this hut how come I can't see them?'

'Because they're both ghosts,' I say.

Zen stares at me. 'And you can see them because . . . ?'

'I don't really know,' I say. Then, realising how strange this must look to Zen, I turn to Bones and ask, 'How come I can see you, but Zen can't?'

Bones scratches his beard. 'Well now, there's a question.

Back in my day there were a fair few folk like you around, those who could see the hidden world and do magic and whatnot, but from what Olive and Elvis have told me, I don't believe there are so many now. You have the gift, Sid, most likely inherited from your mother. That's how it always used to work.'

The gift. What a strange way to describe being able to see ghosts. 'So there's no way Zen can see you?' I ask.

Bones shrugs his big shoulders. 'I don't suppose there is. Not unless he's got the gift too.'

I look at Zen. He's got melted ice cream down his 'I Code Like a Girl' T-shirt that I know he won in an advanced maths competition.

'He's definitely *gifted*,' I tell Bones. 'But I'm not sure he's got the gift.'

And this is when Zen gets freaked out. 'Sid, you do realise that you're talking to a *crate*?'

'Not a crate, Zen. A pirate ghost called Ezekiel Kittow.'

Zen looks seriously worried now. 'Sid, are you sure you're feeling OK? Did you drink enough water on the trip? Maybe you've got sunstroke . . . I think I should take you to see your dad.'

'I'm fine, Zen. I can just see ghosts, that's all!' And I guess I must shout these words because then Zen gives me the look, the one I'm always getting from Owen and the one I've been getting all my life. It's the look my first teacher, Mrs Parr, gave me when I told her that the classroom always smelled of roses just before hometime and it's the look Roundabout Tommy gave me when I asked him why the zebra felt sadder than the other animals. I've even got it from my dad a few times.

In a panic I wonder what I can say or do to stop Zen looking at me like that. I force myself to laugh. 'Sorry. Forget I said anything. I was joking.'

The hut goes very quiet. Zen stares at me and then he stares at the crate. Bones looks right back at him, arms still folded.

After a few seconds, Zen says, 'No you weren't. You were deadly serious. When did your pirate die?'

'Seventeen twenty-one,' I say.

Zen shakes his head. 'No, when *exactly*.'

'Twas a Friday, the eleventh of May,' says Bones, his voice heavy.

'He says it was Friday, the eleventh of May.'

Zen pulls out his phone and starts tapping away. 'What phase was the moon in on that exact day?'

'He's not going to remember that, is he?' I protest. 'It was over three hundred years ago.'

'It was a full moon,' interrupts Bones, 'and it had lit our way home that evening. I thought it was a good omen, until the clouds rolled in and hid her from view.'

'He says it was a full moon.'

Zen looks up, wide-eyed. 'You're right . . . Ask who the governor in Nassau was when he died.'

Bones screws up his face with concentration. 'Well, that is a tricky one. You see, for many years it was a gentleman named Woodes Rogers – we were privateers together, back in the day – only he left Nassau just before I did.' He drums his feet on the floor of the hut as he thinks a bit more. 'I can't know for certain, but I believe a fellow called George Phenney was governor when I left.'

'He thinks it was someone called George Phenney,' I say to Zen.

Zen starts laughing. 'Sid . . . this is *amazing*. No offence or anything, but you're rubbish at history. You thought Henry the Eighth was called Henry the Eighth because he had eight wives. Someone in this room must have told you about Phenney!'

I'm too relieved to feel offended. 'I wish you could see him, Zen. He's a proper pirate, not like the ones we get round here on Pirate Day. Right now he's picking his teeth with his dagger!'

'I've had a bit of salted beef stuck in there since the *Gannet* went down,' explains Bones.

I repeat this to Zen and he says, 'And the map?'

I take it out and pass it to him. 'It's a copy of one Bones died holding. He's got it in his hands right now.

'It's real, Zen.'

CHAPTER FORTY

'Was your mum surprised when you asked for a spade?' I ask Zen.

It's Saturday morning and we're walking along the seafront towards the fishing huts.

'No, she was relieved. Last week I took a sword to the beach. Apparently that's illegal.'

Yesterday, after Zen had bombarded Bones with questions – *How exactly did you die? Have you ever had to walk the plank? Where do pirates go to the toilet? Do ghosts go to the toilet? Have you put fireworks in your beard?* – I told him that the map matched perfectly with Gull Island. Of course, he insisted on coming with us today, so now we're going to meet Bones armed with spades, bottles of water and lots of sandwiches and cake made by Zen's dad.

Bones is waiting outside the fishing hut, pacing up and down. 'At last!' he says, followed by, 'Come on. We need to be off.'

We walk over the cliff path, retracing our route from yesterday. I use the journey to fill Zen in on everything that's happened over the past few weeks. It's amazing to finally be able to tell him all the incredible things that have been going on.

'So you did something that made a pub full of ghosts appear in the graveyard,' Zen says. 'How awesome is that? Can I visit the pub?'

I tell him that seeing as he can't see the door, I doubt it, but he's keen to try as soon as possible. 'I'm not sure that's such a good idea,' I say and then I tell him all about Old Scratch and his ghost dog and how it bit me yesterday.

'I would *love* to be bitten by a ghost,' he says, totally missing the point. 'And you're telling me that Old Scratch is some kind of ancient man who looks about thirty? I want to meet him.'

'No, you don't,' I say. 'He's like a big bony moth, and he smells like damp cellars and Christmas pudding.'

'He sounds cool.'

'He really isn't.'

'Could he be a vampire?' says Zen. 'They live to be hundreds of years old.'

'I seriously hope he isn't.'

Then Zen bombards me with questions, most of which I can't answer. I tell him that I don't know how I let Bones out or why Old Scratch is so old, and that I haven't got a clue what Old Scratch does when he's down in the cellar. In the end Zen turns his attention back to Bones and Elizabeth, claiming he can hear Elizabeth, very faintly.

'I reckon I've got a tiny bit of the gift,' he says. 'If you've got it one hundred per cent, I've got it, like, three per cent.' He looks at my shoulder where I've told him Elizabeth is perched and says, 'Get her to talk again.'

'Hello, Elizabeth,' I croon in my softest voice.

'BUM!' she replies.

'What did she say?' asks Zen.

When I tell him, he laughs so loud Elizabeth takes off into the sky. 'Sid, I cannot believe that you've been going round school with a parrot who says "bum" and you kept it to yourself.'

Next I tell Zen all about the ghosts trapped inside the

Halfway House, or rather, Bones tells me and I pass the information on.

'If we ignore Emma, the most recent fellow to turn up is Dai Hughes,' says Bones. 'Lovely chap. Prefers to be called "Elvis". He was in Fathom for Pirate Day back in 1974. Apparently, the wiring wasn't done right on his microphone. He'd just started singing "Suspicious Minds" when he came a cropper.'

I relate all this back to Zen.

'Hang on,' says Zen. 'If Bones is three hundred years old, how come he knows about microphones and "Suspicious Minds?"'

'I thought you said your friend was clever!' says Bones. 'Remind him that I've been stuck in the Halfway House with plenty of modern folk like you two. Emma the wraith arrived in the year of two thousand and fifteen, only we've not been able to learn much from her on account of how she can only scream "Wayne".'

Next Zen wants to know if there are any famous people in the Halfway House.

'Hey, Bones,' he says to the area around my shoulder (actually Bones is now well ahead of us), 'Have you met Elizabeth the First or the real Elvis or Bruce Lee or Napoleon or Prince?'

Bones makes a grumbling sound. He's obviously getting irritated with Zen's questions. 'Tell your babble-merchant friend that everyone unlucky enough to be inside the Halfway House died close to Fathom.' But then, after a moment's thought, he adds, 'I suppose Beau Fiddler might be considered famous as he was a highwayman, and Mister Holkar claims that he was a famous detective, but he also says he is an Indian prince so I am not sure you can take him at his word.'

'Amazing,' says Zen when I've relayed this to him. 'I wonder if Beau will teach me to sword fight . . . ?' Then he shouts wildly into thin air: 'Hey, Bones! What do you think?'

'NO!' Bones roars back, then he strides on, keen to get to Gull Island the moment the causeway is revealed.

'Look, Sid.' Zen nudges me. 'That girl is watching us again.'

We're just passing Orlig House and sure enough, up in the north tower I can see the same pale face at the window. She's wearing her fluffy hoodie again, only this time she's holding a pair of binoculars up to her face.

Before I can stop him, Zen starts waving his spade around and calling, 'Helloooo!'

Quick as a flash, the girl disappears behind the curtain.

'You scared her,' I say.

Zen shrugs. 'I was only trying to be friendly.'

'Oi!' bellows Bones. 'You two might have all the time in the world to be waving spades around, but I do not!'

CHAPTER FORTY-ONE

Hiding our spades behind our backs, Zen and I pay our entrance fee to get into the Hidden Gardens of Trendeen, then walk down through the valley garden. We go quickly and I try not to think about the moment Snout leaped out of the shadows and sank her teeth into my ankle. But today there's no rustling sounds or panting coming from the bushes. Still, it's a relief when we step out onto the beach.

We're too early. Half a mile of glittering sea still separates us from the lush green of Gull Island.

'I reckon we could swim it,' says Zen.

'With spades?' I ask.

We have no choice but to wait for the tide to fall. Bones strides up and down. Zen and I skim stones. Just after Zen has managed six bounces in a row, he shouts, 'There! I can see it!'

A line of smooth rock emerges from the waves, leading to Gull Island.

Bones is far too impatient to wait until the causeway is clear of the sea. 'Come on,' he says, marching forward. 'Wet toes never killed a fellow.'

Says the man who drowned, I think, as Zen and I take off our shoes and follow him across the causeway.

The water is icy cold, but I like how smooth the stone feels under my feet. Soon we reach Gull Island and we pull on our trainers and hurry after Bones as he disappears into the trees.

The island is a wild place. Roses and honeysuckle scramble between the trees and daisies poke out through the long grass. I'm holding Bones's map, but he seems to know exactly where he's going and he confidently leads us through a maze of trees and weeds.

'Wait for us!' I shout, as he floats through a patch of brambles.

'You'd better not be joking about this whole ghost thing,' says Zen, as we struggle after him.

Just when I'm wondering if Bones actually knows where he's going, he disappears inside a great mound of ivy, then yells, 'Over here!'

The ivy covers a wall and when we've found a gap big enough to squeeze through we realise that we've come out on the other side of the island. We're standing in the ruins of a house. Years ago, it would have faced the sea but now there are only a few crumbling walls left.

A tingle runs up my back. We're surrounded by trees, flowers, sea and sky. This feels like a secret, magical place.

Bones must feel it too because, with a happy sigh, he throws himself into the long grass of the meadow. Zen starts running in and out of the rooms of the ruin. 'A fireplace would have been here,' he says. 'You can see a bit of the chimney. And, look, this would have been a window. Someone would have stood here looking out to sea.'

'But not Bones,' I say.

I'm standing in what had once been the doorway. The door itself is long gone and all that's left is an archway of stone. It's been battered by the rain and wind, but I can just see something engraved on the slab above my head: two entwined willow branches, a shell and the date, 1759.

'Zen, Bones!' I call. 'You've got to see this. Bones's flag is over the door. This must be the farmhouse Mr Lawrence showed us in class!'

They join me and we look up at the engraving.

'Well, blow me down,' says Bones. 'It's my jack!'

'It doesn't make sense,' I say, looking at the date. 'You couldn't have lived here. This house was built ten years after you died.'

'No. This was never my home,' says Bones, turning to look across the meadow. 'But I am certain I have stood on this spot. This place was even wilder back then. There were more flowers, thrift and sheep's bit, and the grass moved like the sea.' He turns and flashes one of his big grins. 'This would be a fine place to live, would it not?'

'Definitely,' I say. 'But more importantly, it would be a fine place to bury treasure. It's quiet, away from Fathom, secret.'

'You're right!' says Bones. 'You two should get digging.'

'What's he saying?' says Zen, tugging at my sleeve.

'That we need to start digging for that cross.'

While Bones lies in the meadow, Zen and I consult the map. We do have some clues: some trees, a stack of rocks and of course the X.

'It looks like the treasure was buried near here,' says Zen, pointing to a spot in front of the farmhouse.

'Let's go,' I say, sinking my spade into the soil.

To begin with, we're full of energy. It's fun – a real-life treasure hunt – but we soon discover that digging is hard work. We stop every now and then to eat cake and sandwiches, or to run down to the sea to splash our faces with water, but we manage to keep going until mounds of earth are dotted all around us.

I wipe my sweaty forehead and look at my watch. We're running out of time. The tide starts to turn in half an hour and we can't risk getting trapped on this island. I'm about to tell Zen that we need to go when he shouts, 'I've found something!'

But all he's found is a tin with *Tucker's Boil Dressings* written on the front.

'I don't think this is Bones's treasure,' I say, putting it in my rucksack along with all the other bits and bobs we've found today: three glass bottles, a shilling coin, a single hoop earring and lots of broken bits of pottery.

My back hurts and I've got blisters on my hands, but I don't complain because I know we've so little time left to dig.

Bones is sitting on a hummock of grass staring at the sea. He looks like a picture that's faded in the sun.

Even Elizabeth seems to be losing energy. She's spent most of the day up in a tree, only occasionally squawking, 'Bully!' or 'Rum!' For a moment, I wonder why Bones isn't urging us to dig faster or deeper – it's like he's given up – but when I go over I realise he's distracted by something.

'Can you see it, Jones?' he asks.

'See what?'

'The ship.' He points at the horizon. 'She's a schooner, I believe, two-masted with sails as white as snow.'

I stare at the distant sea. At first all I can see are clouds, but then, just for a moment, I think that I spot the shape of sails. 'Maybe . . .'

'It's come for me and my crew, Jones. That's how we leave this world – well us sailors, anyway – we sail away to a better place. Don't you think this means we're close to finding it?'

'Definitely,' I say, but when I look at the bumpy meadow, I'm not so sure. We've dug a lot of holes, but far more ground is undisturbed. Can we really find Bones's treasure hidden in this big meadow? And what if it's buried under the house?

I push this gloomy thought away and instead I picture

a gold cross lying just beneath my feet. The emeralds will be dull with mud, worms will be twisting round it, but maybe tomorrow we will lift it into the sun, then dip it in the sea, making it shine again. Bones will stop fading away. His crew will no longer be lost souls and will walk out of the Halfway House. Then, together, they will sail away.

I keep this brilliant thought in my head as say, 'It must be here somewhere. Me and Zen, we've already agreed that we're coming back tomorrow. We'll find it, Bones.'

Zen comes over. 'Where is Bones?' he asks.

'There,' I say, nodding at the patch of poppies where Bones is sitting.

'She's right, we will,' says Zen, doing his best to look at Bones. 'And we'll come the weekend after that too. We'll get membership to the Hidden Gardens of Trendeen if we have too!'

Bones looks at him and smiles. 'He's a good lad, isn't he, Jonesy? You can tell him that from me.'

But before I can say the words, Bones has got to his feet, reached out a big hand and patted Zen on the top of his head.

'ARGHHH!' screams Zen, grabbing his hair. 'What was that? It felt like the ice bucket challenge times ten!'

'*That* was a ghost giving you a pat,' I say.

Zen eyes widen. 'For real? Tell him to do it again!'

And so, because Zen insists, Bones does do it again and again and again, as we walk across the causeway, through the Hidden Gardens of Trendeen and then back along the cliff path. Each time Zen laughs and screams like he's being tickled, and shouts things like, 'Ghosts are real!' and 'Best day ever!' and this distracts us all from the fact that this really isn't the best day ever.

We've failed, and each time I glance at Bones I'm reminded of this fact. When we were crossing the causeway the edges of his coat vanished and his black boots and beard are now as grey as the clouds that have scudded across the sky. It's grown breezy too, and as each gust of wind hits us I worry that Bones might blow away.

'Don't look like that,' says Bones.

'Like what?' I ask.

'Like a carp that's just got hooked,' he says, then he does an impression of me looking big-eyed and worried.

'What's he saying?' asks Zen.

278

'He's telling me that I look like a carp.'

He shrugs. 'Someone had to break the news to you.'

'I look like this because I'm worried about you,' I tell Bones. 'What if we don't find your treasure in time? What if you become a wraith like Emma? Each time I look at you some bit of you has gone. If you become a wraith then you'll be trapped here forever, and your crew will never leave the Halfway House. What if that happens, Bones?'

'*What if, what if . . .* That's a dullard's way of thinking, Jones. Each time I set sail, I knew that there were a hundred calamities that could befall me: drowning, scurvy, getting trapped in the doldrums, running out of water, being on the wrong end of an argument, tuberculosis, dysentery, getting cursed by a witch, getting stamped on by a horse – that, of course, was a land-based calamity – getting eaten by a shark, being lured to my death by sirens. Did I worry? I did not!'

'Why?' I say. 'Perhaps you wouldn't have drowned if you'd worried a bit more.'

'P'rhaps . . . P'rhaps not. P'rhaps, if I'd decided *not* to climb on board my first ship, I'd have walked home, slipped in some muck and bonked my head like what happened to the innkeeper of the Benbow. What I am saying is that we do not know what will happen tomorrow, but we do know about the here and now, and right now you are with friends, strolling by the sea and having a jolly time, are you not?'

And with that he gives Zen a ghostly boot up the bottom.

'AAAGHHH!' yells Zen. 'Ice cubes down my pants!'

I burst out laughing. 'I am!'

'That's better,' says Bones. 'Now you look like a lovely sprat.'

CHAPTER
FORTY-TWO

I'm smiling when I walk into the model village. My fingers might be blistered, and we didn't find the treasure, but Bones was right. We had a jolly time, and we are going back to Gull Island tomorrow. We are going to get there as early as we possibly can, and we're taking plasters for our blisters.

'Dad!' I call out. 'I'm home!' But then I see that the kiosk is empty and the 'Back in 5' sign is propped against the glass.

I help myself to a can of Coke, then walk towards the bench by the cricket pitch. I want to look at Bones's map, see if there's something we missed at Gull Island today.

'Sid Jones.'

The dry voice makes me jump, and when I look up I see that the bench is already taken. Old Scratch is sitting there, arms folded, legs stretched out. The shock of seeing him freezes me to the spot. He stares at me with his tiger eyes. This close, I can see cracks in his lips and the blue veins under his thin skin. His waistcoat and coat look ancient, like they've been pulled out of a dusty trunk, but I notice that the boots he's wearing are just like Dad's. For some reason this frightens me more than anything else.

'What do you want?' I manage to say.

'A friendly word.' His voice sounds anything but friendly. It's cold and hard. I take a step back, but in one swift movement he's jumped to his feet and blocked my path. He points a long white finger at my face. 'You don't know what you have started. This . . . *game* you're playing – running around Fathom with Kittow, playing detectives, looking for buried treasure – is about to take a dangerous turn.'

'You're threatening me,' I say, backing away, looking over his shoulder for Dad.

His eyes narrow. 'No. I'm *warning* you. I don't know how you set Kittow free, but when you did, you unlocked a door to a world of powerful magic. People get hurt in that world, Sid Jones. People disappear. It is not a game!'

He steps even closer to me. His eyes bulge. I try not to breathe in his ancient smell of spices and damp. 'I am giving you one chance. Persuade Kittow to come back to the Halfway House and we can forget this ever happened.'

'No,' I say, shaking my head.

'Then that door that you opened, just a crack,' he lurches forward, shoving his face close to mine, 'is about to blow wide open!'

'What do you mean?'

He holds up his curled fist and squeezes it. I hear a crunching sound and then he opens his fingers and lets something fall to the ground before turning and striding out of the model village.

I'm still standing there, shaking, when Dad walks in.

'You all right, Sid?' he asks. 'Had fun with Zen?'

'Yes . . . it was great.'

'So why are you standing there like a lemon?'

'One of the models is broken,' I say, picking up the bits Old Scratch dropped. 'It's you . . .'

Of course, Dad put our cottage and the model village in

Fathomless, and added a mini Dad and a mini me. Old Scratch has crushed the model of Dad in his hand, snapping off his arms, legs and head.

Dad comes over and I show him what's left.

'It's ruined,' I say. 'It can't be fixed.'

'Course it can,' he says, putting his arm round me. 'Everything can be fixed.'

CHAPTER
FORTY-THREE

On Sunday I don't go to Gull Island.

When Zen turns up to find out where I am, I hear Dad telling him that I feel ill, that I must have got too much sun yesterday and that I've got a headache. He's not lying. I hardly slept last night worrying about what Old Scratch said and did, and wondering what I should do. But if I thought hiding away in my bedroom would make me feel better, I'm wrong.

I try to work on my map, but it doesn't weave its calming magic like it usually does. My mind keeps going back to Bones and the thought of him alone in the fishing hut. We were so close to finding his treasure, but if I keep looking,

Dad could get hurt. That's obviously what Old Scratch was telling me when he crushed the model.

But if I stay away, Bones will never find his treasure and he'll become a wraith. Just the thought of Emma's haunted eyes fills me with panic. How can I let that happen to Bones? And it's not just him. His entire crew is relying on me!

In the end I decide this isn't something I can work out on my own, and I pull on my jumper. I need to find Zen.

When I get to the museum, his mum tells me he's gone to the fishing huts 'to play'.

To talk to a ghost, more like. Sure enough, after I've crept down Fathom's narrow alleyways, keeping an eye out for Old Scratch, I find Zen sitting opposite Bones in the hut.

'Were there really weevils in your ship's biscuits?' he asks the air. 'Tap once for "yes" and twice for "no".' Bones gives him the lightest of taps on his knee, then Zen says, 'What about walking the plank. Did that ever happen?' Tap, tap, goes Bones – then the two of them look up and see me.

'Sid!' Bones cries. 'Feeling better, are we? Zen said your head was aching and I wanted to suggest a compress of cow dung and treacle. It's what my mother always gave me and it worked every time!'

Straight away, I realise that I've got to keep helping him. He looks so wasted and fragile today and his booming voice has become a rasp, but I can save him. 'I'm so sorry we couldn't go to Gull Island,' I say in a rush. 'I know there's not much time left. I should have made myself get out of bed and go.'

Bones waves my words away. 'I've had a grand time with young Zen here.'

'We can go tomorrow after school,' says Zen. 'I've checked the tide times and if we get off the bus at Trendeen we can get in a whole hour of digging and still be home in time for tea.'

'I am afraid I will have to sit this jaunt out,' says Bones. 'Like you, Jones, I'm feeling weary today.' And that's when I notice that his shining cutlass has become a pale smudge. 'But be sure to visit me on your way home and show me what you have found. Who knows? Perhaps you will come running in here holding my cross!'

I push all thoughts of Old Scratch out of my head, and I say to Bones. 'We'll go to the island whenever we can. We'll dig until we find your treasure. I promise!'

But the next day, when we get off the bus at Trendeen, I'm not sure I can keep my promise to Bones.

The bus pulls away, leaving Zen and me alone on the coast road. We're still wearing our school uniforms and clutching spades wrapped in bin bags. All day we've been telling our teachers they're for an 'environment project', and, luckily, they've believed us.

'Zen, are you sure this is a good idea?' I say, eyeing the hedges that line the sides of the road. Old Scratch could be lurking behind any one of them, watching us. He's obviously spied on us before. He must have been here on the day of the school trip when Snout came after me and yesterday he knew we'd been 'playing detectives' and 'looking for buried treasure'. It's an uncomfortable thought, and it's making me want to get the next bus back to Fathom.

Zen frowns. 'I don't get it, Sid. Yesterday you told Bones that we were going to dig until we found his treasure. Now you don't think it's a good idea. What's changed?'

'Nothing,' I say, glancing down the road.

'That's not true! You're jumpy as Skye when Dad lets her eat chocolate spread straight from the jar. Tell me what the matter is and don't even think about lying. We're a team, remember? We're Sid and Zen, the Dead Good Detectives!'

'When did we become the Dead Good Detectives?'

'Yesterday. Bones and I decided it was the best name.'

'That must have taken a lot of tapping.'

'It did. My knee was so cold that I couldn't walk for half an hour afterwards. Now, come on. Tell me what's wrong.'

So I tell him all about finding Old Scratch in the model village and what he said and did.

'I'm scared he's going to hurt my dad, Zen. He could be watching us right now!'

'You're right,' he says, his eyes flicking up and down the road. Then he lowers his voice and whispers, 'I've got a plan. But before I tell you what it is, I want you to follow me, and act normal.'

He turns and strolls into the driveway of Trendeen. I go with him, but we've only taken a few steps inside when he ducks down and darts behind a display of tropical plants.

'What are we doing?' I ask, crouching next to him.

'Hiding,' he says. 'We'll stay here for five minutes. If Old Scratch is following us, then we'll see him go past.'

'That's a good idea,' I say.

'Never underestimate how much TV I watch, Sid. I get all my best ideas from TV.'

As we hide behind our jungle of plants he tells me his plan.

'There are two things we're going to do,' he says. 'One, we're going to keep looking for Bones's treasure. From what you've told me, Old Scratch is one seriously creepy dude, but he didn't actually say he was going to hurt your dad, did he? He just crunched up a model, which is not a nice thing to do, but it's very different from *actually* crunching up your dad.'

I shift uncomfortably. I wish Zen would stop talking about 'crunching Dad'. 'I guess,' I say. 'But he did set his dog on me.'

'His dog that can't actually bite because she's a ghost! Old Scratch is basically a bully and there's no way we can send Bones back into that bully's time-warp pub-prison.'

'I agree,' I say, keeping my eyes glued to the driveway. 'I realised that when I saw Bones yesterday. But what's the second thing we're going to do? How are we going to keep looking for the treasure and stay safe?'

'We're going to do stuff like *this*. We're going to start acting like proper detectives, so he doesn't know that we're still helping Bones. Old Scratch doesn't know we're here, does he? He wasn't sitting on that bus and he hasn't come down the driveway, so we're fine. But from now on, we watch our backs. We're not playing at being detectives, Sid. We *are* detectives.'

And then, being as quiet and sneaky as we can, we pay our entry, go through the garden, and creep across to Gull Island.

We dig furiously for the whole hour, but this time we don't even discover any rusty tins. Before we leave the island, we find a place to hide our spades. Now if Old Scratch spots us back in Fathom, he won't know what we've been up to.

When we come out of Trendeen, we turn away from the coast path and instead walk the long way home, through the woods. 'Change your routine, baffle your enemy!' declares Zen as we follow a path into the trees.

'Did you get that off the TV?' I ask.

'Nope. That's one hundred per cent Zen Moyo,' he says proudly.

The woods might be a change of routine, but they're also quite spooky. To distract ourselves from the swaying trees and shifting shadows, Zen quizzes me about the Halfway House. He's determined to watch me walking inside, to see if it looks like I'm walking through a wall. I promise to let him do this when we're certain Old Scratch isn't around, then he asks me a surprising question.

'Sid, why did you stop hanging out with me? I mean, I know we kept going to the graveyard, but why did you stop coming to my house and playing at school?'

Zen's like this. He doesn't avoid saying or doing things because they're embarrassing. He just goes for it. Straight away, I start to blush as I remember that strange time when everything seemed to change for me.

'It's a hard thing to explain,' I say.

'Try,' he insists.

I break a leaf off a tree and start crumpling it up in my fingers and I try. 'It began with my map.'

'Your map's amazing!'

'That's what I thought. Do you remember how I drew every single thing I saw in Fathom on it?'

Zen nods. 'And not just *things*,' he says. 'You put memories and smells on there and different colours depending on how places made you feel. You made the museum a rainbow.'

'Because that's how good it is. Anyway, when I showed my map to Mrs Lewis, I thought she was going to say, "Wow, that is the best thing you've ever done in your life, Sid!" But she just frowned and asked why I'd made the school green when the bricks were grey. Then, later, I saw her showing it to our teaching assistant, Mrs Sayid.' I take a deep breath because the next part of the story is the bit that makes me feel really stupid.

'Right,' says Zen. 'So what happened?'

'OK, so I could see her holding my map, and I really believed she was telling Mrs Sayid how good it was. I thought, maybe she didn't want to say anything earlier because there were other children around, so I sort of snuck up on them to listen and I heard her say, "When you do the display, don't put Sid's map up, it's . . ."'

'It's *what*?' says Zen.

This next word is hard to say. When I heard it come out of Mrs Lewis's mouth, I felt like I'd been hit in the stomach.

'*Weird.* That's why my map never went on the wall, Zen. It was weird.'

He looks worried. And confused. 'OK, so that was a mean thing for Mrs Lewis to say. But what's it got to do with me?'

'Because that's when I knew *I* was weird, Zen! I mean, Owen Kidd has been telling me for years, but when your teacher says something, it's official, isn't it? Plus there is other evidence of my weirdness. I notice stuff other people don't see, I've got a giant map instead of a phone, and when all the girls in our class started doing TikTok dances I was building dens in a graveyard with you!'

'And there was your cloak,' says Zen, helpfully, 'and you say you can hear trees' hearts beating and you're always telling me what stuff smells like. Oh, and let's not forget when you freed that pirate from the ghost pub.'

'Exactly! Totally and utterly weird, and hanging out with you only made things worse –'

'Because I'm weird too,' he says, looking like he couldn't care less.

'*Yes.* Zen, you regularly pretend to walk into lamp posts

and wear antique clothes, so I thought if I was going to have any friends at all at secondary school, I'd better start acting normal.'

'So I had to go.'

I nod. 'I'm sorry. I thought we could keep being friends out of school, just playing in the graveyard. It was a stupid thing to do.'

'And it was never going to work,' says Zen, 'because out of the two of us, you are by far the weirdest. In fact, if I'd never met you, I'd probably be playing FIFA on the Xbox with Owen right now instead of hunting for a pirate ghost's missing treasure . . . Do you see what I'm saying, Sid?'

'Weird is good?'

He grins. 'Weird is the best!'

Suddenly I remember something Bones said to me when I first met him. 'Do you know, even Bones has called me weird, and he's a ghost!'

'That doesn't count,' says Zen.

'Why not?'

'Because Bones is over three hundred years old and back then weird meant something totally different.'

I stop walking. We've reached a quiet place in the forest.

Trees sway high above us. Leaves crackle. I can hear my own breath.

'What did it mean?'

'Weird meant you could control fate. It's why the witches in *Macbeth* are called "weird sisters". They're not "weird" because they've got beards, but because they can use their witchy skills to change Macbeth's life.' Zen wiggles his fingers in front of my face in a magical way. Then he says, 'Come on,' and starts walking again. 'It will be getting dark soon and I don't want to get lost in the forest with a weirdo like you!'

I follow him. I'm not blushing any more, but there is a warmth beating inside me.

Weird, I think, trying the word out. *I'm weird.*

Then I breathe in the smells of the forest and I run after Zen.

CHAPTER FORTY-FOUR

The next few days feel . . . wobbly.

Change is all around and inside me.

Skull and crossbones flags are being hung around Fathom ready for Pirate Day and a stage is going up on the harbour. Dad adds miniature flags and a tiny stage to the model village. I go to school as usual, and I spend every break and lunchtime with Zen trying to work out when we can get back to Gull Island. He's still doing embarrassing things, like asking teachers where they got their shoes from and fighting invisible things, but I'm not finding it so embarrassing any more. I guess I'm starting to see it was me who had the problem. Not Zen.

Because of school and the tide, the earliest we can get back to Gull Island is Saturday, Pirate Day, but that's no good because the biggest change of all is happening to Bones.

He's disappearing.

The tips of his boots have gone and the green has disappeared from his beard. If he turns his head quickly he looks like a puff of smoke that becomes Bones again a moment later.

Every day, after school, we find him in the fishing hut. Always, his eyes are glued to the sea.

I keep telling him how sorry I am that we can't dig for his treasure, and he tells me not to worry, because his magical cloud ship is still out there waiting for him. And maybe it is, because when I squint my eyes, sometimes I think I can see two sails puffed full of air.

As we can't go to Gull Island, we spend our time talking. If Zen's there, Bones tells us all about his life as a sailor. Well, he tells me, and then I pass it all on to Zen. If it's just me, Bones talks about different things: Margery, his mum and dad (whose name he's finally remembered), about how scared he used to feel during storms because he never learned to swim. I decide all this talking is good because the more Bones talks, the more he is remembering about his past.

When I walk into the fishing hut on Thursday, I find him hunched over on his crate. Today the feathers in his hat only have a trace of colour and his beard is snowy white. Elizabeth, I realise, is so quiet that I don't even jump when she lands on my shoulder and says with a pathetic squawk, 'Sid, bully, rum!'

Bones smiles, then points to the window and says, 'Look, Jones. The ship is there.'

'We can visit Gull Island on Saturday,' I say. 'We're going to spend as long as we can there, even though it's Pirate Day. We'll be back in time for Zen to take part in the parade.'

'A parade of pirates,' he says. 'Won't that be a fine sight! Perhaps you would like me to give you some instruction on how to dress? I found a bit of burnt cork rubbed across my face got me ready for a skirmish, and there were fellows who set fire to their beards. A few rags soaked in tallow and then tied amongst your hair and set alight should do the trick.'

'I'm not taking part in the parade,' I say quickly, and then, because I can say anything to Bones, I add, 'I'd like to. Really, I love dressing up, but when people look at me I go red and get embarrassed, and then I get annoyed with myself for being embarrassed and, well, it's just easier if I stay at home with Dad.'

Bones laughs and says, 'You're like my Willow. When she met a stranger she would cover her eyes with her hands like so,' he holds his big hands in front of his face, 'and hope no one could see her!'

'Who's Willow?' I ask.

For a moment he looks confused, and then shocked. 'Why . . . she was my little girl, Jones.' His eyes light up as he remembers more. 'I met her mother in Nassau and married her during a typhoon. Beth Talleroy was her name and she was the kindest of women, although she had a temper on her you would not believe.'

'I didn't know you had a family.' It's hard to imagine Bones with a baby in his big arms.

He shakes his head in amazement. 'I don't think I remembered myself until now . . . But what sort of a man forgets his own wife and child, Jones?'

'A man who is over three hundred years old?' I say. 'It's not your fault. Your memory has holes in it.'

But he won't accept this and he jumps to his feet and starts pacing up and down. 'That is a sorry excuse. I told you the name of the man I was incarcerated with – Edward No-Thumb – a man I knew for just two days, but I do not mention the name of my wife and little girl? Perhaps I couldn't bear to remember what a terrible husband I was, always sailing off and leaving them alone. Poor Beth and Willow . . .'

Willow. The name reminds me of something . . . Something that I've been wondering about ever since I set eyes on it. I take out my copy of Bones's map.

'Look!' I say, pointing at the willow branches on his flag. 'I don't think you forgot them, Bones. You said the willow branches were supposed to remind you of home: willow branches for your daughter, Willow. You were thinking of her when you were at sea!'

He stops pacing to stare hard at the map. 'But what good is *thinking*, Jones? A girl needs a father who is there to feed her and keep her warm and tell her about the world. A father like yours!' He collapses on a crate. 'Open the window, Jones!'

I open it as wide as it can go and he closes his eyes for a moment and lets the breeze blow over his face.

Then he turns to me and he says, 'Jonesy, I need you to promise me something. If I fade away to nothing and become a wraith, will you keep searching for my treasure? Find it. Take care of it. Keep it safe.' He thumps his chest. 'Just now, the pain of losing it hurts more than I can say.'

'I promise.' Then I touch his other hand and even though it feels like I'm pressing my fingers into snow, I keep them there for as long as I can bear the cold.

And that is the end of the conversation. Bones sits back on his crate and claims he feels 'deadly tired'. It's obvious that he wants me to go.

It's getting late, but as I walk back through Fathom, I find it buzzing with activity as everyone gets ready for Pirate Day.

Tables have been set up outside the Benbow and fairy lights are being strung along the Cockle. There's even a plank being secured to the harbour wall. That's for the moment when the losers in the Yo-Ho-Ho-ing competition walk the plank. Usually I'd love seeing these things happen, but as I walk towards the model village, I'm distracted, troubled by my thoughts of Bones, sitting alone in the hut, his time running out.

Back at home I find Dad has made me a pizza.

'Had a good day at school?' he asks.

'Yeah. It was good,' I say.

The pizza is from the freezer, and Dad doesn't ask me any more questions – he's too busy touching up the paint on Roundabout Tommy's beard – but like Bones said, he's here, with me, and for pudding he's cut me up an orange and he's done it just the way I like it, with all the white bits taken off.

'Thanks, Dad,' I say, after I've put my plates in the sink. Then I put my arms round him and give him a hug. He seems pretty happy about this, even if I do smudge Tommy's beard.

'You look tired,' he says. 'You should have an early night.'

'Maybe,' I say, but I don't go upstairs. It seems wrong to go up to my cosy room when Bones is alone in the fishing hut.

Zen's right. We have become detectives. And the moment I wrote Bones's name on my map I took on my first case . . . a case I'm about to fail.

But this treasure hunt has become so tangled. There's a map that leads to an island that wasn't an island, a ship that went down in a storm, a missing cross, and a forgotten wife and daughter. The only thing I'm certain about is that Bones's map shows Gull Island.

Somehow I've got to get back there so I can keep digging for the cross. I can't wait until Saturday. That might be too late!

The *Fathom Herald* is sitting on the table. I open it and find the tide times. Perhaps I can skip school tomorrow and dig all day? No, that won't work. I'd have to get up at the crack of dawn to get to the causeway, and if Dad found me missing in the morning, he'd be so worried he'd probably call the police.

I need to think of something else.

And then it hits me. There is a way I can get across to Gull Island. Really it's a ridiculous idea: it's risky and foolish and there are so many ways it could go wrong.

I just know Zen's going to love it.

'Dad,' I say, grabbing my coat. 'I'm going to see Zen.'

CHAPTER FORTY-FIVE

At midnight, I slip out of the house and go down the lane that leads to the seafront.

All of Fathom seems to be asleep. Curtains are closed. Lights are off. I can even hear snores coming from inside one cottage.

I find Zen waiting for me in the alleyway behind the Benbow, just like we planned.

'Got everything we need?' he asks, his eyes wide with excitement.

'Torch, snacks, watch,' I say. 'How about you?'

'I've got my phone and a bag of Doritos. Let's go!'

When I asked Zen if he wanted to go on a night-time

trip to Gull Island, the only question he asked was, 'What time do we go?' So now we're creeping along Fathom's many alleyways, making our way towards the coast path. I go first, holding up my hand when I want Zen to stop and then beckoning him forward when I've checked it's safe. We don't talk, and we stick to the shadows. We know that if anyone saw us, they'd take us straight home to our parents, because that's the sort of place Fathom is.

But there is another reason we're being so careful. We don't want to be spotted by Old Scratch. We're sure he won't expect us to be out at midnight, but we're not taking any chances.

It's only when we reach the coast path that we start to relax. No one will be on the cliffs at this time of night.

As we walk along my body tingles. The air is cool and a full moon lights our way. I feel wide awake.

'Sid, I can't believe we're doing this!' says Zen. 'It's the best idea you've ever had, and considering you once made a Flake and banana toasted sandwich, that's saying something.'

I can't quite believe it either, but as soon as the thought of visiting Gull Island during the night popped into my head, I knew I was going to do it. The tide times are perfect: we'll be there by one, have three hours to dig, then be back in our beds by five for an hour or two of sleep. We've got torches (a phone and an LED keyring), Zen knows a way of sneaking into Trendeen and our spades are already waiting for us on the island.

Zen's even got a back-up plan in case our torches die.

Every few steps that we take, he gets a white stone out of his pocket and drops it on the ground. He got the stones from his sister Skye's fish tank. Apparently it's what a customs officer called Daniel Whitworth used to do two hundred years ago when he was patrolling these cliffs looking for smugglers.

'I mean, I don't think he raided his little sister's fish tank for pebbles,' says Zen, 'but he definitely dropped white stones.'

'And you're sure it works?' I ask.

He turns me round and I see a line of white dots leading back towards Fathom. 'See?' he says. 'The stones shine in the moonlight.'

It feels good knowing that the moon will be lighting our way home, and we're both feeling excited when we reach Trendeen. Zen leads me past the locked entrance to a stile. 'It's a public right of way,' he says. 'We're not even breaking in.'

I'm pleased. I don't want to add trespassing to my crime of sneaking out of the house at midnight. We walk down into the garden, then step quietly through the trembling bamboo forest and past the pond fringed with the giant rhubarb plants.

The whole valley is bathed in silvery moonlight. Toads croak, leaves shiver and tiny creatures rustle near my feet. When I'm certain that I can't hear any panting dogs, I start to enjoy myself. I've never been scared of the dark and it feels magical walking through a tropical garden towards the sound of waves.

At the beach we find the causeway already standing clear of the water and leading towards a shadowy Gull Island. We hurry across, and I'm suddenly aware of how visible we must be on the causeway lit up by the moonlight.

Zen must feel this too because he says, 'He can't know we're here, can he?'

He doesn't need to tell me who he's talking about. 'No one knows we're here,' I say. 'Not even Bones.'

Even so we speed up, and we don't slow down until we reach Gull Island. We push through the overgrown bushes and trees until we find ourselves in the ruined farmhouse. Ahead of us, the meadow gleams a ghostly silver.

'This place looks even better at night time,' I say

Zen nods. 'We should camp out here.'

'Definitely. When all this is over and we've found Bones's treasure, let's do it,' I say, then we find our spades and get to work.

We dig in silence and the only thing that slows us down is my torch flickering on and off and then dying all together. The batteries have gone so we have to use Zen's phone whenever we want to look into a hole. But there's hardly anything to look at. A couple of times we get excited, but our two big finds turn out to be the rubbery bottom of a flip flop and a rusty can.

Zen's phone alarm is set to go at three. When we hear the beeps, we know we've got half an hour to get off the island.

Exhausted, I lean on my spade. 'I really thought we'd find something.'

'Me too,' says Zen. 'But we won't give up. We'll come

again on Saturday, Sid. Bones's treasure has to be here. X marks the spot!'

'I know,' I say, trying to hide how disappointed I feel. 'Come on. If we don't go now, we'll be trapped.'

The side of the island where we were digging must have been sheltered because when we reach the causeway we find a wind has built up. It knocks into us as we walk across the slippery stones, and the sea laps over our feet before we're even halfway across.

'We need to get a move on,' says Zen.

Keeping our eyes on the tropical plants of Trendeen we hurry.

Suddenly Zen freezes. 'What was that?' he says, pointing towards the shore.

At first, I can't see anything. Then I catch a glimpse of a shadow flitting across the beach. 'Turn off your phone,' I say. 'It's too bright.'

He kills the torch on his phone and we blink into the darkness. The sea swirls around our feet, trees thrash from side to side and the wind howls . . . but the shadow has gone.

'Might have been a fox?' suggests Zen.

Perhaps. Whatever it was, we have no choice but to keep going. If we go back to Gull Island we'll be trapped there until midday, and I can't imagine how I'd explain that to Dad.

This thought makes me speed up and I bump into Zen. The next thing I hear is a splash.

'My phone!' Zen cries, dropping to his knees. I join him and we feel around in the water, but it's hopeless. The phone has been swallowed up by the sea.

'I'm so sorry, Zen!'

He pulls me to my feet. 'Don't worry about it, Sid. It was so old it should have been in Mum and Dad's museum!'

Zen's got to be one of the most positive people in the world. 'But, Zen . . . It's your phone!'

He smiles. 'At least now you won't be the only person in Year Seven without one.' Then he starts walking again. 'Right now, the only thing that matters is getting off this causeway.'

I follow, pleased that we've got his pebbles to light our way home.

A few minutes later we're safely back on the mainland. Zen wants to have a look round for footprints, but it's just too dark. Instead we hurry back through the gardens not knowing if anyone is hiding in the trees, waiting for us.

We walk quickly and quietly. Zen is ahead of me and I keep my eyes glued to his back as we retrace our steps. I keep telling myself that the shadow was a fox, or a badger, or a cloud drifting over the moon . . . but I don't feel safe until we're out of the garden and walking along the cliff path.

There's nowhere to hide up here, just smooth grass, the cliff edge and far below that, the sea.

At least the wind has died down and Zen's pebbles work brilliantly, guiding us back to Fathom. As we walk, we chat about how much sleep we're going to get tonight (two hours at the most) and how we'll stay awake at school tomorrow.

'I'll get some cake from the museum café and you get us some very sugary drinks from the kiosk,' says Zen. 'We'll have an energy boosting picnic on the bus.'

We get so into planning what we're going to eat that we don't notice the mist. It rolls over the top of the cliffs, thick and silent, until suddenly we realise we're surrounded. Luckily we can still just see Zen's pebbles and we follow them in single file, with Zen leading the way, past Orlig House and then back up to the highest point on the cliff path.

'Thank you, customs man Whitworth!' says Zen. 'He might have died a stupid death, but he's helped us tonight.'

'Why did he die a stupid death?' I ask.

'He was tricked by the smugglers!' Zen says. 'They rearranged his stones so that instead of leading him back to the village, they led him to the cliff edge. His horse rode straight off!'

Then, in a flash, I sense something. The air is colder, saltier. The waves a fraction louder. The wind stronger. Faster than I've ever moved in my life, I reach out and grab the hood of Zen's top.

Just as my fingers close round the fabric, his feet slip out from underneath him and he plunges down the cliff. I throw myself backwards, landing on the grass and I wrap my fingers even tighter around Zen's hoodie. He thuds back against the cliff, but he doesn't fall. I've got him, just.

This all happens in a matter of seconds. Neither of us has time to yell or scream.

'You're safe!' I shout, then I try to pull him up, but he's so much bigger than me and I feel him slipping out of his hoodie.

'Don't drop me, Sid!' he cries. His arms and legs thrash around as he tries to grab hold of something, anything.

'Take my hand!' I shout, and I reach out to him. His fingers wrap round mine and only then do I let go of his hoodie. I hold on tightly to him with both hands as my mind races with panic. How can I pull him to safety? He's so much heavier than me and I can already feel myself being tugged closer to the edge of the cliff. My arm burns. My fingers ache. All I can do it hold on.

But then I realise something. I should have dropped Zen the moment he fell. Normally I couldn't lift Zen off the ground with both arms wrapped around him, but right now I'm holding on to him with one hand.

I'm weird, I think, and the truth of these words washes over me. I feel something hot spark inside me. *I'm weird.* The burning feeling spreads out through my body, tingling, rushing down my arm and into my fingers that are wrapped around Zen's.

'I'm going to pull you up!' I yell.

I feel rather than see him shake his head. 'You can't do it, Sid. I'm scared!'

'*I can.* Stay still!'

I dig my feet into the earth. I tell myself that I'm as strong as a tree, the cliffs, the wind that's pushing against me. Then I close my eyes and I pull.

The tingling in my fingers becomes a rush of energy and with one swift swoop, I lift Zen high enough so that he can grab hold of a clump of grass and scramble up next to me. For a second, neither of us speak. I'm still holding tight to his hand. I'm not sure I'll ever be able to let go.

Then, in a shaky voice, Zen says, 'What was that?'

'He rearranged the stones. Old Scratch wanted to hurt us!'

'I worked that out,' says Zen. 'I meant, what did you just do, Sid? You didn't pull me up the cliff. You *lifted* me.'

'People do strange things when they have to,' I say, finally letting go of his hand. 'Listen, Zen, we've got to get back from the cliff, and we have to be careful. Old Scratch could be anywhere in this mist.' I try to sound brave, but my voice is shaking and so is my body.

Slowly, carefully, we inch backwards, feeling around with our fingers. We keep going until the sound of the waves has faded away and we're back on the smoother grass of the cliff path. Then we sit there, huddled against each other, peering into the mist, listening, watching.

'Seriously, Sid. That was *amazing*!'

'It wasn't just me,' I say. 'You pushed yourself up.' I'm not sure if this is true. I'm not sure what just happened, but Zen's safe, and that's all that matters.

'What do we do now?' asks Zen.

'We wait,' I say. 'We can't walk along the cliff when it's dark. It was stupid of me to ever suggest it. If anything had happened to you, it would be my fault, Zen.'

'No, it wouldn't. It would be Old Scratch's fault. Why did he do it?'

'He wants us to stop helping Bones. He wants him to go back into the Halfway House and he'll do anything to make it happen.'

'But why?' asks Zen. 'Why is Bones so special? He's just a ghost. He can't even pick things up!'

'I don't know, but all that stuff Old Scratch said to me in the model village, about magic and danger . . . I don't think he was making it up.'

Then we stop talking, because we know it's not safe, and we stay like this, silent and still, our hearts thudding, until a pink light appears on the horizon and we can walk back to Fathom.

We say goodbye at the museum, knowing that we'll be meeting again in less than an hour.

'Sorry about your phone,' I say to Zen.

He smiles and shakes his head. 'Sid, you saved my life. We're even.'

I let myself back into the house, kick off my shoes then go upstairs and climb into bed wearing all my clothes, but I don't fall asleep. I lie there watching the golden morning light fill my room and reliving the terrifying moment when Zen stepped off the cliff.

How did I hold on to him? Our science teacher told us that adrenalin can give you superhuman strength and that people can lift up cars if they have to. Is that what happened to me?

'Wake up, lazy bones!' Dad's head appears round the door and I tuck my muddy hands under the duvet. 'Pirate Day tomorrow,' he says with a smile. 'And just in case you change your mind about dressing up, I've got your mum's costume down from the attic.'

CHAPTER FORTY-SIX

Zen bursts out of the museum and comes bouncing towards me.

'Good morning, Sid!' he says cheerfully. I'm expecting him to be bleary eyed, like me, but he seems to have more energy than ever.

'Have you been drinking coffee again?' I ask.

'No. I'm just really, really happy to be alive!' And to prove his point he swings round a lamp post.

All the way to the bus stop he jumps on and off the kerb. He can't keep still, and he can't stop talking either.

'Can you smell the sea, Sid? I can. It smells of rust and mountains and tins of mackerel.' He laughs and throws his arms up in the air. 'And the sky is so blue! It looks like bubble-gum ice cream has been splashed around up there with the odd smudge of vanilla.'

Zen's right: the sky is exactly the same colour as bubble-gum ice cream. But this is the sort of thing I notice, not him.

'Maybe not sleeping gives you energy,' I say.

'In that case I'm never going to sleep again!' he says. Then he runs over to the plastic pirate standing outside the Yo Ho Ho Shake Shack and gives it a big kiss before running back to me and announcing that we're going to Gull Island tomorrow and we're going to find Bones's treasure, 'No matter what!'

I guess not sleeping affects us in different ways, because while I struggle to get through the day, Zen seems absolutely fine. He plays football all lunchtime (scoring two goals) while all I can do is lie flat on my back and stare at the sky. On the bus back to Fathom he is full of plans for finding Bones's treasure, telling me that his dad has a broken metal detector that he's sure he can fix. He's still chatting away about the metal detector when we let ourselves into the fishing hut.

Bones is sitting on his crate. His trousers are grey and his boots have become cloudy blobs. When Elizabeth flies over my head she's a blur of white feathers. She looks so much like Emma that I have to turn away.

'There's my crew!' whispers Bones. 'Now why might young Zen look like he's sat on a weasel?'

I open my mouth to tell Zen what Bones has just said, but before I can say a word Zen cries out, 'I can hear you . . . I CAN SEE YOU!' And he runs over and throws his arms

around Bones's ghostly shape. 'Urgh! Cold!' he cries, but he holds on until he starts shivering so much that I have to pull him away.

'Are you sure?' I say.

'Of course I'm sure! He's tall and his beard is just the most amazing thing I've seen in my life. It's got a crab in it!'

Suddenly Elizabeth flies down from the rafters and lands on Zen's head.

'Hello, Elizabeth,' he says.

'Hello,' she replies. 'Rum, bum!'

Now Zen looks like he might cry. 'I've got a ghost parrot on my head and she said "bum" . . . You did this, Sid. Thank you!'

'What do you mean?'

'Last night, when you were pulling me up the cliff, you did something to me, zapped me with electricity or . . . *something*, and now I can see ghosts.'

I shake my head. 'I don't think so.'

'I'm telling you, you *did*. I've been feeling strange ever since it happened.'

'You've been feeling strange because you nearly fell off a cliff!'

'Will one of you please tell me what is going on?' demands Bones.

So Zen and I tell Bones everything that happened last night starting with my bright idea to visit Gull Island.

'So I was hanging off the cliff and then *WHOOSH!*' Zen grabs an old sack and swishes it through the air. 'Sid pulled me up the cliff like she was Iron Man or something and the next thing I know I can see ghosts.'

'First of all,' says Bones, 'what you two did last night was foolish and dangerous.' He jerks a thumb towards Zen. 'I might expect him to do that, but not you, Jones.'

'I know,' I say quickly. 'We should never have gone.'

'No, you shouldn't,' he says, giving me a dark look. 'But what's done is done, and as to what has happened to Zen . . . Well, Jones, I reckon you gave him the gift last night.'

'No.' I shake my head. 'It was adrenalin. I learned about it in science.'

'You have magic in you, Sid,' insists Bones, 'and last night you gave a bit of it to Zen Moyo, here.'

'Best present ever!' laughs Zen.

I stare at my hands. Was that really what I did? Was the

burning I felt *magic*? It seems too incredible to believe, and also wrong. If I'm so magic, how come I can't find Bones's treasure?

For the next few minutes, while I stare at my hands and wonder if they're magical or not, Zen gazes at Bones and Elizabeth. Then he jumps up and starts running round the hut flinging his hands out and wriggling his fingers and saying stuff like, 'Kabam!' and 'Expeliosis!'

'What are you doing?' I say.

'Magic . . . only it won't work.'

Eventually he gets tired of this and begs us to take him to the Halfway House. 'Please,' he says. 'I want to see more ghosts!'

But I don't want to go anywhere near that place. Not after what Old Scratch did last night, and Bones agrees.

'Surely two ghosts are enough for one day,' I say. 'Plus we've got more urgent things to do.'

'What could possibly be more urgent than going to visit a pub full of ghosts?' Zen asks.

'Saving this one,' I say, nodding towards Bones, and then all my tiredness and worry sweeps over me, and for a moment I think I might cry. 'He doesn't usually look like this, Zen. When we first met, Bones's beard was as black as coal and he had a diamond shining in his ear. Elizabeth was as blue as the sea is right now!'

'Hush now!' says Bones. 'That kind of talk won't help us. Once the *Black Gannet* got stuck in the doldrums for thirty days and thirty nights. We were down to our last sips of water, and they tasted something rotten. The only merry moment I had was winning a chest off Anne Spargo in a game of dice. But what use was that? I could not drink wood! Do you know how we survived?'

'By eating each other?' suggests Zen.

'We were not hungry, you buffoon, we were *thirsty*! No, we spoke as though we were the luckiest fellows on earth. There was no "We are doomed!" or "The wind will never return!". It was all, "I feel a ticklin' breeze! The weather is turning! Tomorrow we shall be flying across the waves!" and, "What a lucky bucko I am to win a fine chest!". Go on, try it, Sid.'

Really, I'm not in the mood for positive thinking. I'm in the mood for feeling sad and sleeping, but because Bones looks so eager I do what he says. 'Tomorrow I will look at your map and see something I have never noticed before,'

I say. 'We will find your treasure and you and your crew will finally be free.'

'That's my girl,' he says with a chuckle. 'Now don't that feel grand?'

I can't help smiling because Bones is right. It does. I take the copy of his map out of my pocket and look at it again, determined not to give up. Something Bones just said to me – 'That's my girl' – seems important, although I don't know why. The words won't go away as I stare at the waving mermaid, and I feel sure she's trying to tell me something.

Eventually, when the light becomes softer, Zen and I know we have to go.

Zen insists on high-fiving Bones before we leave and as we walk down the lane he cradles his hand, saying, 'Sooooo cold.' Then he nudges me. 'Sid, what if the gift you gave me was temporary? What if I can't see him tomorrow?'

I don't say anything. I can't. Because not seeing Bones tomorrow is what I'm scared of too.

Down at the harbour you'd think Pirate Day had already begun. There are people wearing stripy socks outside the Benbow and someone is playing a concertina.

Mrs Ferrari sways from side to side as she arranges an eyepatch on her fibreglass ice cream.

'Evening, you two!' she calls when she sees us. 'Pirate Day tomorrow!'

Zen and I say goodbye outside the museum.

'We'll get to Gull Island the moment the tide goes down,' Zen says. 'We can find Bones's cross, Sid. We're the Dead Good Detectives, remember!'

CHAPTER FORTY-SEVEN

Usually on Pirate Day I wake up with a happy glow inside. But not today.

I lie in bed thinking about Bones and Elizabeth in the hut and hoping we've not run out of time. The tide has only just started to go out, which means we won't be able to get to Gull Island until midday, and that's hours away! What if we're too late?

Before I sink into gloomy thoughts, I remind myself what Bones said last night, and I try to think like I'm the luckiest fellow on earth. I have a map, and clues, and a best friend who wants to find the treasure as much as I do.

I jump out of bed. Zen and I can set off for Trendeen

early, then walk across to the island the second the causeway is revealed.

As I'm getting dressed, I see the cardboard box Dad got down from the attic. At some point he wrote 'Laure's Costume' on the lid, but because he loves making things, he didn't stop there. Using a fat Sharpie he also drew planks on the box, nails and a skull and crossbones, making it look like a real treasure chest.

If only Bones had hidden his treasure in nice big chest that was easy to find!

I freeze in the middle of pulling my jumper over my head. What if he did? What if Bones's treasure is hidden inside something I found right at the very beginning of this hunt? I yank my jumper on, grab Bones's map and head for the stairs. I've got to find Zen.

'Sid, what's going on?' says Zen as he follows me along the seafront. 'There's no point in going to Trendeen yet. The tide is too high!'

'I'll explain when we get to the fishing hut,' I say. Then we dodge round a group of old ladies wearing head scarves and eye patches. Visitors have already started to arrive in Fathom, even though the parade isn't until this afternoon.

Relief rushes through me when we find Bones sitting by the window in the hut with Elizabeth on his shoulder. He turns to look at us through hollow eyes. Overnight he seems to have lost all his remaining colour, and his edges – the three tips of his hat, his shoulders, his toes – have disappeared completely.

'Sid,' cries Elizabeth, faintly. 'Zen!' She's as white and wispy as Bones. She flaps her wings and they vanish for a moment.

'Bones, you've got to come to the *Black Gannet*,' I say. 'I think your treasure might be there!'

His eyes widen and he staggers to his feet. 'My treasure, on the *Gannet*? But why, Jones?'

I pull my copy of his map out of my pocket. 'I've been so stupid. I love maps so much that from the moment I saw this I was convinced it would lead us to the Castile Cross, but I think it was a red herring. When I was in the Halfway House, Jon Pollard said that he saw you hide your cross in a trunk, and last night you told me you won a trunk from Anne Spargo in a game of cards.'

Bones frowns. 'And you believe this trunk is on the *Gannet?*'

'I'm sure it is! Don't you remember what we found when we visited the wreck? Something big and made of wood with AS written on the front!'

'I did say there was treasure at the wreck,' says Zen, smugly.

Bones shakes his head. 'But . . . I am sure my treasure is in Fathom.'

'You keep telling us your memory has holes in it,' I say. 'What if you were trying to get the cross back to Fathom when the storm closed in? It was priceless. You must have been desperate to get it to safety!' Bones still isn't convinced so I add, 'Surely it's worth looking?'

He nods. 'You are right. If there is a chance, we must look.' He points to a pile of my grandad's tools. 'Jones, grab a spade!' Then he strides towards the door, calling, 'To the wreck!'

Soon we're back on the beach and hurrying across wet sand.

It's going to be a hot day, but right now the sun is trapped behind hazy clouds. Mist drifts from the sea towards us and everything is strangely quiet. Even the waves sound muffled.

The tide has gone out far enough for us to clamber over the rocks then run through the tunnel. But when we come out on the *secret beach* the wreck is still covered by the sea.

We have an agonising wait while the waves suck further and further back, until, finally, we see the blackened timbers of the *Gannet* sticking up behind the rockpools.

We run. Bones doesn't seem to notice that his feet have vanished and he's floating over rocks and piles of seaweed. He has a determined, fierce look on his face. 'This chest could hold the answer,' he mutters, 'but there's not much time. Hurry now!'

When we reach the hull of the *Gannet* we split up and search by the timbers for the chest. Panic builds up inside me. The tide turns quickly here. We haven't got long.

Then I spot smooth dark wood poking through the seabed.

I fall to my knees and wipe sand off the wood. I see the rusty lock with the initials AS stamped into the metal.

'I've found it!' I shout, and the other two come running.

Zen laughs. 'It really is a chest! Look!' He scrapes away more sand and the shape of the chest is clear.

The sun burns through the mist, heating my shoulders, and as I run my hands over the sea-soaked wood I feel a rush of happiness. Bones's treasure could be so close!

Waves crashing in the distance remind me that we need to move fast.

I start digging with the spade and Zen grabs handfuls of wet sand and chucks them over his shoulder. The chest isn't big, but it's buried deep. As soon as I get a shovelful of sand away, more trickles into the empty space. But we're determined and we've got Bones giving us orders.

'Put your back into it, Jones. Now heft it away, girl. That's right! Zen, m'lad, you're digging like a little rabbit. Make scoops with those hands. That's more like it!'

Every now and then Zen and I stop digging and try to pull the chest free, but the sand keeps it glued in place. So we keep going, and we don't stop even when our muscles are burning and our fingers are so cold we can't feel them.

As the first foaming waves reach the wreck, we get one corner free.

'Get it out, girl!' cries Bones. 'If you don't get that thing clear of the sand in the next few minutes then we must leave it behind. The tide has turned.'

I'm squatting down in the wet sand, soaked through, sweat dripping down my forehead. 'But what about your treasure?'

'If there's one lesson life has taught me, Sid, it's that no gold is worth risking your life for.'

'He's right. We need to go,' says Zen.

'One last try,' I say, and I throw down the spade and get my fingers under a corner of the chest. Zen takes the other side.

'Ready?' he says.

'HEAVE HO!' bellows Bones.

We pull with all our might.

Finally I feel it: a tiny wiggle. My feet slide out from under me as I try to drag the chest free. And then, with a great slurp, the sand releases its grip.

Zen and I fall back, but the sea that is bubbling around us makes us jump to our feet. Leaving the spade behind, we pick up the chest and stagger back up the beach towards the cliffs. As we go, water streams out of gaps in the wood. Our feet sink into the soft sand and we stumble over hidden rocks, but we keep going.

'That's it. You're doing a cracking job!' cries Bones as he strides alongside us.

'CRACKING JOB!' shrieks Elizabeth.

Zen and I force ourselves to keep going until we're high up the beach. Once I let go of this chest, I'm not sure I'll ever be able to pick it up again.

'Here?' Zen asks.

'Here,' I agree, and we drop the chest with a heavy thud.

We collapse next to it and for a moment I let my aching body sink into the warm sand.

Bones crouches next to the chest. He runs his hands over and through it. I know that he can't wait to see inside.

'Do you think there's something in there?' I say, kneeling next to him.

'I do, Jones, but I'm not sure if that is just desperate hoping.'

'What do you mean?' I say.

'We have company.'

He stares up the beach. Old Scratch has appeared in the mouth of the cave and Snout is by his side.

CHAPTER
FORTY-EIGHT

'Whoa,' says Zen. 'Are you sure Old Scratch isn't a ghost?'

I understand why Zen's confused. With his fraying waistcoat, tattered coat and deathly white skin, Old Scratch looks like a faded photograph. His cobwebby hair blows in the wind and his pale amber eyes stare hard at us. He looks like he's had all the colour squeezed out of him.

'I'm no ghost,' he shouts, making me and Zen jump.

'Whatever he is, he's got good hearing,' whispers Zen.

'I don't like this,' mutters Bones. 'You should both leave while you have the chance. Think what he tried to do to you on the cliff!'

'No.' I start tugging at the lid of the chest. 'We're so close. Help me, Zen!'

Zen tears his eyes away from Old Scratch who is now striding towards us, Snout slinking by his side, and helps me to prise at the lid, but it's stuck solid.

'Mum would kill me,' says Zen.

'Why?'

'Because of what I'm about to do.' He grabs a rock and uses it to bash at the lock. The wood is so soft that it falls away, but it makes no difference. It's like the lid is glued shut.

'Go,' whispers Bones. A small gust of wind makes him vanish, then he's back before my eyes. 'He will hurt you!'

Old Scratch is walking faster, pushing his way through the thin mist. Snout's snarls echo around us. I take the rock and raise it high above my head. 'Move, Zen!' I shout, then I smash the rock down on the lid of the ancient chest. Instantly it crumples inwards.

'Can it be opened?' asks Bones.

Once again we push our fingers under the edge of the lid – only this time when we pull, the lid crashes open and damp, salty air rushes over us.

A snarl makes me look up. Snout has broken away from Old Scratch and is bounding towards us, teeth bared.

'She can't bite, can she?' asks Zen, shrinking back.

I don't have time to reply. The dog hurls herself at me. It's like I've been hit by a block of ice. I slam back on to the sand, my body shaking with cold.

'Get off her!' cries Zen.

He grabs the dog, but of course his hands just slip through her muscly body. He jumps to his feet, shaking from the cold, and starts waving his arms around and backing away.

'Oi, Snout! Do you think you can catch me?' he yells, then he turns and runs away over the sand, adding, 'Then come and get me!'

Snout hesitates, shifts her beady eyes from me to Zen, then leaps after him.

I scramble to my feet, reaching for the chest, but Old Scratch gets there first. He plucks it off the sand as if it doesn't weigh a thing.

'That doesn't belong to you!' I shout.

'*He* belonged to me!' he hisses, jabbing a finger at Bones. 'But you stole him.' His hands tighten on the chest.

'I won't let you steal any more of my lost souls.'

'My crew,' whispers Bones. 'He means to keep them. He knows that if we find my treasure, they walk free.'

Old Scratch laughs, backing away, his arms still wrapped around the chest. 'That's right. I find I don't care much for you any more, Kittow. You're nothing more than a whining puff of smoke. But I am a reasonable man, so I will give you one last chance. Come back to the Halfway House, sign your name and step inside. It is that or become a wraith and be lost forever. Which do you choose?'

Bones opens his mouth to speak, but no sound comes out.

Old Scratch simply laughs, then turns and walks away from us with Bones's chest tucked under his arm.

'No!' I shout. 'There is another way. Bones will find his treasure and be free!'

I run after Old Scratch. Bones reaches out his hands to stop me, but I pass straight through them, the cold cutting into me. I keep running over the sand until my hands slam into Old Scratch's back. The chest flies out of his hands and he whips round to face me.

'I warned you!' he snarls, then he grabs both my shoulders

and lifts me up in the air, holding me close to his face. I smell damp earth and the sickly scent of cloves. 'You will never find his treasure!' he says, shaking me like a rag doll.

'Let go of her!' Bones swipes at Old Scratch, but, of course, his hands do nothing.

Old Scratch continues to stare at me, with a strange, cold expression on his face. My bravery of a few moments ago slips away and now I'm shaking with fear and pain as his hands grip my shoulders, squeezing tighter and tighter.

A yell rips through the air. Zen appears out of the mist and throws himself at Old Scratch's legs. The surprise of his rugby tackle is enough to send the innkeeper crashing to the sand.

I twist away and crawl towards the chest. Behind me, Zen and Old Scratch roll around in the sand. A volley of barks tells me that Snout is coming back.

This is my chance. I shove my hands into the open chest. I'm expecting everything to look brown and mushed up, like the exhibits in the museum, but the things inside have colour. I grab a piece of blue cloth. It's some sort of shirt. Instantly it falls to pieces in my hands. Underneath lies a pouch, a pair of boots, a smooth piece of leather. I pull them all out, tossing them to one side.

The barking is louder now, and I glance over my shoulder to see Snout leap on top of Zen and Old Scratch. This makes the innkeeper furious. He starts bellowing at his dog, but then Zen throws a handful of sand in his face and he starts coughing and spluttering.

Bones hovers close by. Unable to help either of us.

My fingers touch wood. I've reached the bottom of the chest, and it's empty. No . . . That can't be right. The cross has to be here!

Then I remember that Pollard said Bones put the cross in 'a secret place' in the trunk. The bottom of the chest is cracked, but when I push my fingers into the dark space, they don't touch sand. Instead I feel fabric, and something else. Something hard.

'I think I've found it,' I whisper.

Instantly Old Scratch throws Zen away from him and races towards me.

But he's not stopping me now. I take the rock and smash it down on the soft wood. Then I tear the broken pieces of the trunk away until I see a lumpy piece of fabric. I pull it out and feel the weight of it in my hands.

I hold it out in front of me.

Zen appears by my side. He's covered in sand and his hoodie is torn. 'A hidden compartment! I've seen a chest like this before. The bottom flips up.'

Bones joins us. 'No . . . It was the side that came away. I would press down, just below a nail, and it would shift to one side. I remember Spargo showing me how it was done.'

He says all this in a weary whisper. He is white now, all over except for his eyes and mouth which are dark circles. The wind blows over the sand and takes away the feather in his hat. I wait for it to reappear, but it doesn't.

'Open it, Jones,' he says, nodding at the sodden package in my hands. 'Open it quick.'

Old Scratch is watching with a horrified look on his face as I peel back the stiff folds of fabric. Then we see it – the dazzling shine of gold and the glitter of deepest green: emeralds. Bones gasps and Zen throws back his head and laughs. Old Scratch lets out a howl of rage. With trembling fingers, I pull a cross free from its ancient wrapping. I wipe away a layer of algae, revealing the five emeralds as big as blueberries.

'Bones, we did it! We found your treasure. Pure gold,

through and through, and covered in emeralds. This is it, Bones, isn't it? The Castile Cross?'

He nods. 'That's my cross all right. I can remember wrapping it up and slipping it into the chest.' His hand hovers over the cross then falls to his side. The tips of his fingers seem to drift away. Elizabeth opens her beak, but no sound comes out.

'What's the matter?' I say. 'We found your lost treasure. You're free. You can cross to the other side.'

'The cross is mine, Jones, and it's beautiful, but it is not the treasure I am looking for.'

Old Scratch throws back his head and laughs. 'You know what this means, don't you? You are going to become a wraith, in hours, maybe minutes, and when that happens your crew is mine *for ever*. And don't even think about coming to the door and asking to be let in. You are useless to me now.' With a cruel grin, he throws a glance at me and Zen. 'You should have chosen your friends more carefully, Kittow. Did you really think these children could help you?' Then he turns on his heel, his coat swirls out, and he strides into the mist, snapping, 'Come, Snout!'

I push the cross towards Bones. 'Are you sure this isn't

your treasure? It's gold. It has emeralds . . . I'm sure it's priceless!'

'Look at me,' says Bones, holding out his arms. He looks like a sketch drawn with the lightest of pencils. Before my eyes a button vanishes, followed by a finger. 'If I'd found my treasure, then my buckle would shine and my beard would be black as night. Most likely, I'd strike fear into your heart.' He smiles and takes off what's left of his hat. Then he bows and says, 'Jones, I want to thank you sincerely for the help you and young Zen have given me. It was a kindness I did not deserve.' And with this, he stands up tall, puts his hat back on and pulls what's left of it low over his eyes. Then he starts to walk away.

I run after him, my feet slipping in the sand.

'Sid!' Zen shouts. 'What about the treasure?'

For a second I wonder what he's talking about. Then I remember the cross. I turn back. 'Keep it,' I say, 'or chuck it in the sea. I don't care.'

'But it's worth millions!'

He's wrong, I think, as I run after Bones. Really, that cross isn't worth anything at all.

CHAPTER FORTY-NINE

For once Bones doesn't wait for me. While I have to go through the tunnel and climb over rock pools, he simply walks through each obstacle he meets and by the time I reach the beach he's gone.

I stare at the strange sight of a beach full of pirates. I'd almost forgotten it was Pirate Day.

'Sid! Wait up!' I turn to see Zen, wriggling out of our secret tunnel. He jumps to his feet and runs over. He's soaking wet and covered in sand. The cut above his eye is bleeding and he has a graze on his forehead.

'What are you going to tell your mum and dad?' I say.

'I'll probably just say that you and me had a fight with

a three-hundred-year-old dude who goes around with a ghost dog.'

'Seriously?'

He grins. 'No. I'll tell them I fell over on the rockpools. I'm always doing that.'

'You look like a proper pirate,' I say.

He dabs at his lip. 'Shame my beard is going to cover this.'

'You're still dressing up?'

'Definitely,' he says. Then he hesitates before adding, 'Sid, if the cross isn't Bones's treasure, then it must be something else, something hidden at Gull Island, but the causeway will be covered now.'

'I know.'

'We could go later this evening, but . . .'

I shake my head. I don't want him to say the next words . . . *it will be too late.* 'I know, Zen. I made a terrible mistake. We should never have come to the wreck today.'

'We found treasure, but it wasn't the right treasure. You weren't to know that.'

I know Zen is trying to make me feel better, but right now I feel sick with disappointment and worry.

'So what are you going to do now?' he asks.

'I'm going to find Bones and say goodbye.' The tears come out of nowhere. Quickly, I brush them away.

Zen doesn't ask if I want him to come too. He knows this is something I have to do on my own. We walk side by side across the busy beach, then say goodbye at the top of the stairs. Already the band is playing and the harbour is packed with people.

'Let me know if you change your mind about dressing up,' says Zen, then he disappears into the crowd.

I find Bones in the graveyard leaning against his favourite monument.

He looks like he did when I first met him. His eyes are closed and his face is tilted to the sun. Only now there isn't a trace of colour on him. He looks like the hazy mist that hung over the beach earlier today. Before my eyes tendrils of his beard float away and vanish.

Elizabeth is perched on the sea wall watching her master. She opens her beak when she sees me, but no sound comes out.

Bones raises his hat and looks at me. 'I thought we had said our farewells.'

I kneel next to him on the warm gravel. 'How many times have you told me not to think gloomy thoughts?' I say. 'You can't give up yet, Bones. You're here, aren't you? We can walk round Fathom with your map. Tomorrow we can go back to Gull Island and start digging again. We were wrong about the cross, but your treasure could still be there. Maybe it's gold coins or a necklace. X marks the spot!'

Bones listens to me, then shakes his head. 'I don't think I'm going anywhere, young Sid. I think that if I moved from this spot, I'd be blown apart like the foam on a wave.'

'What would Margery do?' I ask desperately. 'She wouldn't give up, would she? I'm going to need another spade, but –'

'No.' His voice is firm. 'This is the end of our caper, and I plan to wait out my time here, breathing the salty air and watching the waves.'

I can't believe that in a few hours Bones, my friend, will be gone and he's just going to sit back and let it happen. 'There must be something we can do!'

'Jones, sometimes we must sail into a storm, no matter how scared we are!'

'I'll stay with you,' I say, my voice pleading. 'We'll look at the map together, see if you can remember anything.'

'Jones,' he says, gentler now, 'you've spent enough time with the dead. It's time for you to leave me.'

My tears come back. 'I'm not going anywhere!'

'Oh yes you are,' he growls, sitting up taller. 'Sidonie May Jones, you are going to go home and put on your outfit and parade through Fathom with the living.'

I shake my head. 'I can't.'

'Why of course you can! I knew you were something special the moment I saw you. Here is a girl who is magic, I told myself. Here is a girl you want by your side!'

I glance towards the gates. People are streaming past the graveyard, heading for the harbour and the start of the parade. No one glances this way. They're all laughing and joking. I can see head scarves and coloured skirts, gold earrings and big black belts.

How can I possibly leave Bones here, get dressed up and join them?

'I can't,' I say.

'Step out with your head held high,' says Bones, 'even when your heart quakes. Do it for me, Jones.' Then he turns back to the sea. 'That is an order.'

He doesn't want me to watch him fade away. So even though I want to stay by his side, I force myself to get to my feet and walk out of the graveyard.

CHAPTER FIFTY

I weave my way through the crush of people heading for the seafront.

Everyone seems to be smiling or laughing. I see babies dressed as parrots and dogs dressed as pirates. I almost fit in wearing my stripy jumper. How can I walk alongside these happy people when I know that Bones is slowly but surely fading away?

Dad is busy selling ice creams in the kiosk so I slip into the house and go upstairs.

In my room I sit on my bed and stare at the cardboard box with 'Laure's Costume' written on the lid in Dad's handwriting. Outside the streets get noisier, busier. The sun moves across my room.

It's a cry of 'Yo ho ho!' from under my window that finally

makes me open the box. One by one, I take out the things carefully packed away in there: a white ruffled blouse, a thick belt, a leather waistcoat, a handful of jewellery, a bright green skirt, boots, and right at the very bottom, a beautifully battered tricorn hat.

The blouse is a bit yellow from being kept in the box. Dad told me that Mum sewed every ruffle on herself. He made the belt and hat.

I lift up the hat and put it on my head. It fits perfectly. I can hear laughter out on the lane. More and more people are pouring into Fathom. Can I put on Mum's costume and join them?

I sit back on my bed still wearing the hat and get out Bones's map.

My eyes move from the mermaid to the tree to the thick black cross he scratched in the middle. Should I put this away and forget about it and join the parade like Bones told me to? I don't want to. I feel heavy with sadness. I want to curl up in bed and wait until Pirate Day is over. Then tomorrow Bones will be gone and my life will go back to normal.

Then it hits me, as bright and clear as the sun pouring through the window.

I don't want my life to ever go back to normal. I don't want to keep my head down as I scurry round the edges of the playground, hoping no one notices me. I cling to this thought as I shake out Mum's green skirt and hold it against me. Dad was right. We are the same size. It's going to fit.

As I get ready, I remember everything Bones told me about going into a skirmish. I polish the buckle of the belt, tangle what there is of my short hair, knot it and tie beads in the twisted ends. I do up the pearl buttons on the blouse with trembling fingers, I tighten the waistcoat, slide the blunt sword into its holder and slip my feet into the boots. My toes wriggle into the dents Mum's toes made. I put the skull necklace around my neck and slip the Jolly Roger ring on to my finger. Finally I find a piece of coal and rub it over my face. Then I look into the mirror.

A pirate stares back at me.

I stare back at me.

One thing is missing. I need a gold earring. I rummage through my jewellery box, but all I've got are a few pairs of studs. Then I remember the hoop earring we dug up on Gull Island. I find the rucksack I took on my trip and shake it out.

All the treasure we found spills out on to the bed, along with the worksheet that we filled in. I find the earring and douse it in surgical spirit. Then, knowing I'm probably doing something very stupid but doing it anyway, I push it into the hole in my ear.

I yelp. There. Now I'm a proper pirate. Bones wanted me to join in with the parade and I will, but that doesn't mean I'm going to stop thinking about his treasure.

Automatically I reach for my map, which I left on the bed.

No. I can't take it. A pirate doesn't wear a map in a holder round her neck! But the thought of leaving it behind makes my stomach squeeze, so I pull it over my head. Then I see something that makes me stop and stare.

A pair of bright green eyes are looking at me from the back of the worksheet. Mr Lawrence has filled it with information about the history of Trendeen. He's put facts and figures on there, along with a portrait of the first owner, a Mrs Willoughby Hawke.

Willoughby Hawke . . . That's the name engraved on the monument that Bones is so fond of. The place in the graveyard that he's drawn back to again and again.

Willoughby . . . *Willow*.

I stare at the lady in the portrait, someone whose eyes are as bright as emeralds. She has brown skin and a smile that lights up her face. Zen and I didn't even look at this when we were on the trip, but I'm starting to wonder if we made a terrible mistake.

I read the information printed next to the portrait. *Unusually for the mid-eighteenth century, Trendeen House was first owned by a woman, Willoughby Hawke. She inherited the land from her from her father and, with the help of her husband, developed it into a small but prosperous*

farm. It was *Willoughby Hawke who planted some of the trees that can still be found at Trendeen. Her fine memorial stands in Fathom graveyard, along with the headstone she commissioned for her father, Ezekiel Kittow.*

I stare at the portrait of Willoughby Hawke. She smiles back at me. It's a beautiful smile. It's a golden smile.

I run out of the room, hoping I'm not too late.

I think I've found Bones's treasure.

CHAPTER FIFTY-ONE

The model village is still swamped with customers, but I slip past them and let myself into the kiosk.

'Dad,' I say, 'if you see Zen, I need you to give him a message.'

He turns round, then blinks with surprise. 'Sid . . . is that *you*?'

He stares at me, two Feasts clutched in his hands. The woman on the other side of the counter gets tired of waiting and grabs hold of them. Dad shakes his head at me. 'Sorry, you gave me a surprise, that's all. You look like your mum!'

I don't want to ruin Dad's special moment, but I've really got to go. Bones could be changing into a wraith right now!

'Listen, Dad, if you see Zen, tell him that *I've found Bones's treasure*.' He looks confused so I try again. 'It's a game we're playing. Tell Zen to meet me in the graveyard.

Tell him I've found Bones's treasure. Got it?'

He nods and smiles. 'You've found Bones's treasure . . . You look great, Sid.'

'Thanks, Dad!'

I'm about to leave the kiosk when something makes me freeze. It's a dry, crackling voice saying, 'One mint Magnum.'

I look up and there, standing at the hatch to the kiosk is Old Scratch. Surrounded by people in fancy dress, his white face and high collared coat don't look out of place.

'Coming right up,' says Dad, turning away.

Old Scratch smiles. I'm not sure who moves first. I throw myself out of the kiosk, dodge round an old lady and run into the lane. I know Old Scratch is coming after me because Dad shouts, 'Hey! Don't you want your Magnum?'

I plunge into the crowd and I'm swallowed up by a sea of mums, dads, teenagers and grannies, all dressed as pirates, and all streaming down to the harbour for the start of the parade.

'Amazing costume!' shouts a lady. 'Can I get a picture?'

'Sorry, I'm in a rush,' I say, ducking between two men.

I look over my shoulder and catch a glimpse of Old

Scratch's domed forehead, but only for a second. There's a roar of laughter and I'm pulled forward. The air around me crackles with energy as drums bang and people call out to each other. Somewhere to my left a baby cries, but the sound is drowned out by the blast of a horn.

'Excuse me!' I say, trying to squeeze between two women. 'Please can I get past?' But it's no use. They form a wall that I can't go through. My heart speeds up. If I'm going to reach Bones in time then I have to get away from Old Scratch!

I wriggle to the left, then yelp. A white face stares down at me. I see more bony faces and white beards and realise I'm surrounded by a group of teenagers all dressed like ghostly pirates. 'Arrrghhh!' one goes in my face.

I duck down and push on, forcing my way through, until, finally, I reach the seafront. I thought it would be less crowded here, but it looks like it's the busiest spot in Fathom. There are stalls serving food and drinks, packed benches outside the Benbow and a sea-shanty band are playing. People are dancing and singing. I'll never get through this way!

Then I spot the narrow alleyway at the side of the pub. I know every inch of Fathom, it's all drawn on my map, and that alleyway is how they get barrels of beer into the cellar of the pub. It runs around the back of the Benbow, joining up with the lane that leads to the graveyard.

If I can get through there I can get to Bones.

'Excuse me! Sorry!' I say as I push my way towards it. I get a volley of annoyed tuts and comments, but I ignore them and keep going until I can slip out of the press of bodies and into the cool, dark passageway.

The buildings on either side of me are packed so close together I feel like I'm in a tunnel. It smells of spilled beer and cooking grease. I'm coming, Bones! I think, as I run along slippery cobblestones towards the rectangle of light.

Then, just when I'm about to burst back on to the lane, a figure steps into the alleyway, blocking my way. I skid to a halt and a familiar face grins down at me.

'There you are!' says Old Scratch.

I look over my shoulder. Can I run back the way I've just come? No, it's too far.

Old Scratch smiles, showing ancient-looking teeth. 'I did warn you,' he whispers.

'Let me past!' I try to sound brave, but my voice is trembling.

He shakes his head. 'I'm not letting you go anywhere near that graveyard. In a few minutes, Kittow will become a wraith and then your adventure will be over.'

I try to dart past, but his hand slams into my shoulder. The shock knocks me back and I land on dirty cobblestones.

'It is over!' he hisses. 'The ghosts are mine!'

I scurry backwards. Then I remember where I am. I've drawn this alleyway carefully on my map. There's an air vent; three gates that back on to gardens, tall and locked; a door that leads to what's left of the Victorian swimming pool – again, locked; and two hatches that go to the basement of the Benbow. One is wide, big enough for barrels to be rolled down a wooden ramp. The other is for coal, and it should be next to me. I glance to my right.

The coal hatch is there. It's small, which is why it's unlocked. But I'm small too.

If I can distract Old Scratch, then I might be able to slip down there. If only Zen were here to help me! And it's this thought that gives me the idea.

'Zen!' I cry, waving madly over Old Scratch's shoulder. He's distracted, just for a second, but that's all I need.

I flip open the hatch and as Old Scratch turns back to face me, I hold on to my hat and throw myself inside.

CHAPTER FIFTY-TWO

I tumble down a dusty chute, landing with a thud on a pile of coal. Dust creeps into my throat and Mum's hat rolls to one side. I slide off the coal, grab the hat and ram it down on my head. Then I jump to my feet. I haven't got long. Already, Old Scratch is banging on the other hatch. I hear wood splintering. He's breaking the lock!

I move further into the dim room. I find a door, but it's locked on the other side. A clatter makes me turn round and I see the doors to the beer hatch being wrenched open. Old Scratch peers in. The next thing I know, he's lowering his long legs down into the cellar.

I dodge behind a stack of crates.

'How long do you think he has?' taunts Old Scratch. 'Minutes? Seconds? Perhaps he's already gone and left you.'

Now I'm in the darkest corner of the cellar. Something whispers on the back of my neck. A draft . . . But that doesn't make sense. I'm below ground. There are no windows back here. Then I remember the smugglers' tunnels! Fathom is full of them, and I've drawn most of them on my map. I step backwards, following the draft. The air gets cooler. My fingers touch a large wooden barrel.

There's a thud and I hear ragged breathing. Old Scratch is coming my way.

I squeeze behind the barrel and my fingers trail along a wet wall. I can smell the sea. I can hear the sea. I want to get out of here, run back into the light, but I force myself to keep walking further into the darkness, my hands stretched out in front of me. I turn a corner and the dim light of the cellar disappears.

Fear sweeps through me. My legs shake and my fingers tremble as I inch further and further along the tunnel. A sob rises inside me, but I squeeze my lips shut. I can't make a sound. Old Scratch will find this tunnel soon. This is my one chance to get away. If only I could see!

Then I remember the skull necklace.

Every few years Dad gets Mum's costume down from the attic. He polishes the leather on the boots and he makes the belt buckle sparkle. Whenever he does this I play with the wooden cutlass and Mum's jewellery. The skull necklace is my favourite because the eyes light up when you squeeze the jawbone.

My fingers fumble as I pull the necklace out from the ruffles on the blouse. Then I hold the skull in front of me. Desperately hoping that the batteries still work, I press on the jaw.

Two red beams of light spill from the skull's eyes. It's not much, but it's enough to show me that I'm standing at the top of a passageway that splits in two directions. Quickly I pull my map out of its holder. My fingers tremble as I open it up. I find the passageway behind the Benbow and the network of smuggling tunnels that I drew on the back with a blue pencil. If my map is correct, then the right-hand tunnel leads to rocks at the edge of the beach and a high metal gate. When the tide comes in, cold water rushes through the gate. The left-hand tunnel leads higher, towards the graveyard.

Footsteps sound behind me.

I pull the necklace off my neck and hurl it down the tunnel that leads towards the sea. Then I take the other one. Seconds later I hear footsteps thundering past. My trick has worked, but Old Scratch will soon realise what I've done.

I run into the darkness, my hands stretched out. I fall over on slimy stones, jump to my feet and keep going. Suddenly my hands slam against wood. I feel around until my fingers wrap around a cold handle. It's a door! I turn the handle, but it won't budge.

That's when I hear footsteps coming closer. At first they're slow, but as I push against the door they speed up.

'I know you're there!' hisses Old Scratch and I catch a glimpse of his face lit up in the red light of the skull necklace's eyes.

I throw myself against the door and it bursts open with a groan. I fall into a dimly lit room. Without stopping to think where I am, I scramble to my feet and slam the door shut. The footsteps thunder closer. I push my body against the door. Somehow I have to stop Old Scratch from getting through! Then I feel something digging into my hip. It's a key. I reach for it just as Old Scratch crashes against the door. The doorknob turns. Old Scratch is fast, but I'm even faster.

I twist the key and with a click the door is locked.

Old Scratch cries out, slamming his fists on the door and kicking it again and again. The wood creaks. The hinges strain.

I turn round. I'm in a small room with stone walls. Dusty hymnbooks are stacked on the floor along with boxes of leaflets. Resting in an alcove is a manger with a plastic baby wrapped in a torn sheet. I've been in the room before, helping tidy up after a Christmas carol service. I'm under the church, which means I'm just down the lane from the graveyard.

I take the stairs two at a time and seconds later I burst into bright sunshine. I lean on the doorway, coughing and wheezing and wiping coal dust from my eyes.

Then I feel a hand on my shoulder. I flinch, but when I look up I see a friendly face peering at me from behind a big green beard.

CHAPTER FIFTY-THREE

'You look incredible!' says Zen. 'Is that cutlass real?'

'No . . . I don't think so. Look, Zen, forget about my costume, we've got to find Bones. I've found his treasure!'

'What is it?'

'There's no time to explain. Come on!'

We run up the lane. 'Our of our way, land lubbers!' Zen yells at the group of pirates in front of us. 'We're on a mission!'

They turn round and I realise the pirates are actually Owen, Kezia and Lara.

Owen stays exactly where he is, blocking our path. He takes in my tangled, back-combed hair, layered skirt and coal-smeared face, and he bursts out laughing. 'Why are you dressed like that? It's Pirate Day, not Halloween!'

Right now, I am in no mood for Owen's comments. I take a step towards him.

'What?' he says.

I step even closer until he's forced back against the wall. Then I lift a finger and press it into his chest. 'If you *ever* speak to me like that again, Owen Kidd, then I will make your ribs into fiddlesticks and use them to beat a rhythm on your heart!'

For a second he doesn't know what to do or say, but I don't back away. I stand my ground, staring at him.

Finally he steps to one side, muttering, 'You're so weird, Sid Jones.'

'I know,' I say, pushing past him and running into the graveyard, 'and you're so boring!'

Zen catches up with me a few seconds later. '*I will make your ribs into fiddlesticks and use them to beat a rhythm on your heart* . . . Sid, what does that even mean?'

'I haven't got a clue,' I say, then my voice trails away.

I've just spotted a white haze hovering in front of Willoughby Hawke's monument.

It's like the last wisps of smoke trailing from a fire. Every couple of seconds, like a flickering film, I can see the faint outline of Bones. His hat is pulled low and his arms are wrapped around his knees. There's a smudge on his shoulder that must be Elizabeth, but she hasn't got a beak or wings.

My huge, bearded pirate has gone.

It's a shock. I feel a pain in my chest and I have to squeeze my mouth shut to stop myself from crying out.

'Is he a wraith?' whispers Zen.

'No.' I shake my head. 'He can't be. Not yet.'

But it's with a thudding heart that I walk towards him.

'Bones?' I say.

Slowly the shape turns and two dark, hollow shapes fix on me. His eyes. The third shape, his mouth, opens and a whisper of a voice says, 'I told you to go!'

It might be thin, and trembling, but it's still Bones's voice and this gives me the courage to run forward.

'I've found your treasure!' I point at the grave behind him. '*She's* your treasure. Willoughby Hawke. Willow, your daughter.'

Bones's face seems to reappear before my eyes as he

stares at the grave. Then he reaches out a ghostly finger to trace the words written on there.

'Willoughby Hawke,' he whispers. 'My Willow?'

'*Yes!*' I say, and I pull the crumpled worksheet out of my pocket. 'Look, I've got a picture of her here.' I thrust the portrait of Willow under his nose – or at least, where I think his nose should be, because once more his face has faded away. 'See, she has eyes like emeralds.'

'Golden girl,' he says, gazing at the picture. Then he turns to me and in a voice filled with anguish he says, 'I remember, Jones. Her dear mother died in Nassau and I arranged for little Willow to be sent ahead of me to Fathom. I wanted her safe, see? But I had one last trip to take, and then I was sailing home to join her. I had promised the *Black Gannet* to my quartermaster. I was giving up my life at sea to make a home for Willow, just the two of us. I was going to build us a cottage. We would have sheep, I told her, and chickens. On stormy nights we would sit as snug as bugs in our home, watching the waves crash on the shore . . . But I never came back. I left her all alone!'

The sadness of this memory makes Bones hide his face in his big hands. His shoulders shake.

'But she was happy,' I say. 'Look!' Once again I show him the worksheet. 'It says that she built the farmhouse just like you planned. She had goats. She planted the trees that are still growing at Trendeen. She lived her whole life there with her husband and children.'

'Children?' Bones says.

'Four. Three girls and a boy.'

But even this news isn't enough to take away the pain Bones is obviously feeling. 'I promised to come back, but I didn't!'

'You tried to,' I say, 'and she knew that.'

Bones shakes his head, refusing to accept my words. For three hundred and one years, he's believed that he abandoned his daughter, and I can see that it's going to be hard to change his mind. But I have to, because his colour hasn't returned and wisps of him are still drifting up into the air.

Then I realise how I can prove to Bones that Willow forgave him.

'Follow me,' I say, using my best captain's voice. Then I march to the top of the graveyard. Zen follows and, after a moment, so does Bones, drifting over the headstones.

376

I stop in front of Bones's own grave, the beautifully carved headstone that I uncovered on that stormy evening just a few weeks ago. Then I take out my copy of his treasure map.

'We got it all wrong,' I say. 'You didn't make your map to show you where you buried your treasure. You made it for Willow, to show her where you planned to build your home. I said it looked like a child had drawn it, and I was almost right. You drew it *for* a child.' I point at the giant sheep and the mermaid. 'You added these for Willow.'

'She loved my tales of sirens,' he says, gazing at the map.

'And she knew you were coming home to her. Listen.'

I read the words that Willow engraved on her father's headstone.

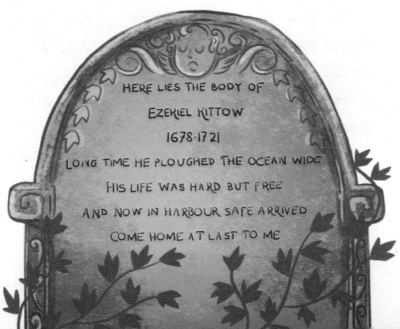

HERE LIES THE BODY OF
EZEKIEL KITTOW
1678-1721
LONG TIME HE PLOUGHED THE OCEAN WIDE
HIS LIFE WAS HARD BUT FREE
AND NOW IN HARBOUR SAFE ARRIVED
COME HOME AT LAST TO ME

Bones stares at the headstone, and then I see it: a patch of blue hovering over his left shoulder. Elizabeth!

'She wasn't angry,' I say. 'She knew you were coming back to her. She built the farmhouse, her home, exactly where you planned it should be built, facing the sea – X marked the spot – and she put your flag above the door.'

Bones turns round and drifts back towards Willow's monument, the one he has been drawn to again and again, ever since he stepped out of the Halfway House. Zen and I follow close behind. He stops by her grave and places both of his hands on the sun-warmed stone.

'Willow,' he says, 'I am here. I have found you.'

And then, before our eyes, Bones appears. His earring shines and his beard becomes a jet-black tangle twisted with strands of seaweed. Elizabeth's marigold yellow feathers burst from her chest and she opens her beak to squawk, 'Bones! Bully! Rum! Bones!'

Bones's shoulders are covered in his thick leather coat. His cutlass hangs from his waist, shining in the sun. Finally, his scarred face turns to look at me. I can't see the sea behind him. He looks solid and real, like I could reach out and touch him.

'I'm free,' he says with his deep growl.

A flash of light out at sea catches my eye. A white ship is sitting on the horizon, its sails full. It's come for Bones.

CHAPTER FIFTY-FOUR

'Captain!'

The shout makes us turn round. A tall blond man is standing at the door of the Halfway House. He steps over the threshold and blinks into the sunshine. 'Wait for us, Captain!' he says with a grin. 'We're coming too!'

Bones runs forward. 'Come out, lads. Breathe the air!'

'Ghosts . . .' says Zen as, one by one, the pirates stagger out into the sunshine. 'So many ghosts. . .' He turns to me. 'Did you let them out?'

I shake my head. 'I didn't need to. It's only lost souls who can be trapped inside the Halfway House. Bones's unfinished business was their unfinished business so now they're free.'

Bones greets each of his crew by name, throwing his arms around their big shoulders. Of course, his hands go straight through them, but they don't seem to mind.

'I'm watching ghosts hug!' says Zen, delighted.

It's a strange sight to see such big strong men (and one small strong woman) fall to their knees to smell the grass and push their hands into beams of sunlight. Tears of happiness run down their cheeks as they breathe in great lungfuls of air.

'Air never tasted sweeter,' cries a stocky man. 'Ain't that the truth, Captain?'

'Never a truer word spoken,' replies Bones, clasping the man's hand and pumping it up and down. 'My goodness, it's good to see you out here, Jon Pollard.'

Jon wanders down to the wall, climbs on to it and throws his arms out wide. 'I can smell the waves, lads. I believe I might even be able to feel them!'

Soon the entire crew of the *Black Gannet* is standing on the wall. Only Bones hangs back, happy to watch his crew from a distance.

The ghosts still trapped in the Halfway House have crowded as close to the door as they can get. Will, unable to stand it, runs forward, desperate to get out. But it's no use. After a couple of steps he smacks into the invisible barrier and is thrown back into the pub. Like the little boy he is, he throws back his head and starts to cry.

'That's a sorry sight,' says Bones.

Peg bends down next to Will and the other ghosts do their best to comfort him. They can't touch him. Not properly. But they go through the motions of patting him on the back and ruffling what's left of his hair.

Olive Buckmore stands at the doorway. 'Pick a flower for me, Master Byron!' she shouts.

'You know that I would if I could, Olive,' he yells back.

'Anne, tell us. What's it like?' calls Peg.

Anne Spargo shuts her eyes for a moment. 'I can feel the sun and smell the sea,' she says. 'Best of all, there's no blooming clocks tickin' and tockin'!'

This makes all the ghosts cheer, but these cheers soon die away when we hear a bang coming from inside the pub. Seconds later the ghosts around the door have vanished and Old Scratch takes their place.

He looks wild and unkempt. His usually pale face and hair are covered in soot. The light-up skull from Mum's necklace is still clutched in his hand. His face darkens as he takes in the scene. The pirates scamper around the graveyard. Some wade through the stream that runs between the graves. Peter Byron is rolling around in the grass like a puppy. Others are simply gazing at their hands, turning them this way and that in the sun.

Old Scratch's hands clench and a look of pure rage crosses his face. His cold eyes meet mine, then, in one violent movement, he slams the door shut.

'He is *not* a happy bunny,' says Zen.

'He is not,' agrees Bones. 'He has just lost sixteen souls.'

Will reappears at the window. Elvis is standing next to him. Peg and Olive join them. They watch the pirates with a mixture of happiness and desperation.

Zen nudges me. 'You could set them free, Sid, and then the DGD can help them find whatever it is they are looking for.'

'Who are the DGD?'

'We are! Sid and Zen, the Dead Good Detectives!'

'I don't know how good we are,' I say. 'It's not like we've got rid of this lot, is it?'

The pirates are still roaming around, bellowing to each

other about 'bloomin' great big daisies!' and egging each other on to climb trees and push their faces into the stream.

Eventually they grow tired of this and gather by the graveyard gates.

'Captain!' calls Peter. 'We're of a mind that it's time to go. You'll see that our ship is ready to sail.'

The white ship is still there, hovering on the horizon.

'Sidonie Jones,' says Bones, taking off his hat and bowing low. 'You have set us free. Will you do us the honour of accompanying us to the harbour?'

'What about me?' says Zen, outraged.

'Well, you too, of course!' says Bones. 'Every captain needs a right-hand man. I have Byron, and Jones has you.'

And with that Bones leads us towards the waiting pirates.

But when we get to the graveyard gates, our path is blocked. The parade has looped through the village and is now making its way back to the seafront. The lane is packed. Drums are thudding, horns and whistles are being blown and someone is playing a fiddle. There are pirates everywhere and the sides of the road are lined with cheering spectators.

'We have to go now, do we?' I say.

'We do,' says Bones. 'But fear not, Jones. You're with your crew.'

One by one, the pirates fall in line behind us.

'Ready?' says Bones.

'Ready,' I say, even though my heart is thudding.

I know that people are going to stare. I'm wearing a magnificent costume and I'm standing next to a boy with a lime-green beard. But I'm also scared because when I get to the seafront I know Bones is going to leave me.

But sometimes we must sail into a storm.

'Courage,' whispers Bones. And seeing a gap in the crowd I step forward, and we are off.

CHAPTER FIFTY-FIVE

My heart thuds to the beat of the drums.

Usually I walk quickly through Fathom, with my head down, taking shortcuts along the alleyways. But not now.

I should hate it. Bones has led me right into the middle of the parade, just in front of a group of teenagers banging drums. A gap opens between me and the people up ahead and suddenly I feel like I'm leading a rebel parade. Maybe the teenagers behind us feel it as well, because they start hitting their drums louder and harder and shouting and yelling too.

The pirates might have been running around the graveyard like children, but now they are serious, marching with their shoulders back and their heads high. Of course, only Zen and I can see them, but knowing they are walking with me fills me with confidence. My shiny boots clip on the cobbles, and my skirts and petticoat sway. My hat makes me feel tall and the weight of my belt round my waist is as comforting as arms around me. Suddenly I know why Mum loved Pirate Day and her costume so much; everything is loud, colourful, free. This was who she was . . . and maybe it's part of who I am too.

People stare, but this only makes me walk taller. I'm proud of what they can see.

When we reach the harbour, everyone spills down to the beach where a bonfire is crackling and the air smells of sizzling food, seaweed and smoke.

'Onwards!' commands Bones, and he marches us towards the Cockle. We step on to the harbour wall and walk along stones rubbed smooth by centuries of feet. The pirates' boots clomp and their swords clank as we walk to the end of the harbour where the setting sun makes a glittering pathway across the sea. Bones takes us down a flight of stone steps. We come to a stop where the steps disappear under lapping water.

'Move to one side now,' says Bones, and Zen and I do as we are told, pressing our backs against the wall of the Cockle so that the pirates can go past.

Zen leans around Bones and says to me, 'Where are they going? Into the sea?'

I haven't got a clue. The white ship is ahead of us, but at least a mile of deep sea separates the pirates from the ghostly ship.

'This is where we leave this world,' says Bones, followed by, 'Go on, then, boys. You know what to do.'

Jon Pollard is the first to walk past. He nods at Zen and me then steps on to the surface of the sea. Following the light of the sun, he walks across the water towards the waiting ship. The other pirates follow, each one pausing to tip their hat or thank us before they walk on the golden path.

Soon only Byron, the quartermaster, is left. Like the others, he bows low. I have a hard lump in my throat because next it is Bones's turn. How can I say goodbye to my friend, knowing that I will never see him again?

Zen must know how I feel because he pats my shoulder clumsily as Byron steps on to the path.

'Let's get that ice cream,' I say to Zen.

'What? Now?' he asks.

I nod. I can't watch Bones go. Already Jon Pollard has vanished into the white haze that surrounds the ship and the others are disappearing one by one.

'Thank you, Bones,' I say, looking up at my friend. 'It's been a magnificent caper.'

He nods. 'That it has, Sidonie May Jones.'

Then, because I can't hug him or shake his hand, I salute him, and he salutes back. Before he can leave, I turn and hurry up the narrow steps.

Zen runs after me. 'Ice cream will cheer you up,' he says. 'It always works for me. Get three scoops and sauce. You deserve it, Sid. You just freed sixteen lost souls!'

CHAPTER FIFTY-SIX

Before I can choose my three flavours of ice cream something amazing happens. Lara grabs hold of me and tells me that I've been crowned Pirate of the Year.

'We've been looking for you everywhere,' she says as I try to take in this incredible news. 'Come on! You need to collect your sash. Everyone is waiting for you!' Then she drags me away from Mermaid's with Zen following close behind us.

If I thought people were staring at me in the parade, now their eyes are positively glued to me. Lara keeps a tight grip on my arm as she pulls me through the crowd, shouting, 'Coming through! I found her!'

When we reach the stage she pushes me forward and I stumble up the steps. I watch in a daze as a red sash is thrown over my shoulders. A cheer rises up. I feel like the whole village is clapping me.

'Well done, Sid!' cries Zen, as I stand there blushing.

Then I spot Dad at the back of the crowd. He's obviously popped down to see the parade and he looks amazed to see me standing on the stage, wearing the sash. And I'm looking shocked and amazed too, because standing by Dad's side is Bones.

I can only escape from the stage after I've muttered, 'Thank you,' into the microphone, and quite a few cries of 'Arghhh!' and 'Shiver me timbers!'

Once I'm allowed to go, I run straight up to Dad and Bones.

'What are you doing here?' I say, trying to keep my eyes on Dad.

'I thought I'd come down to find out who was Pirate of the Year,' says Dad.

'I couldn't leave,' says Bones.

'I'm really so, so very happy that you're here,' I say, to both of them.

Bones laughs his booming laugh and Dad goes pink with pleasure.

'Thanks, Sid!' Dad says. Then he insists on taking me and Zen to get our ice creams before he goes back to the model village.

'Make sure you stick together,' he says once he's bought us triple scoops. 'I want you home in an hour.'

'Don't you worry, Master Jones, I'll look after them,' replies Bones.

Zen, Bones and I sit on the Cockle. We want to eat our ice creams and find out why Bones has missed his chance to cross over to the other side.

'Oh, I am sure another boat will come along soon,' he says. 'I couldn't leave. Not yet. There are others in the Halfway House who need my help, and I believe you two might need it as well. Old Scratch is going to be furious. You cleared out half his tavern when you found my lost treasure.'

'I'm glad you're here,' I say. 'I've got used to having you around.'

'Me too,' says Zen.

There is an almighty squawking above our heads as Elizabeth swoops down and lands on my shoulder.

'RUM! BULLY! RUM!' she cries.

I manage to slip away from Bones and Zen when they are watching the losers of the Yo-Ho-Ho-ing Competition walk the plank.

'I tell you, it never happened,' says Bones, shaking his head. 'If a captain was mean-hearted enough to want a fellow to go in the sea, he would simply toss him in there!'

'I'll be back in a minute,' I say. 'I'm going to get some chips.'

'Get curry sauce!' Zen calls after me.

It's dark now, but I'm not scared as I run towards the graveyard.

I love the dark. I always have.

I am a little bit scared as I walk towards the Halfway House. The lamp still hangs over the wooden door and the window glows a cosy orange. No wonder the lost souls were tempted to step inside.

There's something I noticed earlier that I want to check out. Keeping as quiet as possible, I kneel and read the letters engraved on the step:

LOST SOUL,
step forth into this
timeless tavern

Under the watchful gaze of the gargoyles, I brush away the moss growing there. Just as I thought, more words are hidden underneath. They are much smaller than the others, but they are clearly carved into the stone and they make the message sound a lot less friendly.

LOST SOUL,
step forth into this
timeless tavern
And surrender thyself to me,
by order of the Innkeeper

Suddenly I'm filled with anger. Who does Old Scratch think he is, tricking lost souls into entering his pub and then holding them captive? If Bones had been able to walk around Fathom he might have found Willow, and the other ghosts could have been free too! I remember how Old Scratch chased me through Fathom and the line of white stones that led me and Zen to the cliff edge. Without stopping to think, I jump to my feet and hammer on the door.

For a few seconds there is silence, then the door swings open.

Old Scratch stands there peering down at me, his face ashen. 'What do you want?'

In the gloom behind him, I can see the other ghosts sitting at their tables.

'I've come to give you a message,' I say, standing as tall as I can. 'I set Bones and his crew free and I'm going to free the other ghosts too. You can't keep them here as your personal collection, like your clocks stuck up on the wall. They deserve the chance to resolve their unfinished business and I'm not going to stop helping until every single ghost has left this tavern!'

His strong hands grip the door frame. I think he wants to slam the door in my face, but I refuse to step back. 'You don't know what you're doing!' he hisses. 'Didn't I warn you?'

'You mean the stones on the cliff? They didn't work, did they? I'm still here!'

He snarls with annoyance. '*Stones on a cliff*? I don't know what you're talking about. Stop your idle chatter and listen to me. Terrible things happen when you meddle with magic!'

'Magic?' I say. 'You're not some magical innkeeper. You're just a conman!' I stamp my foot on the step, making him look down. 'You let moss grow over the small print of your spell and you tried to threaten me into giving up. Well it's not going to work. I am never giving up!'

For a moment he doesn't speak. He's still staring at the step. When he looks up, he's smiling. His yellow teeth gleam in the light of the lantern. 'There's one thing you should know, Sidonie May Jones, before you make your bold statements about freeing ghosts. *I* am not the Innkeeper!'

I take a step back. I can't hide how his words have shocked me. If he's not the Innkeeper, then who is?

'Not feeling so brave now, are we?' He crosses the threshold, forcing me back into the graveyard. 'I told you before, you're just a little girl and you shouldn't stick your nose into business that doesn't belong to you.'

I stand my ground and stare back at him. 'You're forgetting one thing,' I say. 'I'm not *just* a little girl. I'm a little girl whose magic was so powerful it broke the spell!'

Then I turn and walk back through the graveyard, my mum's green skirt swishing in the moonlight.

Just before I leave the graveyard, I stop to look out over the still, dark sea. All around me, trees sway and leaves brush against each other. A bat sweeps past. In a blink it's gone. Moths flutter and the ghosts in the Halfway House whisper and murmur.

Magic hums in the air. I close my eyes and, for a moment, become a part of it.

A shout from the lane pulls me out of my dream and I hurry towards the exit. My friends are waiting for me.

Look out for more sensationally
spooky adventures in the next

DEAD
GOOD
DETECTIVES

Coming soon!

CHAPTER ONE

I'm cleaning seagull poo off the roof of Mermaids Café when Zen comes tearing into the model village.

'Sid!' he cries, nearly treading on a tiny camper van. 'A storm is going to hit Fathom in *fifteen minutes* and there's supposed to be lightning. You know what that means?'

I jump to my feet. 'Ghost-freeing time!'

'That's right,' he says with a grin.

Excitement races through me. We've been waiting for a storm for ages. To free a ghost we need lightning, a red gel pen (I've got one in my pocket) and a Crunchie. I did have one of those in my pocket too, but I ate it half an hour ago. Luckily I know where I can get another one.

'Dad,' I say, leaning into the kiosk where he is busy restocking the snacks. 'Can I have a Crunchie?'

'This isn't your personal sweet shop, Sid. You can have one after you've finished your jobs.'

Zen squeezes next to me. 'Please, Jim,' he says. 'It's an emergency!'

Dad raises an eyebrow. 'What sort of emergency has ever been sorted out with a Crunchie?'

I open my mouth to reply, but I don't know what to say. I can't exactly tell Dad the truth . . .

But Zen thinks differently. 'You see, Jim, Sid and I are Detectives for the Dead.' He taps the badge he's pinned to his T-shirt with 'DGD' printed across it. 'And we've discovered this pub in the graveyard full of ghosts. It's our job to help free them and solve their unfinished business so they can pass on to the other side.'

Dad laughs. He thinks this is another of our games. Just last week Zen turned up wearing a crocheted axolotl hat and got me to throw shrimp sweets into his mouth. 'I still don't see what my Crunchies have got to do with freeing ghosts.'

There's a rumble of thunder and warm raindrops fall on my face. I can smell lightning in the air. We've not got much time!

'The Crunchie helps me do a magic spell,' I say in a rush. 'I put it on the grave of the ghost I want to free, write the ghost's name in blood, I mean, red gel pen, lightning strikes and then – boom! – a ghost walks out.'

'And according to my Storm Chasers app, which is eighty-nine per cent accurate,' adds Zen, 'lightning is going to strike in twelve minutes.'

'So we really need that Crunchie,' I say, then I make my eyes go big and add a long drawn out, 'Pleeeease.'

Dad glances at the dark clouds gathering in the sky, then he hands me a couple of Crunchies. 'There you go, one each. Make sure you don't annoy anyone in the graveyard.'

'We won't,' I say. 'Thanks, Dad!' Then I turn towards the bench by the miniature cricket pitch and yell, 'Bones, come on! We're going to free Dai Hughes!'

Ezekiel 'Bones' Kittow lifts up his shaggy head and drops of water scatter to the ground. He's a pirate, one of my best friends and he also just happens to be a ghost.

He leaps to his feet, his pistol clanking against his cutlass. 'To the graveyard!' he cries.

ACKNOWLEDGEMENTS

I'm lucky to be published by Farshore where my books are in such kind and creative hands. Thank you to Cally Poplak, Lindsey Heaven, Sarah Levison, Olivia Carson, Pippa Poole, Ben Mallet, Aleena Hasan, Lucy Courtenay, Olivia Adams and Ryan Hammond for believing in this story, helping me, and for making sure it reaches lots of children.

Thank you to Laura Bird for her beautiful design work and thank you to Liz Bankes for being not only an awesome editor, but also lovely person who laughs at all my jokes.

I am incredibly lucky that Dead Good Detectives is illustrated by the fabulous Chloe Dominique. Thank you, Chloe, for bringing Fathom alive in such spectacular fashion.

Thank you to Julia Churchill who – I always feel proud to announce – is my agent.

Thank you to my early readers: Mum, Dad, Nick, Gemma, Eric, Audrey and Helen Dennis. Your advice was brilliant and your kind words kept me going during the long editing days.

Finally, an Ezekiel Kittow-sized thank you to Ben, Nell and Flora. Shiver me timbers there is a lot of us in this book: a lovely dad, a magical girl who notices everything, a salty seaside setting, and a massively annoying pirate ghost (that's me).

ARE YOU READY FOR ROAR?

Believing
is just the
beginning

DEAD GOOD DETECTIVES

JENNY MCLACHLAN

Illustrated by Chloe Dominique